hard to love series

P. DANGELICO

**WRECKING BALL** (Hard to Love Series #1)
Copyright 2017 P. Dangelico

ISBN-13: 978-0692834831
ISBN-10: 0692834834

Published by P. Dangelico
All rights reserved. No part of this book may be reproduced or transmitted in any form, including
electronic or mechanical, without written permission from the publisher, except in the case of brief
quotations embodied in critical articles or reviews.

This is a work of fiction. Names, characters, places, events, and incidents are either the product of the
author's imagination or used in a fictitious manner. Any resemblance to actual persons, living or dead,
or actual events is purely coincidental.

This book is licensed for your personal enjoyment only. This book may not be re-sold or given away to
other people. If you would like to share this book with another person, please purchase an additional
copy for each person you share it with. Thank you for respecting the author's work.

Cover Design: Najla Qamber, Najla Qamber Designs
Proofreading: Fiona Dreaming
www.pdangelico.com

# ALSO BY P. DANGELICO

<u>Romantic Suspense</u>
A Million Different Ways (A Horn Novel Book 1)
A Million Different Ways To Lose You (A Horn Novel Book 2)
Cold Hard Winters (Coming Soon)

<u>Romantic Comedy</u>
Wrecking Ball (Hard To Love #1)
Sledgehammer (Hard To Love #2)
Bulldozer (Hard To Love #3)  2018

Baby Maker
Heartbreaker
Game Changer

# CHAPTER ONE

CAUTIONARY TALE LADIES, NEVER MARRY a man who quotes the movie *Wall Street* like it's his Bible. If Gordon Gekko is his idol, it's time to pack your bags. Trust me, I wish somebody had given me the heads up.

"Sign here and here—" instructs the vulture also known as the federal prosecutor, "and this case will officially be closed." He pushes the stack of papers across the conference table. I grab the pen my lawyer hands me and pause.

"What about the money in my checking and personal savings accounts?"

"Claw back." He always delivers the worst news in a soft, gender-ambiguous, yet effectively scary voice. I know it well by now. A filthy smile tips up the corners of his mouth. My steady glare convinces him to put a lid on it. Then I glance askance at my overpaid lawyer who, as usual, has nothing to add. "Mrs. Blake, the more we recover, the better this will go for you in the event a civil suit is filed."

"Let me get this straight," I say, exasperated beyond measure because after living this nightmare for three years, I have no patience or filter left. "Even though my husband never used any of the investors' money for our personal use, you can still confiscate every single thing we own?"

"Mrs. Blake—" he says very softly.

"But he was only covering losses!"

"Mrs. Blake—your husband could've stopped after one, two, even three years. But he didn't. He ran this Ponzi scheme until his unfortunate demise. And had he lived, there's a very good chance he'd still be running it. In the last five years of his life, he didn't earn an honest dollar. Who do you think owns all that stuff?"

I swear if he says 'Mrs. Blake' one more time I'm going to take this pen and drive it into my carotid artery. He has a point though. The management fees Matt had been charging hadn't been honestly earned when all he managed to do was lose money for his clients.

"Like I said, there's still a very good chance the victims will file a civil suit," he repeats, delivering this precious gem with a gleam in his hard eyes.

*Breathe in, breathe out, breathe in, breathe out…cannot have a panic attack now.*

The last thing I want to do is to reward the sadistic turd. I check my mental Rolodex for a soothing image to focus on and get a momentary flash of my husband instead.

*Breathe in, breathe out, breathe in, breathe…breathe, bitch, breathe before you pass out.*

It's incomprehensible to me how Matt could have done such a thing. Matthew Edward Blake was my high school sweetheart, the love of my life, the yin to my yang. He was the man I shared my first dance, first kiss, first everything with. He was also the man that had been lying to me for years. And I didn't have a goddamn clue. You can't blame me. We didn't lead an extravagant life. Idyllic, maybe, but not extravagant. That is, right up until three years ago, when on a cold winter night the police showed up at my front door to inform me that my husband's car had to be fished out of the Hudson River, along with his body, and the course of my life was forever altered.

That was just the beginning. The investigation came next.

Ambition was a facet of Matt's personality. That was never in question. So he liked bright shiny objects, so what. Matt wasn't greedy. He was always kind and generous with those around him. Hence, I chose to see it as a positive. My ambitions were of a different nature. Being a good wife. Making sure every child that entered my third grade classroom received the best education possible. That's all that has ever mattered to me. Did I have aspirations that included becoming a CEO of a fortune five hundred company? No. Did I dream of winning a Pulitzer? No. Qualifying for the Olympics? Mmmnnno. And if that sets the feminist movement back fifty years, then so be it.

For a while, I considered getting a Masters in child development. Until Matt persuaded me that I would eventually be too busy raising our children. There was nothing ever unreasonable about what he wanted. He never gave me cause to doubt him. Therefore, as a good wife, I supported my man. I'm a team player after all, loyal to a fault. If Matt wanted the house in Connecticut that we really couldn't afford, I went along with it. When he got me the BMW I said I didn't need or want—well, he was just being generous. Things are nice, but I had family, friends, and the love of my life. Matt always wanted more. It was never enough. There was a certain *restlessness* in him that I never cared to look at too closely. In hindsight, I wish I had—I'll forever be sorry I was too much of a coward to deal with it—because something keeps needling my conscious like a splinter I can't see yet can feel every so often. And now that he's gone, I'll never know where it all went wrong.

"We'll give you three days to vacate the premises. If you remove anything other than your clothes we will bring you up on charges," the vulture informs me. My carcass has officially been picked clean.

Now if this was a sassy romcom, this would be the part of the story where I mount my comeback. Complete with a super cute montage of me going to the gym and sweating like a pig, me cleaning out my wardrobe and refrigerator, and me getting a new job. Playing in the background would be an ass kicking soundtrack featuring Chaka Khan in which she sings about how strong and powerful this new me will be. Spoiler alert: nothing of the sort happens.

"What about my cat? Am I allowed to take my cat? Or is he being clawed back as well?" My whole life has been dismantled by no fault of my own, and the rage that had been steadily simmering up, finally hits the boiling point.

Exhaling his irritation loud enough to be heard in Alaska, the prosecutor steeples his salami like fingers and says, "You may take your cat and nothing else."

Frigging cat hates me. I'm taking him on principle alone.

\* \* \*

"Did you take out the garbage?"

"Yes, Ma."

"Did you pick up the milk?"

"That's the second time you asked—yes, I did."

"The two percent? Not the skim, right?"

*Holy mother of...* "Yes. Now can I finish what I'm doing??"

"No need to get hostile. I'm just askin' a question."

She bows her head and wrings her hands as she walks the short distance from our small dining room to the kitchen. Cue the eye roll. Nobody plays the victim better than Angelina DeSantis. She could make Mother Theresa feel like a villain.

My eyes return to the screen of my father's ancient laptop, which doesn't support Flash, which of course makes it

## WRECKING BALL

incompatible with nearly every website on the planet. I've resorted to scanning the job listings in the most arcane, back alley sites. Sites that include job listings like *'seeking female massage therapists between the age of eighteen and thirty at the Happy Day Spa'* and *'receptionist needed at a gentlemen only club'*.

Gentlemen, my ass.

'Stay busy,' everyone said. 'Go back to work. It'll keep your mind off your troubles.' Top of my troubles—not being able to get a frigging job. Piecing my life back together will without a doubt be a long and arduous process. And I'm harboring no false illusion that it will ever resemble what it once did—minus the scandal and the thieving husband, of course. I just never thought it would look this hopeless.

After my last visit to the federal prosecutor's office in Manhattan, I went home, dropped my cell phone into the trash bin, huddled under the covers, and cried like I did it for a living. I mourned not only the loss of my lover and best friend, but also the death of everything I believed to be true. All those years…all those memories were a lie. My husband embezzled millions from anybody willing to trust him with their savings account. I lived it and it still sounds like the bad plot of a *Lifetime* movie to me. Unfortunately, though, it is not a *Lifetime* movie, it is the steaming pile called my life. I have the paperwork to prove it.

I emerged from my cocoon of despair not a beautiful butterfly, but rather a woman harboring more rage than was healthy. And it was all directed at one gender. Then I packed my bags and my cat, and made the pride-crushing journey back to my parents' house in a yellow cab because my BMW had already been repossessed. Four months have passed since I've lost my home and my job. The house holds too many memories; I wasn't entirely sad to see it go. The job is a different matter altogether. That hadn't been my decision to make. The department of education thought it best for all parties involved if I just fucked off since some of the parents of my third graders had invested with Matt.

"Any luck, Punkin'?"

My father places his calloused, knobby hand on my shoulder. I love my mother, I really do, but I'm my father's daughter. I pat his hand and look up into sympathetic brown eyes. The same eyes as mine. Although he's still handsome in a rugged way, Thomas DeSantis seems to have aged exponentially since the proverbial shit has hit the fan. Lately, he's looking older than his sixty-six years.

I'm an only child, a miracle baby. I've heard the story a billion times. How I came along after ten years of marriage, long after my parents had stopped hoping to conceive. So to say that they have all their hopes and dreams in one basket is not an exaggeration.

"Nothing yet," I say, my voice hitting a strange high note that sounds like the worst attempt at optimism ever.

"And the agency?"

I can't even answer in fear my voice will crack. I resort to a quick head shake. You would think that with a double degree in psychology and early childhood education, I wouldn't have too much trouble finding a decent job. The problem is that my husband's crime has been well publicized in the Tristate area, along with my face, and since I can't afford to move elsewhere, anywhere that I won't be easily recognized, finding a job has become a torturous experience. I've resorted to scraping the bottom of the barrel. Basically, I'm ready to consider the receptionist position at the gentlemen's club—if they'll have me, that is.

"You'll find something, I know you will. And I can always ask Bill if he needs another secretary."

Bill is the owner of the plumbing business my father runs.

# WRECKING BALL

He's also the lech that insists I call him uncle while openly grazing my boobs at holiday parties every chance he gets.

No thanks.

I always thought my father should go into business for himself. His excuse is that he didn't want to do that to Bill, who had given him his first job after trade school. Truth is, my father and I are a lot alike. Translation: he doesn't need much to be happy, and he has everything he needs in my mother and me. As he constantly tells us.

"How you doin' with money?"

"Fine, Dad, really," I answer quickly.

It's a total lie of course. At this point, though, I'd rather turn tricks than take another one of their hard-earned pennies. My parents are working class folks, scrupulously disciplined savers, as 'old school' as it gets. They're even suspicious of credit cards. It took my mother years before she finally caved and started using an ATM. And I still see her hit the cancel button like ten times before she walks away because she's convinced that somehow the next person can get into her account without a card.

With the way the economy has been going in the last ten years, their income can no longer cover their expenses. Lately, they've had to dip into their retirement fund. A retirement fund that has been decimated thanks to all the legal fees I incurred proving that I had nothing to do with Matt's business.

The fancy float in this shit parade is that Matt never suggested my parents invest with him, not once, leaving their retirement fund intact when so many others had suffered terrible losses. Did he do it on purpose knowing I needed that money to prove my innocence? I'll never know. In the end, everybody lost. That's why I can't ask them to loan me any more money. The situation has officially become dire. Just then, by some miracle, my cell phone rings. The name of the agency I signed with a month ago flashes on the screen. It's the first time they've ever called.

"Hello," I answer enthusiastically.

"Ms. DeSantis?"

Yup, I've learned the hard way that it's best to use my maiden name. The name Blake seems to inspire looks of total disgust once the person interviewing me places where they've heard it. Of course, they all assume I was an accomplice at worst. Or, at the very least, fully aware of what my husband was up to. Never mind I was cleared by two government agencies. I don't even want to entertain the notion of what would've happened if I didn't have the money for a decent lawyer.

"Yes?"

"We need you to come in tomorrow. A job listing has come up that you qualify for."

Saved by the bell.

\* \* \*

"The position requires you to live on the property."

Sitting across the lady from the employment agency, Mrs. Marsh, I wait patiently for her to continue. She takes the pen from behind her ear, pokes it through her teased up, gray bob, and scratches an itch on the side of her head. My eyes follow the dandruff that sprinkles down onto the shoulder of her black blazer.

"Is that going to be a problem? It pays extremely well—don't think about it too long."

I stare at her blankly, waiting for the bomb to drop, any bomb. This employment opportunity seems too good to be true, and after what my handsome and loving husband has done, I'm a born-again skeptic. Everything seems too good to be true.

"Where's the property?"

Truth: I have $48.77 sitting in my checking account. If the property is in the Sudan, I'll be on the first flight out.

"Alpine, New Jersey."

"Alpine is only a ten minute drive from where I'm currently living."

"If you can't reside on the property, they won't even consider you. And quite frankly, Ms. DeSantis, we haven't been able to find any employer that's willing to overlook the trouble that your notoriety will bring. Nobody wants the headache." She finishes with a shrug, her expression tight in a manner that makes her look constipated.

"I don't understand why they're willing to consider me then?"

"The job is listed under child care and education. You're the only one on my roster qualified."

This is the lucky break I desperately need. Children are my passion.

"They know who I am—right?" The first job in months with any real promise and I'm trying to talk her out of it. Someone needs to punch me in the face. Mrs. Marsh raises an over-plucked, penciled-in eyebrow.

"Not yet," she says, guilt drawn into the firm purse of her thin lips. And the burgeoning hope I was nurturing only a minute ago withers away in an instant. "They'll find out eventually. When they run a credit check. I'm hoping by then you'll have made a good impression. Besides, beggars can't be choosers." The last few words she mutters under her breath, though I catch them all the same.

"Meaning?"

She sighs heavily before answering. "I hear through the grapevine they haven't been able to keep anyone for very long.

I won't sugar coat this for you, the client is a *difficult* man to work for. Thus, the salary."

*Ah yes, here it comes.*

"You have to sign a nondisclosure agreement, abide by a tight set of rules, and take a full physical exam."

"Why?" I ask with what I am sure is a horrified look on my face.

"Make sure you're not carrying any contagious diseases."

"I guess that explains the difficult part." By nature, I'm an extremely easygoing person; my anger threshold is incredibly high. And I tend to be non-confrontational. Which means I will apologize to diffuse a situation whether I'm at fault or not. Don't get me wrong, I'm no pushover. But my desire for peace always upstages my desire to win any silly argument. The thing is, events over the last three years have tested the integrity of my patience and left it significantly weakened. If this guy is into public displays of humiliation, this is not going to work.

"Do you want to interview, or not?"

My thoughts shoot straight to the gentlemen's club. An image of hairy, sweaty men with toothpicks hanging out of their mouths staring at my ass and calling me 'doll' crops up.

"What's the address?"

# CHAPTER TWO

IN A STRANGE TWIST OF fate, the town I grew up in, the town where my parents still live, is only three towns over from the address the employment agency gave me. Economically, though, they couldn't be any farther apart. Where as my little town is staunchly working to middle class, Alpine consistently ranks in the top two most expensive zip codes in America. Once upon a time, names like Frick called Alpine home. Now names like Combs, as in Sean, Cece Sabathia, and Chris Rock rub elbows with some of Wall Street's highest earners.

    I drive my mother's twenty-year-old Camry slowly as I search in vain for a house number that matches the one on the piece of paper I'm holding. Alpine is not your typical wealthy enclave. Nobody that lives here advertises their wealth; they're notoriously private. Sprawling mansions hide behind high walls and heavily wooded landscapes. If you drove through it accidentally, you would assume it's just another country town.

    I finally locate the correct number on a plain wooden gate and drive up to the black security box, press the intercom, and announce myself. The gate doors peel back slowly, revealing the landscape of the estate. Yes, it's a bonafide estate. The winding gravel driveway extends past the woods and rough winter lawn, all the way to a large white farmhouse with a glossy black door and matching shutters. Unexpectedly, my throat pinches as I note that this house resembles mine. The style that is, not the size. This house could swallow three of mine. Or what had once been mine and is currently property of the U.S. government.

I check my face in the rear view mirror. As usual, I've harnessed my pin straight, dark hair in a bun. Also, as usual, small pieces have started falling out. The only makeup I'm wearing is mascara. My complexion is medium, tanning easily, the same shade as my father's, and I have a smattering of very distinct freckles over the bridge of my nose. Coupled with my full lips, makeup tends to make me look like a Broadway performer or a drag queen, so I generally avoid everything except mascara and lip-gloss. Let me be clear, every woman that grows up in New Jersey does *not* look like the *Housewives of New Jersey*. Personally, I prefer season tickets to diamonds, sunscreen to makeup, and flats to platform heels. But that's just me.

After straightening my gray Theory blazer and brushing a piece of lint off my slacks, I ring the bell and send up a Hail Mary. I'm not a religious person, by any means, however, at this point I'm ready to try anything other than sacrificing live animals to secure a paycheck. The door eases open, and my mind draws a complete and total blank.

*Someone get the paddles—I think my heart just stopped.*

Josh Duhamel apparently has a doppelgänger because I'm staring right at him. This dude may actually be better looking. He's uterus-clenching handsome. His are the kind of looks that turned Neanderthals into homo sapiens with perfect DNA. Long lashed, almond shaped brown eyes compliment a bone structure so symmetrical it inspires poetry.

"Ms. DeSantis?" He smiles warmly and extends a hand. For whatever reason, he seems very excited to see me. I stand there unresponsive, silently staring at him for far too long. His

# WRECKING BALL

brow quirks in confusion.

"Ah...yes." It comes out sounding like a question.

*Wow, promising start.*

Shaking my head at my faux pas, I reach for his hand. It's surprisingly rough and calloused.

"Excellent, come on in," he says, stepping aside for me to enter.

I follow him through the house. It's completely empty, no furniture. We finally end up in a large living room, which is also empty except for an insane television/entertainment system that takes up an entire wall and two armchairs that look new.

"Have a seat please," says Mr. Perfect DNA. He takes the chair opposite me and sits with his legs spread apart, an open file on his lap, eyes downcast on said file.

*Did he tell me his name and I didn't hear him?* I flip through my mental log and find...nothing. "I'm sorry, I didn't get your name?" I ask sheepishly. *I'm really killin' it so far.*

"Once you sign this NDA, I can answer any and all questions you may have," he says with a casual smile. Weird and cryptic, though I don't have the luxury to debate this. After scanning the paper lightly, I sign my name.

"Ethan Vaughn. As his lawyer and manager, I conduct all preliminary interviews for Mr. Shaw."

"So I won't be working for you?"

"No," he says, smiling when he notices me sigh in relief. Even if I have sworn off men for eternity, this guy would have me running into walls all day long.

"You'll have to excuse my ignorance, the only information I was given is that this position requires me to live on the property and involves childcare."

His mouth purses. Choosing his words carefully, he says, "Mr. Shaw is in need of a teacher and caretaker for his eight year old nephew." I hold my breath as he speaks, excitement without a doubt sparking a slightly maniacal glint in my eyes. "You've taught third grade for three years, I see." There's a strange inflection in his voice. With his eyes glued to my resume, however, it's impossible to get a better read on him.

"Yes."

"Sam will have a say in whom we hire, although Mr. Shaw makes the finally decision." Mr. Perfect's expression is suddenly tense. "Are you a sports fan, Ms. DeSantis?"

Sports fan? That's putting it mildly. I played softball up until my senior year at Boston College. Until my shoulder couldn't take it any longer and it was either live with chronic pain, or quit. If there are balls involved, I'm a fan…get your mind out of the gutter, you know what I mean.

"Uh, yeah…why?"

Looking disappointed, he sighs heavily. *Shit, wrong answer.* "Because when I say Mr. Shaw, I mean Calvin Shaw."

I grow very still as I process why that name sounds…*holy hot bawls*. The starting quarterback of the NY Titans.

"Is this going to be a problem?" he asked warily.

"No," I reply with a little more kick in my voice. Because it won't.

I have zero interest in celebrity. It starts and ends with the fact that I've had my fair share of unwanted fame lately. This is a simple case of survival. I need to get paid. If the celebrity in question were Jesus, I would wash his schmata and polish his sandals regardless of how many Facebook or Twitter followers the man has. I need this job more than I give a single shit who pays my salary. As long as he isn't a white supremacist, pedophile, who likes to kick puppies in the head for fun, and has ties to ISIS, I am good to go. Besides, I'm a loyal fan of the other New York team.

Across the open living room, over Perfect's shoulder, I

notice a large man with a towel hanging around his neck walking down the hallway. When I say large, I mean easily six four and all of it muscle. I know this because his sweat soaked, white t-shirt is painted to his torso, highlighting every swell and curve. His hair is dark, nearly black, and long. Much longer than it is in the publicity shots and billboards around the city. And it's pulled back in one of those ridiculous man buns that no man has any business wearing. It also looks like he hasn't shaved in over a century.

*Auditioning for Duck Dynasty?* I mean...I know it's the offseason but God almighty—for the sake of hygiene alone.

He wipes his brow with the towel, and when he opens his eyes, he's staring directly at me. Even from across the room, they're the iciest gray eyes I've ever seen, cold and unforgiving. A strange feeling sweeps through me. As if I just stuck my finger in an electric socket. The experience is not a pleasant one. I scowl. Then he scowls. Then he turns away. *Ugh, this is not good.* I'm feeling the heebeegeebees and slightly bummed at this inauspicious start.

A little at a time, I recall bits and pieces of news I picked up over the years. Shaw has a reputation for being closed off. He went from number one media darling when he was drafted, to Mr. Guarded in recent years. He's been known to flip off hecklers and refuse autographs. Not a good look in the largest media market in the country. If he hadn't won a Super Bowl for the Titans already and so beloved by the fan base, he would've definitely been run out of town by the ruthless New York media machine.

"Okay, the details. This job has an expiration date lasting ninety days." Perfect's voice brings a sudden halt to my musings. I can feel all the giddy excitement I was drunk on only a while ago bleed out of me. "For your services, you will be compensated a hundred thousand, provided all goes smoothly."

"Did you just say one hundred thousand? For three months of childcare?"

"Yes," he says with a completely straight face. And the maniacal spark is back in my eyes.

"With a stipulation, however. There will be three payments made. One at the end of each month—assuming you last. I mean, you remain in Mr. Shaw's employ."

*Oh right, he's difficult.* For a hundred thousand, I could deal with it. Just as long as he didn't marry me…and lie to me…and run a Ponzi scheme under my nose for five years.

"Agreed. When do I meet Sam?"

"Right now," he informs me, rising from his chair.

Perfect leads me to a large upstairs bedroom with a playroom attached. A little boy with floppy, sandy brown hair is kneeling in front of an enormous Lego train set he's meticulously assembling. When I walk over to him and sit down on the floor cross-legged, he glances up with large gray eyes that look somewhat familiar, before timidly returning his gaze to the messy pile of Lego pieces in between us.

"Did you do this all by yourself?"

Once again, he glances briefly at me. Then he shrugs and nods.

"Cool." For the next twenty minutes, we don't say another word. I search for pieces on the instruction manual and hand them to him while he assembles.

"All that's left now is for you to meet Cal—I mean, Mr. Shaw," says the hot guy that will thankfully not be my employer. "Have a seat and I'll see if he's available," he adds once we're back downstairs.

I sit there patiently for ten full minutes staring at the bare, ivory walls. Toes tapping, I clench my knees together and fight the urge to visit the bathroom as long as I can. Five minutes

## WRECKING BALL

later, I finally cave and go in search of one. As I'm rounding a corner, I hear masculine voices. Sounds like an argument.

"No." The voice is deep and smooth. It's the sexiest voice I've ever heard and I don't throw that word around casually. The kind of voice that spawned phone sex because this guy could get someone off by simply reciting the alphabet.

"What do you mean, no? Did a barbell fall on your head? We talked about this."

"I mean *no*, find someone else."

"Be reasonable for one fucking minute, Cal. She's more than qualified, willing to work a temporary job, and I'm pretty sure Sam likes her."

"Did Sam say something?" His voice is instantly softer, concerned.

"No, he didn't have to. I saw it myself—he took to her."

"Get her out of my house."

Whoa…difficult? This guy is far from difficult. He's a total, unmitigated jerk. The first doubts about how long I can last begin to creep in. *How many others have there been before me?*

"Listen, the last seven perfectly qualified candidates have quit within a week. We're out of options," Mr. Perfect asserts. Great. The odds are not in my favor.

"E—get that fucking cow out of my house *now*."

In my mind, each word is spelled out separately and slowly, followed by a high pitch ringing in my ear.

*Get. That. Fucking. Cow. Out. Of. My. House. Bzzzzzzz.*

The son of a bitch didn't even bother to whisper. He might as well have thrown a matchstick on an ocean of gasoline. All the resentment that has been festering beneath the surface for the past three years ignites in a blaze of glory. I don't even take the time to think, I just react. Hundred thousand be damned. With my purse firmly tucked under my arm and my chin lifted, I make my way to the front door. As I pass the kitchen, I step into the doorway and wait.

They both turn to look at me. My face is a mask of stone cold indifference, the one I perfected during countless interviews with the FBI and SEC. Perfect's face drops, suddenly stricken with embarrassment when he reads my expression. Shaw doesn't flinch. He continues to glare with those icy, lifeless eyes of his. There are a million things I want to say, the vitriol sourly coating my tongue, however, in the end I just walk out. No way am I allowing this irredeemable prick to see how upset I am, to take the last shred of dignity I possess. He doesn't even warrant the effort it takes for me to be angry. But I am, unimaginable so. He and his unhygienic beard can go to hell.

# CHAPTER THREE

"BELVEDERE ON THE ROCKS, RUM and Coke, top shelf, and two Heinekens," I shout over the din of the crowd and the mellow hum of hip-hop music playing in the background. Amber jumps into action immediately. Amber Jones, all around badass and my best friend since the fifth grade when Jimmy Murphy pegged me in the face during a game of dodgeball. While I stood there crying like a little bitch, Amber Isabelle Jones, half my height and weight, tightened her side pony, sauntered up to him without a word, and punched him in the nuts. After that, we were inseparable—my sister from another mister.

She's the hot flash and I'm the slow burn. When I need someone to kick my ass into gear, she's the fire in my belly. And when she needs to be talked off a ledge or to be stopped from committing a felony, I'm her voice of reason. We suit each other perfectly. When I told her what had happened with Shaw, she was on her way to my house with a dozen rotten eggs before I'd even finished telling her the story. Amber has the brass balls to do all the things I just fantasize about. God, I love her. She's an actress. With limited success so far. But with her beauty, brains and talent, it's just a matter of time and perseverance before she makes it big. In the meantime, she works as a bartender at one of the most exclusive bars slash lounges in the city. On any given night, One Maple Street is filled with a who's who of celebrity entertainers and star athletes. After some finagling, and a lot of heavy flirting with the new manager, she scored me a couple of shifts as a cocktail waitress, thank heavens, abating my monetary worries—for now.

In the two weeks since cowgate, I've received a number of emails from Mr. Perfect. After apologizing extensively on his behalf, which I believed, and on Shaw's behalf, which I didn't, he offered me the job. I accepted his apology, harboring no ill will against him; I heard it for myself how hard he'd lobbied for me. However, I've officially reached my limit. My fragile pride can't survive one more beat down. I know this for a fact. So I didn't need to think twice about it when I respectfully turned down his offer. Then I cried a day and a half for the loss of the hundred grand.

I know what you're thinking, that I'm in no position to turn down an offer like that. Not unless I'm required to commit a crime or bend over, both of which I'm not yet desperate enough to do. However, when you've had every piece of your life dissected, trampled on, or taken away from you, you cling to the meager remains as if it's a matter of life or death. As if giving up what little is left of your dignity, you may in fact cease to exist altogether. At least, that's what it feels like to me. Bottom line, claiming my power to say 'no' felt dang good, and I haven't had a heck of a lot to feel good about lately.

*Cow. Ugh.*

Truth: every time my head hits the pillow at night that word rattles around my head like loose change…and every morning since that day, I've awoken in a craptastic mood. No, I'm not a delicate snowflake. Standing a robust 5'9", however, does not make me a *cow*. Granted, I'm less fit than when I was

# WRECKING BALL

playing softball in school, but I still work out regularly. I'm curvy, always have been. Tits and ass that I used to be ashamed of until I hit high school and realized boys seemed to like it. More importantly, Matthew Edward Blake, most popular senior of Norwood High School, loved it. And that's all that ever really mattered to me. Do I sometimes struggle with my self-image? Of course, I do. Especially when I'm shopping for jeans—show me a woman who doesn't. But a cow? Mmmmno.

Amber loads my tray with the drinks I ordered. Glancing beyond my shoulder, her hazel eyes narrow when she says, "Someone just sat down on table twelve. Please inform *The Mountain* that the table he's occupying is reserved."

Turning, I spot the large man sitting in the VIP section. The tables in that area are always reserved for people who go by acronyms. This dude does not look like JLo. From what I can tell through the heavy Thursday night crowd, he's alone and dressed inappropriately for this place. He's wearing a rumpled white button down and a weathered ball cap with the curved rim riding low over his eyes. My eyes slide down to the Duck Dynasty beard and an electric current zaps my spine, the feeling an unpleasant one.

*Jesus, Mary and Joseph…*

"Earth to Camilla…Cam?" Amber snaps her fingers annoyingly close to my face. I glare at her and she points to the tray. The bar is packed, three rows deep, and she's right, she doesn't have time for this crap.

With dread snaking up my throat and my heart staging a near riot inside my chest cavity, I slink toward the table to deliver the drink order with my eyes trained on Duck Dynasty. He looks completely out of place and painfully uncomfortable about it. I can't get over the shock of seeing him here and what a strange coincidence this is. Then again, this is my life, a perfect shit storm. For whatever reason, I keep getting more than my fair share. I place the drinks before the group of early twenties Manhattan professionals as slowly as I possibly can without looking like a completely incompetent moron. Across the room at table twelve, Sarah, one of the other cocktail waitresses, taps him on the shoulder and says something to him. As I breathe a sigh of relief, he shakes his head at her. Then Sarah's head pops up and I watch her scan the crowd… until her eyes land on me. She waves me over.

*Damn it. Who did I murder in a past life to deserve this?*

Plastering a mask of cool indifference on my face that I'm not feeling, I wipe my now sweaty hands on my black jeans and walk slowly to table twelve. When Sarah sees the expression I'm wearing, her casual smile melts right off of her face. I treat her to a death glare, and she returns an awkward shrug. Then she pivots on her heels and scurries away. *Frigging traitor.*

He doesn't look at me, the rim of the cap hiding his eyes, and I don't say a word. It's like showdown at high noon, time suspended by silence and a palpable tension. His massive shoulders are hunched, his elbows rest on his well-worn jeans, and his large hands are clasped in a single fist.

"This table is reserved," I inform him, finally deciding to cut to the chase.

"For Titans players," he counters without missing a beat. I feel my full lips thin in blatant annoyance. *Gawd, I so strongly dislike this dude.* He finally tips his head up and deigns to look at me. His cold, gray eyes scan my face for an amount of time that I deem inappropriate. And then they descend down the length of my cowish body.

*Fucking cow…get that fucking cow out of my blah blah blah.*

My ears are suddenly on fire as those words play on a loop in my head. "What can I get you?" My eyes move off in a

# WRECKING BALL

totally bored expression. I get nothing in return, not a frigging word. "Hello? This *cow* has things to do," I say, jabbing a thumb at myself. "What. Can. I. Get. You?"

His eyes snap up to mine. He looks…startled? Okay, weird. Slowly, he stands, my eyes following his face until it's looming over me. I have no idea what the heck to expect when his expression—that is what I can make of it from under the cap and beard—changes from indifferent to painfully uncomfortable. He stuffs his hands in the front pockets of his jeans and shrugs up his big shoulders.

"You," he mumbles.

"What?" I practically shout. Clearly, I haven't heard him correctly.

"I came for you."

\* \* \*

"He's back," Sarah says, nodding in the direction of the man sitting at table twelve. White button down and ball cap, again. I roll my eyes in exasperation. I'm really not in the mood for this. The Friday night crowd is always louder and more demanding than Thursday's, so I've been running around for the past two hours. My feet are aching and my voice is hoarse from shouting over the racket. I decide to nip this in the bud immediately. Clearly, I wasn't sufficiently rude last night because he didn't get the message that nothing would ever entice me to work for a crude, entitled bastard such as himself.

This is how that melodrama played out.

Him: 'I'm offering you the job.'

Me: 'Thanks, but no thanks.'

Him: 'No? What do you mean *no*?'

Me: 'No as in denial, refusal, an explicit rejection. If you've never heard the word before, let me be the one to introduce you.'

Him: Looking over my head to a point in the distance. 'I shouldn't have said what I said.'

Me: Confused look on my face. 'I couldn't care less what you do, or don't say.'

Him: 'Shouldn't have said it.' Finally looks me in the eye.

Me: Yup, no remorse in that cold, lifeless stare. 'I don't give a single crap. Are you ordering something to drink, or are you going to continue wasting my time?'

Him: Silence. Then, a scowl that should've killed me, followed by more silence. Spins around and stalks out of the bar.

Me: Self-satisfied smirk.

Marching over, I plant a hand on my hip and glare. "I don't work here for sport or hobby. You're taking up a table that could be earning me money. Now, what can I get you? Because if you're not here to drink, I can go speak to the manager." I watch the refined nostrils of his straight nose flare. I can tell he wants to let me have it, but he choses to stare me down instead.

"Bring me a bottle of champagne," he mutters.

I hold out my hand for a credit card and he fishes a black Amex out of the wallet he's removed from his back pocket. I stalk back to the bar and wait as Amber pours five shots of tequila for some Wall Street hotshots that are leering at her reed thin body and shouting indecent proposals. She verbally spars back and forth with them, and the more insulting she gets, the more the morons are lapping it up. Go figure.

"How about you let me show you a good time, sweetheart?" says moron number one.

"A two pump hump in the men's bathroom is no one's definition of a good time, Slick, except your mother's. That certainly explains your fondness for it," is Amber's quick reply. Morons number two through four double over in hysterics. Ignoring the suits, she turns to me and tilts up her chin.

"He's here."

"Do I need to handle this?" Amber regularly forgets that she's 5'5" and a buck nothing.

"What's your most expensive bottle of champagne?" I ask.

"The Krug—4 grand."

I'm loving the devious look in her hazel eyes. "Let's do it."

"Coming right up," she says smirking. I don't feel even the least bit guilty.

I drag the bucket with the Krug on ice back to table twelve and place it on the table. He's blasting me with that chilly stare of his. I can practically feel the frostbite forming on the side of my face. Then, before I can retract it, he gently grips my wrist. A ripple of awareness climbs up my arm and fills my stomach with icky sludge.

"Sam likes you." It takes me a minute to realize he's speaking about his nephew.

"I liked him, too," is all I say because it's the truth. Then—nothing. Those crystalline eyes search mine for something. What for? I haven't got a clue. But the intensity of his examination makes me lean away.

Just then three, very tall men walk up to the table and stare at Shaw as if they've just witnessed a Kardashian receive a Nobel prize in Physics. I tug on my wrist and he lets go.

"The fuck?" says one. "Dude," says the other. And "No way," says the third. Shaw tenses visibly. I get the impression that it's rare for them to see Shaw at this sort of establishment. Tall, slim black dude starts laughing and says, "Who's your stylist, man? The grand wizard of the Klan?"

I do a quick up and down of slim, black dude. He's wearing a royal blue suit of expensive wool gabardine perfectly tailored to the swells of his body. Accenting his impeccable suit is a colorful bowtie that would look foolish on anyone else, though on him looks amazing. He's easily the best dressed guy in the room and that's saying a lot in this crowd. In addition, his build, skin color, and wide bright smile also make him devastatingly handsome.

"Shut up, Brandon," says a sulky Shaw. *Brandon?* The name jars something in my memory loose. *Brandon Meriwether, all-pro cornerback.*

Three hundred pounds plus white dude sits next to Shaw and the whole couch sinks under him. He grabs the bottle of Krug and his rust colored eyebrows crawl up his forehead. "Shaw-shank, you sure got expensive taste for a cracker from Jacksonville." Without waiting for permission, he pours himself a glass.

Shaw's eyes shoot to mine, glinting with something... dangerous, while I manage to keep a totally impassive expression. "Expensive, you say? How expensive, Pop?" His icy glare remains trained on me. *James Popovitch, nose tackle.*

Popovitch scratches his red, stubbled chin pensively and says, "'Bout four grand." Then he raises the champagne glass and drains it. I can't keep the corners of my mouth from lifting just a little bit.

"Not like you can't afford it," says the third Titans player. I recognize him immediately as Grant Hendricks, star linebacker on the team and one of the most beloved players in Titans history. He runs an extra large bear paw, I mean hand through his floppy golden hair. His brand of handsome is of the Iowa corn-fed variety. His shrewd gaze moves between me and Shaw, assessing the situation. I catch a cynical smirk that belies his squeaky clean persona. Tugging up his gray slacks, he sits on the couch with his legs spread apart, opposite the other men. "You hanging around 'til the other guys get here?" Hendricks asks Shaw. Shaw shakes his head and Hendricks

## WRECKING BALL

answers with, "Didn't think so."

I suddenly notice that I've been standing silently for far too long and find my voice. "Gentlemen, can I get you anything else, or should I close out the bill?"

In unison, they all answer something different. Shaw scowls at them and tells me to close out the bill.

"Be right back."

Standing, Shaw says, "I'll come with you."

"Not necessary," I answer as I turn and walk away. When I briefly glance over my shoulder, I see he's following me. No surprise there. Is it all the blows to the head he's sustained or hearing loss, I wonder?

At the bar, as I'm waiting for one of the bartenders to charge his card, I watch Shaw part the crowd three rows deep like he's Moses. He walks up to me and stands way too close, close enough that I know he's doing it on purpose. Then he places his large, tan hand next to my elbow on the bar, a mere breath away from touching me. Like I said, I'm not a small woman by any means, and yet at the moment I feel dwarfed and crowded. If he steps one inch closer, I may have to "accidentally" kick his shins. His intense gaze bears down on me from his lofty height. While I look everywhere but up, my heart starts to pump heavily for reasons which I can't figure out.

"What's it going to take?" he murmurs in that insanely smooth baritone. It's another perfect example of the heinous injustice of life that this guy has such an amazing voice. His pushiness raises my hackles. I've felt so powerless over the last couple of years, robbed of the ability to make choices about the trajectory of my life, that his attitude launches me from irritation into rage. It doesn't take much for the devil in me to make an appearance.

"Something you don't possess—a time machine," I say

27

and hand him the bill one of the male bartenders has dropped off. He opens the folder, signs his name with a flourish, and hands it back to me. Without another word, he turns and disappears into the crowd. A momentary pang of guilt hits me that I may have hurt his feelings. It doesn't take much for me to shake it off, however. All I have to do is remind myself what a self-centered jerk this guy is. Absently, I open the folder with the signed slip and my eyes bug out. He left a two thousand dollar tip on a four thousand dollar bill—and he never even touched the champagne.

* * *

The rest of the week flies by uneventfully. I don't give Shaw more than a cursory thought. I have more pressing issues to consider. If I don't get another job soon or pick up more shifts, I'll be broke once again after I pay my medical insurance. This feeling of hanging on the edge of a cliff by my fingernails, I realize, will become a constant unwanted companion for the foreseeable future and the urge to become an alcoholic grows stronger. Too bad I can't handle my liquor. I usually get a migraine before even the slightest buzz takes hold. *Once again, shortchanged by life.* An image of the hundred grand flashes through my mind and I decide to go for a run. I need to clear my head before I start smashing things I don't have the money to replace.

The lifeless, taupe gray landscape matches my mood. I run to the point of exhaustion to block out the million emotions I'm not ready to deal with. Entering through the back door, I'm shrugging out of my Patagonia jacket when I hear my mother's shrilly laughter emanating from the dining room. Angelina DeSantis, a woman who has been happily married for forty years, positively melts around attractive men so I know there's one in the house by the tone of her voice. I walk into the room to find her having coffee with none other than Ethan Vaughn. *Wow. She broke out the linen napkins and good cookies.*

"Cami, Mr. Vaughn has been waiting for you for twenty minutes," she scolds, as if somehow I'm the one that forgot the appointment. Mr. Perfect hands me a friendly smile. Then, turning the power of those hypnotic brown eyes on my mother, he says, "Has it been twenty minutes? I've been enjoying our conversation so much I must've lost track of time."

I throw up a little in my mouth while my mother titters like a teenage girl. "I'll walk you out, Mr. Vaughn," I announce, my voice clipped, and get both their blank stares.

"Camilla Ava Maria DeSantis—" she says in a hushed voice. And I'm instantly five again. "That is not how I raised you to treat guests."

"He's not a guest, Mother, he's a lawyer."

She plants a hand on her chest like I've just mortally wounded her. "Did you know that Mr. Vaughn went to Harvard?" Her dark blue eyes bore into mine.

And it all comes back to me. Her little quirk. I've been part of a couple for so long I forgot all about it...my mother's obsession to land me a husband with a Harvard degree. My mind follows that line of thought to its logical end and immediately grasps onto the fact that I am no longer part of a couple. Instantly, a cold sweat sweeps over my skin and I'm laboring to breathe. *Oh my God, am I having a panic attack*? I try to swallow the fist of pain clogging my throat with no success. *I can't be having a panic attack...can I?* The urge to run out of the room, shrivel up under the covers, and cry is overwhelming. The walls are closing in on me. *Air. I need air.* I know I have to get rid of Mr. Perfect before I start to break down. Thankfully, he sees the look on my face and gets the clue.

"I've already taken up too much of your time, Mrs. DeSantis. Ms. DeSantis, if you could show me out?" Without waiting for him to even finish the sentence, I'm already marching to the front door. Meanwhile, he thanks my mother profusely and promises to come by again for coffee sometime soon.

Outside, the cold air hits me in the chest and the shock settles my nerves a bit. I walk in a circle with my hands planted firmly on my hips, all my attention focused on measuring each breath and not hyperventilating.

"Are you okay?" Vaughn sounds genuinely concerned. I'm *this* close to snapping, 'do I frigging look okay?' but I don't want to incur Angelina's wrath—I'm almost positive the nosy woman is eavesdropping as I speak—and keep those words locked up in my mouth. Motioning him away from the front steps, I make sure she's no longer within earshot to lay into him.

"How the hell did you get my address? If the agency gave it to you, they are f…they are going to be sorry." His friendly demeanor falls away and I'm introduced to Mr. Vaughn the lawyer, his perfect brow knit in determination.

"Ms. DeSantis, I appreciate your reason for refusing our offer, really, I do, but I think there's room to negotiate. If you would only listen to what I'm proposing—"

I hold up a hand. "Stop, stop this instant." I'm mildly amused when he actually does as I ask. "Find someone else."

"Can't do that," he answers, his head shaking vigorously. I keep walking toward his car in the hope that he's following me and gets the hint to leave. If not, I'm more than ready to stuff him inside myself.

"Why not? I can't possibly be the only qualified applicant in an area twenty four million people inhabit."

"Sam likes you…he doesn't take to many people." Turning

swiftly, the look on my face shuts him up real fast. I did like the boy. Silence ensues as I reflect on this fact.

"Why not?"

Vaughn looks off into the distance and exhales heavily. "Remember you signed an NDA," he warns. That earns him a glare. "He's really shut down since he came to stay with Cal, Mr. Shaw, and Cal just doesn't know how to handle it."

My scoff is loud and immediate. "Yeah, well, if his behavior toward me is any indication I can see why."

He looks pointedly at me and says, "Sam really needs someone like you." I want to tell him that he hasn't got a clue who I am but I let it slide. I need him gone, and a lengthy debate with a *Harvard* educated lawyer would be counterproductive to my goal.

"Why ninety days?" I know I shouldn't, that any sign of interest will only open the door to more stalking, however the curiosity is killing me.

"His mother's in rehab again. What do you say, Ms. DeSantis? Will begging do the trick? Because I'm prepared to get on my hands and knees if I have to," he pleads, batting his long eyelashes. This has less than zero effect on me—of the good variety. Overly flirtatious men have always made my ovaries shrivel.

"That nonsense only works on my mother, so stow it if you want me to consider your proposal." A bright grin spreads across his face. "Besides, nothing's changed. Your client is still a jerk and I'm still offended."

All of a sudden, he looks uncomfortable. "Yeah, about that, you see…Cal's had a tough time lately."

"A tough time??" I interrupt, looking at him askance. "He's had a tough time? No, don't say another word. Just get in the car and give me a couple of days to think about it."

I have absolutely no intention of thinking about it, and feel zero guilt for letting him believe otherwise.

"Great!" he says all chipper and gets into his Audi.

"I'm not promising anything."

He reverses out of my driveway, his elbow hanging out of the open driver's side window. "So I'll expect you in a couple of days?" he continues undaunted.

"I said, I'm not promising anything."

"Right. See you soon." He's speeding away before I can argue further.

# CHAPTER FOUR

"Oh, this is a good one," Amber announces cheerfully. She pulls a Law of Attraction book off the shelf and holds it up for my edification.

I was all set to put on my 'no chance in hell I'm getting laid' sweatpants and spend the day in bed feeling sorry for myself...and then I answered the phone. Mistake. Huge mistake. It took Amber all of five minutes to talk me into meeting her in the city for brunch. After drowning my sorrows in a large order of French toast and two mimosas, I'm feeling marginally more optimistic. That's why we decide to hit up the bookstore on our way back to her place. I'm in desperate need of guidance on how to resurrect my life from the ashes it's presently in, and at this point I'm ready to try anything.

I'm busy scanning various titles when Amber hands me a book. I read the title out loud, "How To Reclaim Your Life And Your Orgasm." If only that was my problem.

"I'm not looking for sexy times, dude. Look for a book titled *'Your Husband Was A Crook, Your Life Is In The Shitter, This Is How You Fix It'*."

When I try to hand it back to her, my outstretched hand goes ignored. She pulls another book out by the spine. "I don't have this one. How do I not have this one?"

My part bloodhound/ part Italian nose picks up a scent.

"Ambs, you haven't heard from Parker, have you?" Parker Ulysses Gregory, all around POS. Also her ex-fiancé, but that's not my story to tell.

"Nope," she answers without looking at me.

The orgasm book goes right back on the shelf. "If you have all of these, why don't I just borrow them from you?" At the silence I'm met with, I glance her way.

"Have you officially lost your mind? If you end up losing or forget to return one, it will damage our friendship beyond repair…nope, can't chance it."

"Have I ever told you how weird you are?"

"All the time."

Arms loaded with my new books, we get in line to pay. A middle aged woman with spiky red hair and dark burgundy lips struts by. She comes to a sudden stop and turns to face me.

"I know you." The woman's voice is loud enough that it garners the attention of everyone else waiting in front of us. Anxiety swamps me, a film of cold sweat breaking out over every square inch of my skin. I'm frozen in place while Amber starts inching closer. "You should go to hell for what you did." I rear back as spittle flies out of the woman's mouth. My face is suddenly on fire. She points a painted black nail at me. "Stealing all that money from those poor people—shame on you."

Amber grabs the stack of books from me and plunks them down on a display table. Then she laces her fingers through mine. "Yeah? Why don't you save us a seat when you get there, you decrepit bitch." Then she takes my hand and drags me out of the store, empty handed but with a heavy heart.

\* \* \*

"How do you feel?" A week later and Amber's still wringing

her hands and watching me with concern in her big eyes.

"Victimized—what else is new." We grab our coats out of the employee lockers in the back.

"You want to crash at my place tonight?"

"No. I'm taking the ferry. I have Angelina's Camry."

"How is Ange?"

"Earning an Oscar nod for martyr, I mean mother of the year," I reply with a sly grin. Amber chuckles because I don't need to elaborate. She knows my mother well; she practically grew up in my house.

I don't know when it started, this friction between my mother and me. Maybe it was when my father started spending all his free time following my softball career, maybe it was always there and steadily grew over the years. Regardless, my mother has always had a stealthy, passive aggressive gift for making me feel like I'm at fault for something, like I seem to constantly come up just short of her expectations.

"The bawls on him."

I know exactly what she's referring to. "Yeah, didn't see that coming."

Shaw actually looked remorseful the other night. These days I'll take every single microscopic bit of satisfaction where I can get it. Watching that well developed ass squirm in discomfort was like early Christmas. We walk out the employee entrance and huddle closer, a blast of unusually cold March air chilling us to the bone.

"Aren't you a little tempted?" Her hazel eyes are all over me, patient and kind.

I come from a long line of women that take stoicism to a whole other level. My parents never got to see how bad things really were for me. I tried as best I could to shield them from the worst of it. For them, I kept it together, while my deepest anguish, I reserved for Amber. She's the only one that knows the magnitude of the damage inflicted. She's the only one that knows about the anger and guilt I still carry around.

"Who wouldn't be tempted by a hundred thousand...I could pay back my parents," I say wistfully. "But how long would I have lasted, really?"

"I wish you would've let me have a little chat with him." The devious look on her face makes me chuckle...and gives me pause. Amber knows no reasonable boundaries when it comes to protecting the people she loves.

At the street corner, Amber raises her arm to hail a cab. I'm about to walk in the opposite direction, to the bus stop, when a white Range Rover with black tinted windows pulls up in front of us. After exchanging curious glances, we both fish the pepper spray out of our purses. The black window slides down and my suspicion is confirmed.

"Can I give you a ride?" Shaw's laser focused stare is directed straight at me, which feels like he's digging into my brain with an icepick. I want to glare back. I really, really do. But I can't hold the eye contact. Like the coward I am, I look away first.

"No," I snap, bristling with irritation. "I told your *boyfriend* I need a few days to think about it." With more courage than I'm feeling, my narrow-eyed gaze returns to him. He looks confused. Whatever I just said seems to have gone straight over his head—too many concussions, obviously.

"I'll give you a ride. It's cold."

As if I haven't noticed the snotcicles hanging from my nose. Amber's golden eyebrows nearly reach her hairline.

"Hey fucknugget, the cow said *no*." Amber spits this out while hooking a thumb at me. I have to give him credit, I really do. While my eyes are as big as dinner plates, he doesn't even blink.

## WRECKING BALL

I can see the momentum of where this is headed and it may or may not involve me bailing Amber out of jail, so I grab her arm and pull her closer to the corner. Cupping her face, I fight to keep her eyes on me while she tries to crane her neck in Shaw's direction. "Amb—Ambs look at me. It's fine. You did great. Now get in a cab before this gets ugly."

"I can't leave you at the bus stop with this guy lurking around." She steals another suspicious, furtive glance at him. "I'm getting a murdery vibe from him."

"He's not dangerous, just annoying. I have my pepper spray and phone," I assure her even though I know they won't be necessary. Reluctantly, she nods and turns to glare one more time at the bearded man watching us intently from his car. He rubs his chin and does a little four finger wave at Amber that is sure to set her off. Just then, by some stroke of luck, a cab stops before us. As soon as the last passenger exits, I shove her in.

"Text me when you get home so I know he hasn't cut you up into little pieces and stuffed you in his wall," she shouts for all of Seventh Avenue to hear. I wave as the cab pulls away. Then I take a deep breath and walk over to the open driver's side window of the Range Rover.

He's removed his ball cap and his black hair is back up in that ridiculous bun again. Everything about this guy is a total turn off. I can feel a frown developing on my face as I stare at it.

"What do you want?" I do nothing to hide my exasperation. "It's two a.m. I've been running around all night, and I'm tired."

"I apologized *three* times," he says, his jaw in danger of shattering. *Yeah, real genuine.* Somebody needs to tell this guy he's not the injured party in this scenario.

"Because you want me to work for you. Because you've

already run off every other qualified applicant in the Tristate area, and now I'm your last hope. Well tough noogies, Mr. Shaw. This time you don't win. I win and *you* lose." And I realize I'm beginning to shout. His eyebrows, two black slashes making his eyes look even paler, rise up. Then the most unexpected thing happens. Those cold, unforgiving eyes turn into crescents and a burst of laughter explodes out of him.

"Tough noogies?" His laughter is deep and rich and it bothers the hell out of me, one more slight to my already bruised ego that I refuse to tolerate. My patience has officially run out.

Through clenched teeth, I grind out, "I don't mean to be critical—but you're an insufferable a-hole!" and walk away. I take three steps and feel a huge, warm hand grip my upper arm. In a knee jerk reaction, I wheel around and whisper-hiss, "Don't you dare touch me."

He instantly releases his grip and holds up his hands in surrender. Then he stuffs them in the front pockets of his jeans, and shrugs up his massive shoulders in a posture I've seen him assume when he's uncomfortable.

Despite that it's well past midnight and colder than a witch's tit, the streets of the city are teeming with people. As they walk past us, they curiously turn to watch without breaking stride. It takes a lot more than a mountain of a man, famous or not, and a woman with smoke coming out her ears to get their full attention. One lingers longer than necessary.

"Nothing to see here," I growl. My glare convinces the onlooker to skedaddle.

"I'm sorry," he says. His voice is soft, his tone earnest. My attention immediately returns to him. I almost can't believe my ears. He rubs the back of his neck, his eyes avoiding mine. "I'm really, really sorry—I was havin' a bad day." A light southern twang hangs on the last few words. "I'm in a real bind...my nephew..." His voice trails off. His eyes are back on me, suddenly warm and searching. And for the first time since we've met, I may not hate his guts.

We stand there awkwardly, studying each other for ten agonizing minutes until he looks away. I'm freezing my butt off and I'm wearing a down jacket—all he's wearing is a button down. Biting on the inside of his cheek, he says, "What if I paid you a hundred thousand up front—not in three payments. You can walk away any time you want, after three days or three months, and you still get to keep the money." He doesn't look at me, choosing to stare at the brick wall of the building next to us instead. I watch the warm air he breathes out form clouds around him as I mentally picture giving my parents back half of their retirement fund. My shoulders begin to sag under the weight of defeat, guilt eating away at the entrails of my pride. I don't have the strength to turn him down one more time.

"You can drive me to the ferry on the west side."

His head whips around and his eyes slam into mine, questioning if this is a tacit agreement to his offer—which it basically is. Without a word, I walk slowly to the passenger side of his car. I hear a *thump, thump, thump* right behind me and turn abruptly. Only to have my face almost crash into the wall also known as his chest.

"Jezus," I say half horrified at the thought of touching him in any way, shape, or form. Surprisingly, he remains quiet, never taking his alert gaze off of me. Before I can reach for the handle, he opens the car door. I slide in and buckle up without looking or thanking him because part of me is bitter as all get out that I've lost once again. Not my best moment, I know, but I'm tired and cold and feel like I've just relinquished the last bit of my self-respect. I can't be nice right now...I just can't.

He gets in and starts the car. I don't dare look at him. God forbid I find him gloating, the next phone call I place will be from county jail. The car is warm and quiet, a cozy, luxurious cocoon. And admittedly a much better way to travel than the ferry bus. Now that my nose has thawed, a subtle masculine scent hits me all at once. It reminds me of my husband.

My memories of Matt are complicated by the push and pull of conflicting emotions. How much I miss him, how mad I am at him, the guilt I still carry, the overwhelming amount of shame. Suddenly, I'm on the verge of tears and bite the inside of my cheek hard enough to break skin. Adding to my discomfort, he drives slowly down the West Side Highway. On purpose, I wonder? I certainly don't put it past him.

"Sam likes you," he blurts out. This is all he keeps repeating. But I get it. Sam seems to be the only thing we agree on—a safe topic.

"And I like him, which is the only reason I'm considering doing this."

His bunned head turns toward me. "Then you'll do it?"

No point in arguing further. "Against my better judgment, Mr. Shaw, I'll do it."

I notice his massive shoulders sag. He settles deeper into his seat, one big hand rubbing his thigh. "Good."

"With some major stipulations." I turn a little in my seat to watch his reaction. I find him staring straight ahead, his expression in deep freeze...clearly bracing for the worst. "One more insult, one more slightly off color remark and I'm gone." He nods a little too quickly at this. I doubt he can last more than a day, however, I'll let him prove me right. "And I want the full amount in my checking account the day I move in." I expect him to give me grief about it, but get another short nod instead. "And I want to keep my Thursday and Friday night shifts at One Maple."

"No." No explanation, just a hard *no*.

# WRECKING BALL

"Yes. I don't know how long I can last, considering your track record, and I don't want to lose the only dependable job I have. I'm keeping those two shifts." He blows out an exasperated breath. His grip on the steering wheel tightens.

"Fine," he says through gritted teeth. *Wow, that looked painful. He must be seriously desperate to be agreeing to this.*

Pulling up to the ferry terminal, he puts the car in park. I'm ready to jump out and tug on the door handle. It's locked. Tug, tug, tug. Still locked. My eyes slide over to him. He's tense. I would even venture to say a little nervous, though I could be mistaken.

"When can I expect you?" *Is he planning on holding me hostage until I sign in blood?*

"Day after tomorrow." Now that the decision's been made, why delay. I get another one of his brief nods. The sound of the doors unlocking prods me into action. Without a backward glance, I'm out in a flash. As I'm slamming the door shut, I hear a quiet, "Thank you." I'm already walking away when I grasp what he's said. *Whatevs.* I'm too tired and broken down to care.

\* \* \*

"You have to live with him? But he's a bachelor." In confusion, I stare at Angelina across the kitchen table. For a moment, I wonder if she's being serious. And then I remember. It took a full year for my mother to accept that my living with Matt before we were actually married was not a black stain on the family name. I load two more chicken cutlets onto my plate and dig in.

"I think so. I'm not sure...who cares." I look at my dad for help. He doesn't meet my eyes. *Coward.*

"I care," she says.

"Don't worry, my honor is not in jeopardy." I have to

forcibly stop myself from snorting. I have no intention of explaining the animosity between Shaw and me because my mother will somehow spin it as my fault.

"Why do you always have to be so sarcastic?"

"Ma, the house is huge. He probably won't be there much, these guys travel a lot in the offseason. And there's an eight year old boy living there as well." And I intend to stay as far away from him as possible, which shouldn't be too difficult knowing how he feels about me. That, I keep to myself.

"Have you met the boy yet?" My father finally decides to join the conversation. *Welcome to the party, Tom.*

"Yes, he's lovely. Very quiet, shy. His mother's in rehab."

My mother's eyes go butter soft and she tsks. "Poor baby, bring him over for dinner." My mother is convinced that everything can be fixed with food. I can almost hear her thoughts as she considers what she'll cook for him.

Angelina has been hounding me for grandchildren since the day Matt and I got married. We always thought we had time…and now I've suddenly lost my appetite. I push the baked eggplant around my dish. Grief is uniquely tailored for every individual. For me, it lies beneath the noise of everyday life, cropping up at unexpected moments. And I'm not talking a gentle nudge either, more like a blindsiding slap across the face…like right now. It just occurred to me that I may never have children and the pain is more than I can bear. Because falling in love again and getting married is so far from the realm of possibilities for me that I can't imagine any scenario where that could happen.

"Sure," I grumble. "I have a surprise," I say desperate to change the subject. My parents look at me with sheer terror in their eyes. "Relax, it's a good surprise this time." Suspicion hangs around a little longer. "You'll be receiving a check from me this week…for a hundred thousand dollars."

# WRECKING BALL

They don't look happy. You would think a hundred grand would put a smile on their faces.

"What kind of a joke is this?" my mother says.

"It's not a joke. He's paying me a hundred thousand *up front.*"

"To babysit?" she says, her tone riddled with skepticism. I briefly glance at my father and find him as still as a mummy.

"Good grief," I mutter. Leave it to my mother to suck the joy out of this, too. "To take care of Sam and home school him. I'm a teacher, remember?"

"A hundred thousand," my father repeats. I finally recognize the expression on his face...it's *relief.* He's relieved that he'll get his money back. And in that moment, I know I did the right thing accepting Shaw's offer.

"The job is only for three months." They both look confused. "I'm assuming Sam will go back to live with his mom when she gets out. He won't need me after that."

"A hundred grand for three months work?" dad asks. His voice sounds far away, unmitigated bewilderment in his tone.

"Yup." I watch my father take a small sip of his red wine, his face unreadable. "What are you thinking, Dad?"

Without missing a beat, he says, "That I just became a Titans' fan." That's saying a lot. Dad has been a diehard fan of the other NY team all his life.

# CHAPTER FIVE

"Where's the rest of your stuff?"

Mr. Etiquette is standing in the doorway with his hands on his hips, wearing a white t-shirt so completely soaked in sweat I'm surprised he's not leaving a puddle. I look up with displeasure and watch a deep v carve itself into his forehead. Between the black slashes of his eyebrows and his bunned up hair, he reminds me of a Samurai warrior—or the Prince of Darkness.

My gaze does a cursory slide down the length of his body. The pictures really don't do this guy justice. He looks much more imposing in person. Especially this close. When my eyes climb back up to his face, a narrow-eyed, gray glare is bearing down on me. Nothing has changed. As soon as I'm around this guy, my hackles give me jazz hands. He barely steps aside to let me in. His nipple is practically poking me in the eye, a clear sign that he's standing way too close, but does he step out of my personal space? No. I swear everything he does is orchestrated to irritate the shit out of me.

Forced to squeeze past him, I scrape my shoulder blades against the doorjamb in an effort to avoid touching him in any way. For that cordiality, I reward him by sniffing the air for body odor and even though I get only soap and deodorant, I still make a face. Practically on cue, he volleys back his most

## WRECKING BALL

menacing glare—no doubt meant to give me frostbite. All this transpires in the span of ten minutes. If this is any indication, I'm pretty sure I won't be here long.

"That's everything," I say, shrugging. Should I antagonize him? Probably not. However, something about him brings out the worst in me, couple that with the fact that my tolerance for bullshit has been reduced significantly, for men in general but especially for entitled bullies, and you get me behaving badly.

His eyes swing from the suitcases back to me. His brow is wrinkled and his eyes watch me expectantly, like he's waiting for me to elaborate. Which of course I don't. All this guy needs to know is my name, where to wire my money, and that I have a clean record. Finally, he snaps out of it.

"Follow me." Before I can reach for them, he grabs my seemingly weightless suitcases and leads me through the empty house.

"Who's your decorator? Love what she's done with the place." His reply to this is a half-assed grunt. Without pausing, he continues upstairs to a large bedroom. *Wow. I mean...wow.* It's beautifully decorated in neutral tones. The king size bed is swoon-worthy. Add to that the elegant furniture and the large flat screen television on the wall, and I've just moved into the Ritz. This, I can get used to—how long I get to use it is yet to be determined.

"Where's Sam?"

"In the playroom down the hall. Do you want to get settled, or see him now?" After placing my bags down, he walks to the doorway and hovers. I don't fail to notice how uncomfortable he seems. *What a weirdo.*

"I'd like to see him now, please."

As I follow Shaw down the hall, we pass another doorway and he points and says, "My room."

Like I care. The only reason for me to know which one is

his is if he goes missing and a smell of decomposing organic matter drifts out. And even then, I'm not sure I'd care. Before we enter Sam's playroom, I tap him on his gigantic sweaty tricep. *Yuck.*

"Listen, I forgot to mention that I don't have a car." I meet him gaze to gaze. The insufferable ass looks at me like I'm a cockroach scuttling across his kitchen floor. Holding steady, I don't look away—high-fiving myself for that one. Only fifteen minutes have passed and I'm already exhausted.

After an agonized sigh, he says, "You can use one of mine. I'll call the insurance company in the morning."

Inside, Sam is kneeling in front of another intricate Lego creation. I walk over and drop to the floor close to him. Without looking up, he hands me the instruction booklet to the village he's building. Shaw's eyes are all over me. I can feel them burning a hole in my back. Stealing a glance over my shoulder, I find him leaning against the doorframe, arms crossed in front. He doesn't bother to hide the fact that he's staring. *Jerk.* My attention returns to Sam, and for the next hour and a half, we work without speaking.

*  *  *

"Mercedes?"

"Si?"

"I can't find the white bean soup I made yesterday," I say as I rifle through the massive refrigerator. "The potato and string bean salad I prepared last night is also gone. And I can't find the strawberries I bought at Whole Foods."

Mercedes is Shaw's housekeeper/estate manager/keeper of his secrets. She's the only person that lives on the property, and was assigned to watch Sam before I came along. Shaw is OCD level fastidious about keeping the house clean. Really, it's just too large a house for one person, but

## WRECKING BALL

apparently the Prince of Darkness doesn't trust anyone other than his beloved Mercedes. Overworked and exhausted, I can safely say that Mercedes was probably the happiest person in the house to see me move in. Ergo, Mercedes and I bonded instantly. She gives me a puzzled look. My thoughts immediately shoot to Shaw. I swear I'll murder him in his sleep if I find out he's been throwing out my food.

"I'm making bucatini with fresh tomato sauce, would you like some?" Mercedes informs me that she's going to dinner at her daughter's house, and departs shortly afterward.

In the refrigerator, I push aside all the containers of his food. On day two, I found out that he gets his meals prepared and delivered. A plant based diet with a ridiculous list of ingredients that he can't consume because they cause "inflammation" in his hundred million dollar body. No tomatoes, no mushrooms—ever. No eggplant. No peppers. And God forbid you cook with olive oil. Basically, every Italian on the planet is screwed. Including, yours truly. And the list goes on and on. No coffee, no caffeine, not to mention sugar and flour. Fine. Whatevs. I get why he's so cranky all the time now.

Tonight I'm making a fresh tomato sauce with artisanal bucatini for dinner. Super inflammatory. Sitting at the counter, Sam watches me intently for a while. Until I ask him to join me in the kitchen, where he proceeds to help me smash up the ripe vine tomatoes while wearing a big fat smile on his face. In just a few days, he's already started to open up. I'm finally getting a vocal, albeit softly spoken, *yes* and *no* from him, and quite frankly couldn't be happier with the progress we've made.

After the pasta is cooked and drained, I pour the sauce on while Sam sets up the plates and utensils on the island counter since there isn't a kitchen table for us to sit at. I have no idea

47

what the routine was at his mother's house, but I suspect there weren't many family meals.

"Sam, did I mention that my mom makes the best chocolate cake ever?" He looks up bright eyed from the pasta he's busy devouring and says an actual 'no.'

"Would you like to go to my parents' house for dinner sometime?" His enthusiastic nod makes my heart hurt.

Shaw stalks into the kitchen, his expression thunderous. "Who the hell is *Camillia Blake*?" The jerk actually mispronounced my name.

Instantly, Sam's whole demeanor changes. He retreats back into his shell. Which pisses me off beyond measure. Me, I'm no shrinking violet. And I grew up in New Jersey. If men shouting and throwing around macho bravado bothered me, I would've been confined to a padded room ages ago. However, I can only imagine how intimidating this growling, hairy beast must seem from a child's perspective. I throw the shackles off my tongue because the hundred thousand is already sittin' pretty in my bank account and that pleasurable golden nugget is always at the forefront of my mind.

"That'd be *moi*, Calvin." His scowl deepens. "Although, I'd prefer it if you didn't butcher my name. It's pronounced *Camilla*. Or is that too much information for your brain to process at once?"

His eyes go wide. "My office," he snaps, stalking out of the kitchen without waiting for a response.

Sam's big gray eyes flicker to me in worry. I run my fingers through his chestnut hair and smile.

"Eat your supper and we'll read a book as soon as I'm done talking to your uncle." The doubt on Sam's face makes me want to throat punch Shaw into tomorrow.

When I walk into his office, Shaw is standing with his extra large hands planted on his hips. For the first time in my life, I consider what it would feel like to be hit by hands that size, and my stomach does a flippy thing. I immediately play offense.

"You've just undone all the hard work I accomplished in three days." I go for broke and point up at him aggressively. "He shuts down immediately when he senses your anger. Or have you been hit in the head so many times that you haven't even noticed?" My tone sets him back on his heels. He looks unsure how to respond. "I suggest you either see a shrink, do some yoga, or get on medication. In other words, chill the heck out." He's shocked at my fortitude. *Mission accomplished.* I turn to leave.

"We're not done. I ran a credit check," he very calmly states. Turning, I cross my arms under my ample breasts. When his eyes flicker down to my chest, I drop them immediately, chalking this up to an involuntary reflex in all males because, God knows, he couldn't possibly find udders on a cow attractive. His attention goes straight to the paper he's holding.

"It says here that—"

No way am I going to allow him to rummage through the charred ruins of what used to be my life and dance on its ashes.

"It says that I was married. That I'm a widow. It says that everything I've ever owned has been repossessed, or impounded by the U.S. government. It says that I currently own nothing. Except for my dignity. And that, Mr. Shaw, cannot be taken from me without my consent. What it doesn't say is that it took every penny I possessed for me to prove that I had zero knowledge of what my husband was up to when he embezzled millions of dollars. It also doesn't say that I was a very good teacher before I was run out of the Connecticut district where I taught." At his blank stare, I continue. "If you have a problem with anything I just told you, I'll pack my bags. But I like Sam. And I think I can help him, so I would like to stay."

I wait for him to say something. And wait...and wait some more. I start to sweat under his close examination of my person.

"How long?"

"How long, what?"

"How long have you been a widow?"

The question takes me by surprise. Usually, people are interested in how much money my husband embezzled. As if the amount somehow determines how big a scumbag he was.

"Three years."

Nodding, he shoves his hands in the pockets of his sweatpants and shrugs up his big shoulders. His pants get pushed dangerously low. Inadvertently, my eyes gravitate to the flat band of tan skin and trail of dark hair below the hem of his t-shirt, just above the waistband of his pants. *Gawd, he's not wearing underwear.* I force my eyes back up to his face. *Awkward.*

"Do you have any more surprises for me?" he murmurs quietly.

"Nope."

More silence.

"You think Sam's scared of me?" He's inspecting his bare feet as he says this, half sitting on the back of his desk and gripping the edge. Just as quickly, he crosses his arms in front. The cut muscles of his wide chest pop up in stark relief. Even with his t-shirt hanging loosely, I can tell he's ripped.

"He's afraid of your temper." That gets his attention. His eyes meet mine. "I don't know what that boy's life has been like up until now, but I think I can safely assume that if his mom is in rehab, it couldn't have been all rainbows and unicorns. You need to make a conscious effort to control your emotions around him…it would also benefit your blood pressure."

This earns me one of his signature scowls. "Anything else?" he asks gruffly.

"Yeah, it would be nice if you could purchase some furniture." I get a hum of approval. That went better than expected. "Are we done?"

After another nod from him, I head for the exit, my feet carrying me out the door as quickly as possible. I wouldn't want to give him time to come up with more grievances. He's got that look about him, the one that says he's keeping score of every little indiscretion.

Sam is quiet for the remainder of our meal. I've already figured out not to push him with questions when he shuts down, and just allow him to work out of it at his own pace. After I clean up, we go upstairs because, of course, there's no furniture in the family room, and watch television together in his bedroom. A sitcom. And it pays off. It doesn't take long for his little boy giggles to fill the room. Once he's tucked in bed, I pull out my copy of *The Box Car Children*.

"Cam," he says in a quiet voice. Our first day together, I insisted he call me Cam, Ms. DeSantis sounding too formal for our arrangement. I explained that all my friends call me Cam, and since I consider him a friend, it would be okay if he did as well. Besides, he isn't the type of child to be disrespectful, or take advantage.

"Yes." I wait patiently for his solemn gray eyes to meet mine.

"Are you staying?"

"I'm staying as long as you are."

"Promise?"

"Yup," I say and watch a brief smile appear on his face.

The sense of accomplishment I feel at making one little boy smile is ridiculous. Sitting on the bed next to him, I read until he drifts off to sleep.

# CHAPTER SIX

BY THURSDAY, WE'VE SETTLED INTO a pretty comfortable routine. After breakfast, I start the lesson plan and Sam and I work straight through until lunch. After lunch, we explore more creative subjects. Some days art. Other days music. By early afternoon, we both need some fresh air so we head off to the park if the weather is decent. As promised, Shaw lent me a car to drive. That went well...insert eye roll. If he was expecting me to lose my shit over his collection of expensive cars, he would have to wait an eternity. I don't give a single crap about cars. As long as it's running properly, I'm good. Inside his six door garage, he led me past one exotic sports car after another as if we were in an episode of *MTV Cribs*.

"You can drive this," Shaw announced, motioning to a Yukon XL. The look on his face was...dare I say eager. What did he expect me to do? Fall to my knees and kiss his feet for the use of this gas guzzler?

"Don't you have anything smaller?"

At my query, he leveled me with a narrow-eyed look of utter disgust. "Sorry ma'am, all out of compacts this morning." Then he threw me the keys and stalked out. Needless to say, after driving my mother's Camry for the last few months, driving this monster truck has been a trying experience. It's fully decked out, with every upgrade imaginable. So to say I'm nervous that I may get a scratch on it and that I drive around like I got my license yesterday is an understatement.

By five, I have to be on my way to the bus stop if I'm to get to One Maple on time. I go in search of Shaw and my first stop is his gargantuan sized gym. I won't even begin to list all the top of the line gym equipment. I'm not even sure the team facilities are this well equipped. It's empty. *Huh.*

"Hello?"

"In here," that deep, smooth voice answers.

Following the voice to its source, I peek into one of the rooms attached to the gym and...o*oopsy*. Shaw is on his stomach—with like, a *hand towel* draped over the pronounced globes of his behind. He's in the middle of getting a massage from a petite blonde that looks like she weighs about as much as one of his arms. I duck my head out quickly and place my hands on my cheeks. My face feels blowtorched.

"Umm, I'm leaving—just reminding you," I shout, keeping my back to him as I speak.

"Reminding me of what? Where are you going?" Then I hear a muffled, "Ahhh, Natalie take it easy."

"I'm leaving for work. Sam's dinner is on the stove. Just heat it up for him. Do you think you can do that?" Silence. "Hello?"

"How are you getting there?" he says gruffly. And once again, he seems pissed for absolutely no reason.

"Bus. I gotta get going. I should be home around two." As I turn to leave, I suddenly feel a large body right behind me.

"Hold up." His voice sounds awfully close. Turning, I'm met by a wall of lightly tanned skin, and the blast of heat he's throwing off. Instinctively, I freeze. I'm no prude, far from it, but there's no safe place for me to look. Aesthetically speaking, his body is a work of art, sheer perfection. His muscles are thick and defined, the heavy bones of his six foot four stature perfectly proportioned. My eyes fall and are met by the sight of a very large appendage tenting the scrap of towel he's wearing. *Good grief.* And he's not even hard. I almost feel bad for his girlfriend...or girlfriends. Who the heck knows—or cares, for that matter. My gaze snaps up. His expression hasn't changed. And yet, I swear there's a smile in his eyes. My face is on fire—again. You could cook an egg with the heat radiating from my cheeks. I go for neutral and stare ahead, at his chest, the one smattered with fine dark hair, the one that apparently has the power to render me speechless.

"How are you getting there?" *Huh?* I shake off my scientific study of his nonexistent body fat. "Well?"

His voice prompts me to look back up at his face. "Bus."

"I'll drive you."

"What? No, no, *nooo*," I say, fervently shaking my head. "That's not necessary. I gotta get moving, or I'll miss my bus."

His mitts are on his hips now, a deep v etched between his brows. "I have a hundred grand invested in you. I need you in one piece. Go tell Mercedes to watch Sam." Without waiting for a reply, he stalks off. "Meet me in the garage," he throws over his shoulder.

An investment. Right. It was the height of insanity to believe for just a second that this self-centered jerk could possibly be doing something for anyone's benefit other than his own. We've barely said two words to each other since the office incident, and now I have to sit in a car with him for the thirty minute ride over the George Washington Bridge to Manhattan. Problem is, I don't have time for a debate.

Fifteen minutes later, I see him eating up ground as he walks over to the Range Rover I'm standing next to. He's wearing a Titans hoody and sweatpants and...oh dear, it doesn't look like he's wearing underwear again. And now my eyes want to go ahead and double-check to be sure. In the front seat, I force myself to stare at the road. *Eyes ahead, eyes ahead, damn it!* Have you ever tried that? Yeah, it never works. With my eyes roaming everywhere other than to the man on my left, I briefly catch sight of the gate doors closing in the side mirror of the Rover.

"Rotten eggs."

"What?" I say, startled at the intrusion of his voice.

"Someone threw rotten eggs at the gate." I remain quiet for fear that my voice will crack and give me away as the vandal. "Probably a disgruntled fan," he adds casually.

"That sucks." My voice is weirdly high and loud. *Holy hell, did I just say 'sucks'?* I don't dare face him in spite of the fact that I can feel him watching me. My pits start to sweat in an unladylike manner. I need to get some air circulating under there, can't show up for work stinking like a goat.

"Is it hot in here?"

"No. What time does your shift end?"

I hazard a look and find him staring ahead. For the first time, I notice his profile is finely drawn, his nose straight and slender. Who knows what the rest looks like since it's buried under all that facial hair—other than a vague memory I have from pictures.

"One."

Even if it is for his benefit, as he so rudely informed me, I have to give him credit for going through the trouble of driving me. It's a serious inconvenience for him. And honestly, the thought of freezing my butt off waiting for the bus when there's still snow on the ground is far from appealing.

"I'll pick you up."

"No, no, absolutely not." He still doesn't look at me. And he doesn't say anything else for the rest of the ride. The silence in the car is tense. Neither one of us does or says anything to change that until he pulls up to the employee entrance of the club.

"Thanks," I say, feeling awkward. I mean, here's a guy I can barely stand to be around, the feeling clearly mutual, and suddenly he's chauffeuring me to work? Still looking straight ahead, he nods. These small nods seem to be his preferred choice of communication. *Anywho.* I'm out the door and in the club a minute later, an unsettled feeling pecking at me.

\* \* \*

"He did what?" Amber's eyes are huge, swallowing up her delicate features.

"He drove me here." I grab another glass from behind the bar and wipe it down. "Not like it was for my benefit. He's protecting his investment."

"He said that?" Ambers voice is filled with disgust. She moves around quickly and efficiently, setting up the bar for service.

"Yup."

"What a douche. So, did Ange get her panties in a bunch over a gently bred young lady such as yourself living with a confirmed bachelor?" The overly dramatic British accent she uses makes me chuckle.

"She sure did. However, Tom was visibly relieved to get his money back, hence I'll take whatever Angelina is ready to dish out." My curiosity is suddenly piqued. "Is he?"

"Is he what?"

"A confirmed bachelor."

"According to TMZ he is." At my eye roll, she adds, "What? I had time to kill between auditions. Apparently the divorce was nasty."

She has my undivided attention. "And?"

"What happened to the eye roll and the self-righteous look ya just gave me?"

"Amber," I growl.

"No kids, the divorce was contentious, dragged on for two years. Which is no surprise since there was a hundred million at stake. They settled out of a court for an undisclosed amount."

"How long was he married?"

"Eight years." I know he's thirty-three because I remember watching SportsCenter when the analysts were arguing the merits of the Titans offering him another five year contract. Shaw married young—like me.

The rest of the night goes smoothly. I'm so busy I don't spare Shaw another thought. With a number of professional athletes and music industry moguls in the house, the tips steadily pour in. By midnight, most of my tables have closed out their tabs and the crowd is thinning. I'm behind the bar, closing out a number of my checks, when a tall rangy guy approaches the bar in a loose-limbed walk. He's movie star quality handsome—and young. Twenty-three at the most. His thick, brown hair is cut short and disheveled in a way that looks carefully thought out. He smiles at me, and the white grin that stretches across his face produces two dimples. Yeah, I'm not affected at all.

"Hey gorgeous," he says with a southern accent I can't place. And now I'm affected, instantly annoyed. The cringe skates up my backbone. There's nothing I hate more than pet names from strangers. God help him if he calls me sweetie, sweetheart, or anything else in the confectionery family.

"What can I get you?" I'm all business.

"You can help me settle a bet," he says, staring at my boobs. They're hardly on display. I'm wearing a black, stretchy turtleneck with my black jeans; the dress code for everyone at One Maple. But it is tight, outlining my Ds perfectly. I stare back blankly, no amusement on my face to invite him to continue. Though this obtuse pretty boy obviously lacks wits because he barrels ahead. "Puerto Rican, right?" I look around his shoulder and notice his friends looking back at me expectantly.

"No."

"Dimples, you drinking, or is your pretty ass just taking up space at my bar?" Amber shouts from a few feet down the bar. She places two cosmos in front of a group of thirty something, expensively clad women that look like they're celebrating a promotion, dries her hands on a towel, and lifts her chin at him. Everyone turns to stare at Dimples.

I bite my bottom lip, fighting the urge to laugh at his expression. He's clearly taken aback, and has no idea what to make of this sharp tongued, fiery little blond. *Welcome to New York, Dimples.* The group of women snicker as they watch pink creep into Dimples' cheeks.

"Another round," he finally mumbles.

"Great. Why don't you take those sweet, tight buns of yours back to your table, and I'll be right over with your order." His chocolate brown eyes flicker to me and after a slow two-finger salute, he walks away.

One of the thirty something women shouts, "Come back, sweet buns, we'll entertain you," and the rest of them break out in drunken fits of laughter.

For the next hour, we work quickly, cleaning the bar and our stations. I have to admit that keeping busy seems to do the trick. I haven't had a panic attack since the scene at my house, and memories of Matt are easily kept at bay when I'm running around and physically spent. Sidling up to me, Amber asks, "Taking the bus home?"

I nod and she tells me to get going, that she'll finish the rest. Without argument, I get ready to leave since I have to be up by seven to make Sam's breakfast. I see it as soon as I step out the door of the club. White Range Rover, black tinted windows, black hubcaps. The driver side window slides down as I walk up with my hands stuffed in the pockets of my down jacket.

"You ready?" His voice is toneless, his expression bored. It crawls right under my skin.

"How long have you been here?"

"Not long. It's cold, get in." I'm sensing this cold thing is a big deal for him. By the time I'm buckling up, he's already speeding up Sixth Avenue.

"I'm sensing this cold thing is a big deal for you." This displeases him, my idiocy so egregious it doesn't even warrant a reply. Instead, he pins me in place with one of his signature icy glares. "You can't keep doing this. I intend to keep working there, and you can't drive me in every week." Again, I get nothing. The silence rolls on. "Don't you have a life? A girlfriend to take shopping or make a sex tape with or whatever it is you people do—" My words are cut short by a sharp, annoyed exhale.

"Don't you ever shut up?"

Okay, maybe I went a little too far. But his inability to take a 'no thanks' from me is making me nuts. We ride the rest of the way in complete silence. Only a few feet separate us, though we may as well be on different planets. Or more precisely, I wish we were.

# CHAPTER SEVEN

"WHO WOULD WANT TO FUCK a werewolf?" My eyes are glued to the latest episode of *Penny Dreadful*. "Ugh, can you imagine the smell? Hold on, don't go anywhere," I tell Amber, and rearrange my cell phone on the other shoulder so I can dig into my comfort tub of Ben and Jerry's cookie dough ice cream.

"I would, that's who. I would definitely fuck a werewolf if he looked liked Josh Hartnett."

Leaning against the tufted headboard of my king size bed, correction Shaw's guest bed, I give her words careful consideration. "Long hair or short?" Always in sync, we both add, "Long hair."

"I'd fuck a bear too while we're at it—at least one of those shape shifter type bears," she continues after a thoughtful pause.

"What about vampires?"

"Sure, why the hell not. How about you?"

"That's a definite yes. They're beautiful, sensual and ancient. They gotta have some serious moves in bed. Don't you think?" In tandem, we say, "Alexander Skarsgård."

"Did I mention that he has every available channel on the planet? That alone makes up for the verbal abuse."

"Just mickey his water bottle with a few eye drops," the lunatic also known as my best friend suggests.

"Sure, inmate 2267. Not only is that a myth, but you can actually kill someone that way."

"Really? Bummer," Amber adds with a sigh.

My stomach gets a little queasy and I know I've officially crossed the line. There is such a thing as too much B&J ice cream. "Ambs, gotta go, dairy emergency."

After hanging up, I make my way down to the kitchen to put the rest of the ice cream back in the freezer. All I'm wearing is my thin lounge pants and a white tank top with no bra but it's past eleven and Duck Dynasty usually retires to his room around eight thirty. On Friday night, I found him out front waiting for me. He drove me in—we said nothing. He drove me home—we said nothing. I've come to accept that arguing with him is pointless because in the end he always does what he wants anyway.

As I pass by Sam's room, I peek in and find him sleeping soundly. Every time he gets ready for bed, something in his expression tells me that wasn't always the case, that he's had too many sleepless nights for a boy his age, and I can't help but be mad at his mother. Where his father is, is a mystery I have yet to solve.

I continue down the stairs and into the spacious and well laid out kitchen. It's a real chef's kitchen and my favorite part of the house. Ivory custom cabinetry, Calacatta oro marble countertop. There's a massive island in the middle with a sink and cooktop on one side, opposite the gas stove, and seats up to four people on the other. Did I mention how much I love the kitchen?

I'm already well inside, practically standing next to the island, when I notice that the door of the SubZero refrigerator is wide open and one tall man is standing behind it.

My footsteps come to a screeching halt. Very quietly and very, very slowly, I start…retracing…my steps, backing out the same way I entered. I *reeeeally* don't want to be in the same room with him if I can help it. Everything about him makes me uncomfortable. From the pale emotionless stare he usually directs at me, to his gruff demeanor. All of it makes me self-conscious. And quite frankly I haven't gotten over the whole *cow* thing yet. I don't know why it bothers me, why I give a shit what he thinks, but it does. Which aggravates me to no end.

Just a few more steps and I'm safe. All of a sudden, the door closes and I see he's holding the left over pasta primavera I made for dinner.

*Wait a cotton pickin' minute...*

He shovels a fork full of cold pasta, *my* pasta, into his mouth and closes his eyes. The look on his face is positively orgasmic. I don't know what's more fascinating, the fact that the man I've come to know as having only a single emotion, anger, or none at all looks like he's high off of a dish of cold pasta, or that I just caught him cheating on the "anti-inflammation" diet when I've seen him openly turn up his nose at the food I cook as if somebody took a shit and forgot to flush. Then I remember all the food I've been missing—the food I thought he had thrown out because the smell bothered him.

His whole body stiffens with awareness. And all at once it dawns on me that he's only wearing a pair of threadbare, stretched out boxer briefs.

*Dear God, please don't let his junk be hanging out. I'll be good, I promise.*

He turns slowly to face me, blinks twice, and sighs. It's the most defeated, pathetic sigh I've ever heard in my life and I have to curl my lips between my teeth not to burst out in laughter. His eyes flicker down to my braless tank top and my amusement fades, drops right off my face. I can only imagine what he's thinking—*cow*. I'm almost one hundred percent certain he dates women that peel the skin off their grapes and measure their protein intake with a thimble. Needles rake up my neck as I see my body from his judgy perspective. His body, by the way, is frigging perfect—according to anyone's definition.

Watching me intently, he puts the bowl down on the counter. "Go ahead."

*Huh? Did I miss something?* "Excuse me?"

"Your victory dance. You caught me."

I realize then that he's truly embarrassed, and as sweet as revenge sounds right about now, being a jerk doesn't come as naturally to me as it does to him. I will only feel worse afterward.

Moving very quickly, I walk by him and put the ice cream back in the freezer. I don't need to look to know his eyes are glued on me; I can feel them giving me a third degree burn.

"Do you want me to heat that up for you? If you're going to blow your diet, you might as well do it right."

*Jezus Christ, did I just say 'blow'?*

Without a reply, he very tentatively hands me the bowl. His hands are not only large, but the fingers are long and his knuckles even, the nails clean and short. He has beautiful hands. Then I notice he can't straighten his pinky all the way.

I turn the gas burner on low and pull a flat pan out of the cupboard. After dumping the pasta in, I cover it. Braving a look, I find him leaning that spectacular six foot four frame back against the edge of the marble countertop with his fingers curled around the edge. He and modesty are not on friendly terms. He doesn't seem to care a lick that he's basically naked. Those tissue thin boxers are not concealing much from what I can tell in the periphery of my vision.

*I will not look. I will not look. I will not look.* So of course, I look.

"What happened to your finger?"

He holds up the pinky and flexes it. "Broke it—didn't have it set right away and it healed like this." My gaze lifts to his and I'm surprised to find it open and warm, the corner of his lips slightly lifted.

"Is that your throwing hand?"

"Nope," he answers, his head shaking slowly.

"Why didn't you have it set right away?" I check the pasta and turn the heat off, the scent of butter and cream infusing the room. After pouring it into a dish, I turn to hand it to him and am met by his intense, unblinking gaze. I'm already uncomfortable around him and this level of scrutiny makes me want to curl up like an armadillo to protect what's left of my already shredded ego. That ice cream is not sitting well in my stomach right about now.

"No money." He's moved to sit at the counter and is heartily digging into his midnight meal.

"What does that mean?" The question rolls off my tongue inadvertently. At present, he doesn't seem to mind, so I go with it.

"I broke it in college, couldn't afford to go to the emergency room. I didn't have a dollar to my name until I was drafted." He watches me intently while I absorb this information. I know he was drafted second over all. That money must've been a windfall for a penniless young man. "I've also broken four ribs, lacerated a kidney, torn an mcl, and had two concussions that I know of. And that's not counting the day to day bumps and bruises."

*Jesus, Mary, and Joseph.* "Sounds like you've been to war. Ever consider retiring?"

He scowls as if I just called his mother a whore. "They'll have to carry my dead body off the field."

The thought is a jarring one. I feel the beginnings of a panic attack creep up on me. "Don't say that, not even as a joke." Taking the now empty dish from him, I turn and begin to wash it and the pan in the sink, scrubbing aggressively while I struggle to tame my racing heart. A large, warm hand lands on the exposed skin of my shoulder blade and my breath stutters. I stiffen and the warmth is gone just as quickly.

"I didn't mean—"

"It's all right," I interrupt, suddenly anxious to end this conversation. "I know you didn't, Mr. Shaw."

"Enough of that."

Drying my hands on a paper towel, I turn and take him in, a mere few feet separating us. He's standing against the counter again with his arms crossed, pecs bulging over his forearms. I try like hell to keep my eyes from wandering.

"What are you proposing?" I ask, mustering a weak smile, my spirits lifting at the change of topic.

"That you call me Cal…what should I call you?"

*Cow?* Yes, that's right. That's the first word that pops into my mind as I'm standing there staring into the clear gray eyes of a man that, before this evening, never had a nice word to say to me. And I swear on all that's holy that he knows exactly what I am thinking because I see the edges of his mouth wanting to lift. Standing in the presence of all that…whatever that is that's coming off of him…manliness? Manthing? I feel a pressing need to clear my throat.

"Umm, Cam or Camilla. Definitely not Camillia."

"Well, Cam, thank you for the delicious meal," he says quietly. Then he walks around the island and moves toward the stairs. "Y'all have a good night."

I stand there for a full twenty minutes before returning to my bedroom. I can't, as of yet, figure out how it happened, but I'm hoping I made a friend.

# WRECKING BALL

* * *

I have not made a friend. Not even close.

The gruff demeanor is alive and well. And he's always home—always. This house is probably around ten thousand square feet. Mathematically speaking, it should be easy for me to avoid him. But it's not. You know why? Because he's always frigging home! I get up to cook breakfast—he's in and out of his office. I cook lunch—he's in and out of the gym. I cook dinner—he's in and out of his office. I don't get it. Is he on house arrest? Most guys travel during the offseason, go on vacation. Shaw? Nope, he's home.

I made braised pork chops for lunch. Thankfully, Sam isn't a picky eater. So far everything I've cooked for him has gotten his approval. Just as we sit at the island to eat, I watch Shaw, freshly showered after his morning work out, stride into the kitchen and open the refrigerator. He removes his containers of 'death to inflammation' food and places them on the counter. I glance at Sam and notice his gaze is downcast as he eats, avoiding eye contact with his uncle. Shaw's eyes flicker to my plate, then his containers.

"I made some extra if you want." I point to the covered pan on the stove. He looks torn. When his eyes return to my plate, however, there's a hunger in them that makes me want to laugh. It's like I offered a diabetic a box of Krispy Kreme doughnuts. Not waiting for a response I may never get, I go to the stove and fix him a plate, and set it down with utensils next to Sam's seat. Then I return to mine. Shaw slowly sits down and begins to eat his meal.

The silence is stifling.

Most days during lunch, Sam chatters about the afternoon lesson plan. He's a sweet, curious child. An only child, he's told me. We haven't spoken much about his mother; it's still too soon for me to press him on that sensitive subject. But I now know that he loves trains, building things, and animals. I know he's not very athletic, although he's tall for his age—a Shaw gene, no doubt. He loves to read, but his favorite subject is mathematics. And of course he's naturally introverted. So it's not surprising that he's intimidated by the gruff hairy giant sitting next to him. Today he's completely mute. I don't know how this chasm between these two started, but I know I have to find a way to bridge it.

\* \* \*

"Knock, knock," I say from the open doorway of his office. Shaw pauses the game footage he's watching on a flat screen television. His desk chair is tipped back, legs crossed at the ankles, feet propped up on the edge of the desk. His head turns to me and I watch his eyes shamelessly work all the way down the length of my body.

If I didn't know what he really thinks about me, this wouldn't be an issue. But I do. My ears are suddenly on fire. I'm wearing work out clothes. Black leggings and a body skimming, technical shirt. Nothing sexy, nothing's hanging out. The fact that I've never been self-conscious wearing these clothes before and now am because of one man makes my blood boil.

"Where are you going?" The warm baritone, a voice that on anyone else I would find panty torching, is 'nails on a chalkboard' level annoying on him. There's an accusation in his tone, something snide in the way he says this. I cross my arms because if I don't, I may take my sneaker off and throw it at his head. Where did I get the idea that I could actually befriend this beast?

"To the strip club, for my shift. Where does it look like I'm going?"

# WRECKING BALL

"Out for a run when it's dark out."

*Huh?* "It's five thirty," I feel the need to point out.

"And dark out. It's dangerous. Use the gym," he says and hits the play button on the game footage, his attention returning to the screen. I walk into his office and plop down in the armchair in front of his desk.

"I can appreciate your *obsession* with my safety, Mr. Shaw—" At the word *obsession*, I get a cynical, sideways glance. Then his eyes return to the game.

"Calvin."

"Calvin...Willie, whatevs." His head swivels to face me again, his expression genuinely confused.

"Willie?"

"Robertson. Your fashion idol."

His black eyebrows lower, lower again, his lids grow heavy. I may have just gone too far but the die has been cast.

"You think I look like Willie Robertson?"

*You think I look like a cow*, pops into my head, though thankfully it does not come out of my mouth. His lips twitch, and twitch again. Then they curl up ever so slightly. He strokes his beard.

"You don't like my beard."

"I'm sure the vermin that call it home *luv* it."

"Is this what you came in here for?"

"We need to talk about Sam."

The mild amusement drops off his face, his expression suddenly uncomfortable. "What about him?"

"Did something happen between you two that I should know about? He shuts down around you and I'd like to know if there's something more to this besides your super duper charming personality."

"Nothing's happened," he says. I don't miss the way his muscles tighten. His feet swing off the desk and hit the floor with a thud, his posture now defensive. I'm confused. My gut tells me that there's more to this story, though I don't press. I recognize the mulish expression on Shaw's face. It looks just like the one Sam wears when he's having trouble with a math equation.

"God, you two are so much alike some times." Shaw looks surprised at this. "If you're not busy this week, I would like for you to join us at the park. Or maybe you can throw a ball around with him?" I casually suggest.

"No," he spits out. *What the heck?* The strength of his refusal gets my attention. My eyes snap back to his face. He's glowering again.

"Why?"

"I pay you to teach him, not play psychiatrist. Do your job and mind your own business." He turns the television back on and ignores my stare. Good grief, I need a happy pill to deal with this guy. He's right. I'm not a psychiatrist. However, he certainly needs one.

# CHAPTER EIGHT

MOTHER NATURE HAS NOT GOTTEN the memo that it's finally April and already spring. It's cold, and the rain has been steadily coming down for a few days. A pressing need to burn off some nervous energy has me pacing the house like a caged animal. Until I remember he said I could use the gym. Around three o'clock, while Sam is busy with a new Lego set, I decide to sneak in a forty minute run. I walk into the gym holding my breath and exhale when I find it blessedly empty. After stretching and doing a five minute warm up on the treadmill, I start jogging lightly. Kings of Leon are singing 'Comeback Story', my new anthem, and I'm starting to get a little bit of a runner's high. I've settled into a comfortable pace when two very tall men walk in, stop, and stare at me. The double take gives me whiplash.

Shaw and his trainer. *Damn it*. Without breaking stride, I smile tightly and wipe my sweaty face with a hand towel.

I consider myself an athlete. No, I'm not doing an Ironman triathlon any time soon. However, when I run it's not for vanity, it's for fitness. That's why a large dose of anger pumps through my veins when I suddenly become conscious of all my bouncing flesh. I can literally feel my boobs go up and down, up and down. My thighs are now two slabs of beef rubbing together, and my butt feels like it has its own zip code.

*Who cares what this asshole thinks*, I say to myself and try to concentrate on Kings of Leon. No such luck. I'm reduced to stealing furtive glances across the room, my eyes tracking them as they move from machine to machine like I'm some insecure teenager.

The trainer is almost as tall as Shaw and handsome in a nondescript way. He gives me a friendly smile with no heat as he passes, and in return, I offer another constipated smile. Shaw pretends I don't exist, which is more than fine by me. Trust me, I wish he didn't exist either. He goes to the wall and presses buttons 'til the music comes on. Some country western song I don't recognize. Then he walks to the mats and starts stretching. They're talking in hushed voices, saying something I can't hear, and it's making me nervous…and now I'm becoming paranoid. I really need to get a grip.

Turning it up, I pick up the pace, running much harder than I usually do because their sudden appearance has managed to compound the tension I'm already feeling. My eyes flicker to Shaw on and off. In between his bench presses, I catch him scowling at me. *Wonderful*. He's pissed I'm intruding on his work out. I can't win with this guy.

Twenty minutes later, my thighs are on fire because I NEVER RUN AT THIS PACE. I don't know who I'm more mad at, myself for being an idiot that's so easily intimidated by a man that means nothing but a paycheck to me, or him for being such an ass.

I finally hit a wall and reduce my grueling Olympic marathon speed to a comfortable walk. Time to cool down. The exhaustion makes my mind go thankfully quiet for a nanosecond. Shaw walks into the bathroom attached to the gym and I'm left alone with the trainer. He's setting up the next machine for Shaw when my treadmill shuts off. Without Shaw's judgy glare searing me, I scurry over to the mat and

## WRECKING BALL

begin stretching. I'm lying on my back with my feet planted on the ground, when the face of the trainer floats above me, into view. He's hovering, saying something I can't hear because I've got Kanye West singing that 'what doesn't kill you makes you stronger' and I'm thinking *bullshit,* but whatevs. I take out my ear buds and give him a questioning look.

"You want help stretching out your hamstrings?"

*Shit, I hope he's not coming on to me.* I search his eyes for a sign and find none. "No, I'm good, thanks."

I barely get the words out when a booming voice from across the room shouts, "Steve, I pay you to train me, not to hit on the help."

*The help?* The help? Steve looks at me and shakes his head, leaving me to attend to 'the master of the house'. I'm officially done. I couldn't care less what this man, or any man for that matter, thinks of me or my looks. I'm too tired, too disappointed in life, too disillusioned to care anymore. And it's enormously liberating. A shit ton of weight is suddenly lifted from my shoulders. I don't even care if I get a Charley horse that lasts a week. Without finishing to stretch my already sore legs, I get up and hobble out. Maybe Kanye is right after all. Maybe I am stronger.

\* \* \*

"You have to admit, he's kinda hot," Amber says as she wipes down the bar. All my tables are empty. The club was unusually slow tonight. It's almost one and I'm ready to head home. *Home?* That's weird that I would think that way about Shaw's house.

"A few weeks ago he was murdery. Now he's hot?" *Benedict Arnold.*

"So was Ted Bundy. Those two things are not mutually exclusive."

"Honestly, I don't see it," I say, shaking my head. "I mean, his traps are a thing of beauty, but I just can't get past his totally shitty personality."

"Tall drink of water at twelve o'clock," Amber mutters, her heavy-lidded eyes glued to a spot over my shoulder. "Gonna bust my vibrator tonight."

I turn to take in the object of her blatantly sexual interest and come face to face with a familiar set of dimples. He walks up to the bar and takes a seat directly in front of us. Amber's mouth curves into a crooked smile that means only one thing—trouble. Leaning on the bar, I prop my chin up with my hand and settle in to watch the fireworks.

"Dimples, what can I get you?" she practically sings. Actually, this guy seems harmless. He smiles good naturedly at her.

"Jäger, please," he answers with a heavy sigh. His soft, brown eyes go back and forth between us. "How are you ladies doin' tonight?"

"You sound a bit down, sweet cheeks, what gives?"

Raising the shot glass in mock cheers, he tips it back, drains it, and slams the empty glass on the bar. "You wanna know?"

"I'm a bartender. I hear more confessions than a priest."

"I got dumped. She said she doesn't trust me to stay faithful to her livin' so far away," he explains dejectedly.

"How far away is the little lady in question?"

"Tennessee."

"Is she right?" I ask. A stubborn wrinkle appears on his forehead. He shakes his head vigorously. "Well you *are* kind of a flirt, Dimples."

"Harper," he says as he pats his chest. I have a feeling Dimples has had more than one shot tonight. "Justin Harper. And that's just me, she should know that well enough by

# WRECKING BALL

now." For some strange reason, I believe him. "I don't mean nothin' by it."

While Amber listens attentively to Justin's tale of woe, I take off to grab my stuff from the locker. Justin is closing out his tab as I walk past the bar on my way out.

"I'm off," I say and Amber nods back. I'm halfway to the door when I feel a tap on the shoulder.

"Can I speak to you for a minute?" Justin Harper looks uncomfortable. My suspicious glare makes him smile. "Just a minute. I promise," he says with his hands up in surrender.

"Fine," I grumble, tired and anxious to get home. "Walk me out." As we walk out the door into the cold dead of night, he says, "I just want to apologize for last week. That was outa line, and I don't want you thinkin' I was being disrespectful is all." I look up into his face and find a sweet, embarrassed earnestness that makes me smile. This is a pleasant surprise.

"Apology accepted."

"Harper, what the hell are you doing here?"

That voice, that frigging voice is drawing closer. I turn to the left to see Shaw getting out of his car. Harper looks totally confused. His gaze shifts back and forth from Shaw to me. Walking up to us, Shaw grunts out, "Are you ready?"

"You two know each other?" Harper asks hesitantly.

At the same time I answer, "I'm the help," Shaw answers, "How do you know her?"

"Time out. How do you know him?" I ask Shaw.

"He's the new wide out we just traded Tennessee for." *Talk about a small world.* Shaw is killing young Harper with his glare.

"Justin, a pleasure meeting you. Shaw, let's go," I say, not even bothering to look back to see if he's following me to the still running car.

In the Range Rover, I crane my neck to find Shaw still

talking to Harper. He's pointing a finger aggressively in the younger man's face. Eye roll. A minute later, he's buckling his seat belt and driving down the street with the same scowl plastered to his face. The former me would've stayed quiet, wouldn't have caused a ripple. Everything's changed now, however. "I can't do this anymore." His head turns swiftly in my direction, something strongly resembling fear crosses his face and his body braces. "I can't live day in and day out with someone that is about as pleasant as a nest of riled up hornets. Life's too frigging short!"

He squirms a little in his seat. His expression turns pensive, the lines of anger on his face going smooth. After blowing out a deep breath, very quietly, he says, "I'm sorry... I've got a lot on my mind lately."

*Wow. I mean, wow. An apology? A genuine one? And he just admitted I wasn't the instrument of his pain.* Maybe there's hope for him yet. "What are you stressed about?" Helping people, if it's in my power, is an instinct I cannot curb or deny. That will never change. If he wants to talk to someone about it, I'm a great listener—except I really don't expect him to answer.

"For one thing, my contract expires after this season."

More honesty. It's official—hell has frozen over. "You're in your prime and you had a top five total QBR last year."

He glances briefly at me. By the look on his face, I think it's to make sure I'm the one that spoke those words, and not some other random person who has somehow hitched a ride with us in the last ten seconds.

"You watch football?"

Should I be offended? Not only am I big fan of professional football, I can recite stats as well as any dude. I watch all three days of the draft and check Bleacher Report every couple of days for breaking news. This, he does not need to know because I've never been a big fan of the Titans, or him for that matter, and I have a tiny suspicion that he may take this as a personal insult. When I give him a sly smile, his brows lower in understanding.

"Whose jersey do you own?"

"That's for me to know and for you to wonder about," I say, chuckling at his annoyed expression.

"Top three," corrects Mr. Modesty.

"Under Brady," I counter. His face scrunches up in mock anger.

"The year before he was two below me." I laugh at this. *I laugh.* Holy cow, we're actually laughing together. Well—technically he's not laughing. But there is a ghost of a smile on his face. And it feels good. So damn good.

I glance his way and his face has transformed. Even with the beard, he looks much younger when he lets go of all that angst. Brooding intensity is only sexy on a man if your own life isn't filled with shit that makes you broody and intense.

"Are you really worried? You've won a Super Bowl and appeared in another, you've been voted league MVP I don't know how many times…you're indispensable to this team."

Taking his eyes off the road again, he turns to look at me. I notice that his handsome face wears gravity well. Yes, handsome. For the first time, I get a glimpse of it.

"Nobody's indispensable," he says quietly. A meaningful silence hangs between us.

"Calvin." His name sounds pleasant on my lips—and strangely familiar. He makes a humming noise and his smoky gray eyes hold mine. "I don't want to be at odds with you. I've had my fair share of crap this year and I…" *What am I trying to say? Take mercy on me?*

"I get it," he says. "I don't mean to pile on."

"I'll be out of your hair soon enough. Can we call a truce?"

"Yeah," he says, nodding slowly. After that, a comfortable

silence settles between us. I find myself smiling the rest of the ride home. As we pull into the driveway, Calvin's the one to break the silence.

"I have a thing, a team sponsored event coming up on Saturday. Do you think Sam would like to go?"

"I think he'd love it if you asked him. He worships you, you know." Still no smile. "I'll go see my parents."

"You don't want to come?" he casually asks, more like a question framed as a statement.

When I don't answer right away because I'm SHOCKED, he takes that as a *no*. "It's fine." He's already mad. Good Lord, this guy is wound tight.

"Jeez, give me a chance to answer. I'm just getting used to you not growling the question." His lips want to curve up. I know they do. Making this guy smile is becoming a worthwhile pursuit. That's why I answer, "I'd love to come."

*  *  *

Around lunchtime, Shaw makes an appearance. That seems to be happening more and more lately. We've reached a fragile detente in our tolerate/hate relationship. I don't even bother to ask. I place some of my *looks-fried-but-it's-really-baked-chicken* on a plate along with fresh grilled vegetables and roasted Yukon potatoes sprinkled with rosemary, and set it down next to Sam in the hope that these two males might relax around each other over a good meal. Maybe I really am my mother's daughter after all.

One quick glance at Shaw tells me he's having an orgasm over the chicken and my spirits lift. I'm thinking that should take the edge off of the grumps, until he opens his mouth.

"We have an event to go to on Saturday at team facilities."

Not a question, not a, "Hey, how are you doing Sam?" Nope. A command. *A command* that leaves no room for further

# WRECKING BALL

discussion, given to a eight year old that's already completely intimidated. What does he do for fun? Drown kittens? Now I'm fuming.

"What your uncle means, Sam, is that there's a team event that he needs to attend and he would love for you to go with him. It helps kids that are sick. Would you like to go?"

In the periphery of my vision, I see the deep v etched on Shaw's brow. All those warm fuzzies he's usually oozing are directed at me over Sam's head, which I do my best to ignore. In the mean time, I'm telepathically flipping him off. Without looking once at his uncle, and in a small voice that breaks my heart, Sam says, "Are you coming?"

"Sure. Where you go, I go." His eyes brighten and he gives me a short nod. Shaw's full lower lip looks tight with (surprise surprise) displeasure, although he wisely chooses to remain quiet. I return to my now cold lunch. The rest of the meal is painfully conducted in silence.

# CHAPTER NINE

THE EVENT SATURDAY IS TO benefit a local children's hospital. Children's organizations are often the beneficiaries of the Davis', the Titans owners, charity efforts, which I believe stem from the fact that, sadly, they lost their only son to cancer. Shaw informs me that there will be carnival-like games set up for the children and the players to compete in, therefore, to dress casual. Sam and I are waiting in the kitchen, me in my dark designer jeans and a black v neck wool sweater with a pair of black flats—my go-to outfit when I don't know what to wear—and Sam is in a nice blue button down and khakis.

What I'm not prepared for is the sight walking down the stairs. He's dressed in a pair of artfully distressed designer jeans, a blue and white checkered button down shirt, and Italian leather lace up boots that are pretending to look worn and used, though probably cost a small fortune. *Seriously?* It looks like he mugged a mannequin in a Barneys window. He also trimmed the beard. It's super short and neat. Basically, it looks like he spent more time on his appearance than I did. Not that that's too difficult; I'm no fashionista. His pale eyes meet mine and for the life of me I can't look away.

Pretty boys have never appealed to me. Ruggedly handsome is my preferred style. I've always had a private fetish for the working class hero. For guys who know how to use their hands and come home sweaty and a little bit grimy and say things like, "Let me wash up first." Ironic since my husband was solidly white collar—a shrink would have a field day with that one, but I digress. And now I remember why Shaw never did it for me. If he was any less of a brute, if his brow wasn't plagued by a perpetual scowl, he would be prettier than most women. Those large, gray eyes are framed by a crowded fan of lashes so thick and black it looks like he's wearing eyeliner. And the slender nose coupled with those sensual lips? All I have to say about that is he's lucky he has a strong jaw and sharp cheekbones otherwise he'd be a Disney character.

I must be glowering because he says, "What?"

"A haircut wouldn't kill you." It's still in a man bun. This earns me a half-assed grunt. The unhygienic beard is gone—not the obnoxious personality. He does a quick sweep of my person and his mouth pinches.

*If this peacock even thinks about criticizing my clothes...*

"Let's go."

In the car I put on a video for Sam to watch in the backseat. Shaw remains quiet, his eyes on the road ahead. It doesn't bother me as it once did. I know now that's just him.

"Is there anything you expect Sam to participate in? Pictures? Anything I should know about?"

Okay, I'm babbling. I tend to do that when I'm nervous and it just dawned on me that we'll be in public, most likely surrounded by reporters, and someone might recognize me. *Crap. Double crap.* Shaw's eyes flicker to my leg, which is beating nervously against the floor of the car.

"Didn't you hit the can before we left?"

*Charming.* "Yes, I did."

"Then what's the deal? You nervous?"

How much do I explain? I have no frigging idea. "Yes," I

answer, going with the truth. He's staring like he expects me to elaborate. I'm having a hard time with this clean shaven version of the Prince of Darkness who looks deceptively like Prince Charming. Between that piercing gaze of his and my frazzled nerves, I'm starting to unravel. My chest feels tight. "Stop staring at me like that. It's rude," I snap, and watch his eyebrows climb up his forehead. After a backward glance to make sure Sam isn't listening, I whisper, "I'm scared someone will recognize me."

"So what?"

"So I tend to inspire nasty behavior in whomever recognizes me." His expression hardens. Even with those pretty features, he suddenly looks dangerous.

"What kind of behavior?"

I sigh heavily and moderate my oxygen intake because the last thing I need right now is to hyperventilate, and there's a really good frigging chance of that happening.

I hate talking about this—with anybody. There's so much shame attached to it. Do I want to tell him about the time someone waited outside my house for two days only to spit on me when I took the trash out? Do I want to explain that I had to drive an hour away just to grocery shop for months because I had an orange thrown at me at my local grocery store? No. I really don't.

"Shouting and swearing, sometimes pushing and shoving," I mumble. When the silence continues, I chance a glance in his direction. He's staring ahead, his jaw locked, his mouth stretched in a grim line. We ride the rest of the way in silence, the atmosphere tense. I think I may have just driven the last nail in my own coffin. He's probably mad that may happen around his nephew and I don't blame him. He parks the car and I'm about to jump out when he grabs my wrist.

"You don't have to worry about that shit happening

anymore."

What's that supposed to mean? Before I can ask, he's out of the car.

* * *

Inside the indoor practice facility, the entire field is covered with carnival themed games and food stands. A lot of the guys on the team are in attendance, most with large families in tow. When I realize how many of them have young kids, it makes sense that they would still be in town until school lets out. As soon as we walk in, Sam's eyes go wide and a smile spreads across his face.

"Sam, why don't you walk around with your uncle so he can introduce you to some of the other players on the team?"

This question is answered with a little boy scowl that's a carbon copy of the one Shaw gives me when I've done or said something to displease him, which of course is often.

Shaw starts to walk away. "Let's go, Sam." Sam shuffles after him, dragging his feet, his shoulders slumped. And I almost feel bad pushing him.

The next hour passes slowly. I hide in a corner, away from a bevy of reporters and photographers, and watch Shaw and Sam from a distance. They aren't saying much to each other, but it's more time than I've ever seen them spend together since I moved in. I guess that's something to celebrate.

"Whom are you hiding from?" I look sideways and find Ethan Vaughn scanning the crowd suspiciously.

"No one…what about you?" The exasperated expression he gives me puts a smile on my face.

"Short brunette, loud voice. Give me a heads up if you see her coming this way."

"You badger me relentlessly and now you expect me to help you?" I say mildly amused.

"How is Angelina, by the way?"

"Infatuated. Add another heart to your trophy case." For that comment, I get a strange quirk of his brow. His beautiful eyes follow the path mine take, straight to Sam.

"I knew you would be good for him," he says, those chocolate orbs glimmering in triumph.

"How would you know anything about it?"

"Cal's been raving about you. He says you've worked wonders with Sam." *Say what?* "Oh shit—just go with it."

"Go with what?" Before I can get another word out, Vaughn swings an arm around my neck and huddles closer.

"Vaughn, if you don't remove your hand from the vicinity of my breast area, I will break off every single one of your digits," I say in the same voice I used to employ on my unruly third graders.

"Look over my shoulder and make sure she's gone," he whispers. Fighting a smile, I glance over his shoulder and spot the busty brunette staring at us with her head tilted and a pout on. Behind her, I catch a glimpse of Shaw.

"What is she doin…aaaaaahhhh." Vaughn is pried off of me by an angry ogre with a firm grip on his ear.

"You're hurting him, stop it." Shaw lets go. While Vaughn is busy rubbing life back into his cherry red ear, I lift his hand and inspect the ear. "You'll survive."

"Fuck, Cal. What the hell's wrong with you?" Vaughn looks pissed. I get the feeling this is strange behavior even for Shaw.

"Nothing's wrong with me. What the hell's wrong with *you*?" Shaw snaps back. Ethan narrows his eyes. There's a lot of bewilderment there.

"Where's Sam?" I ask, suddenly worried. Pointing behind him, I get a grunt from Shaw. Sam is standing there looking unsure and awkward. "Way to go, *hero*." Stepping around them, I grab Sam's hand and we walk off.

* * *

"Oh crud. You beat me again," I say, feigning disappointment. Sam giggles so loudly I may have to throw ten more games just to hear it again. We've been playing a beanbag toss game for the past half hour.

"Can I play?"

Both Sam and I turn around at the sound of the deep voice. I don't think I've ever seen Shaw look quite this uncomfortable. He's standing there with his hands shoved in the front pocket of his jeans like the last kid on the playground to be picked for a dodge ball team. Do I let him disrupt the happy vibe we've been surfing, or turn him away and possibly cause more problems down the road? With a warning glare at Shaw, I say, "You can take my turn." I don't miss the worried look that crosses Sam's face.

A short while later, even though the excitement has fallen a notch or two, Sam still seems to be having fun. I can't deny that part of me is surprised. I didn't expect Shaw to make this much of an effort. Maybe there's hope for him yet— although he made sure to win at least half the games so the jury is still out. *Jerk.* I just hope these two have turned a corner.

"Now you take my turn," Sam says, surprising me. I glance at Shaw and the smug look on the arrogant ass' face makes my spine go laser straight. *So he wants to play does he? Fine by me.* Should I mention I was the pitcher on a championship winning softball team? I'll keep that little beauty to myself. By the tenth game, Sam is openly cheering me on and I have to forcibly stop myself from doubling over in laughter. Shaw has smoke coming out of his ears. The Super Bowl MVP doesn't like to be upstaged by a girl apparently. Not that either of us are winning; it's a dead heat even after he stopped taking it easy on me.

"One more, or are you done?" I taunt and watch those chilly eyes narrow. "That killer glare doesn't work on me, Calvin." The sound of his name on my lips makes his twitch. He wants to smile, I know he does, and yet…nothing.

"A picture, Mr. Shaw?" We turn to find a photographer armed with a massive camera already poised to shoot.

"Not now," Calvin answers.

"Just a quick one," insists the photographer and begins snapping pictures of us. Calvin's entire body stiffens. All except for the good parts.

"Unless you want to be banned from team facilities for life, I suggest you erase the last three pictures." His voice is deadly calm and his face a frozen mask. This is not his game face, one I know well from the hundreds of games I've watched him play over the years, this face holds malicious intent. The photographer smartly tunes into the serious threat. He nods slowly and begins scanning the screen on his digital camera. Stepping closer, he shows me the last pictures on the screen. I give him a tight smile after I confirm the absence of our images.

"Are we cool?" the young man asks Calvin.

"We're cool."

As soon as the photographer is gone, I turn to Calvin. "What was that about?"

His gaze stays on the beanbag he tosses in the air and catches. "I saw the look on your face when he took the picture." Then he drops it and walks away without sparing me another glance.

All the action makes Sam and me hungry. Heading over to the food stands, we decide on a couple of hotdogs and something to drink. Then we find an empty picnic table on a quiet side of the field to eat.

# WRECKING BALL

"Fancy meetin' you here," drawls a friendly voice. I look over my shoulder to find Justin Harper loping in our direction. His crooked, carefree grin provokes one on my face, too. When he reaches us he swings a long leg over the bench and straddles it.

"Sam, this is Justin Harper, the new wide receiver for the Titans. Justin, I'd like to introduce you to Sam McCabe, Calvin Shaw's nephew," I say, heavy emphasis on the last few words.

"Nice to meet you, Sam." Harper thrusts out a hand that Sam shakes with a smile, instantly taken by Justin's sunny demeanor. Leaning into me, Justin whispers, "I have a question for you." My whole body braces for the worst. Looking a tad self-conscious, he asks, "Is your friend single?"

It takes me a moment to realize he's asking about Amber. The smile this incites almost breaks my face in two. "Dimples—what about the girl you were crying about?"

He screws his face up in an adorable scowl. "She's already datin' someone else, damn it."

"Are you sure about this?"

I mean, I love Amber more than I love myself, but she'll devour and spit him back out before he realizes he's lunch meat. I feel the need to at least give him the opportunity to save himself.

He nods vigorously, eagerness sparking in his light brown gaze.

I'm thinking, 'it's your funeral', even though I answer, "Yes, she's single."

"We're going," a deep voice shouts.

Justin narrows his eyes and we both turn in its direction—along with all the other thirty some odd people in the general area. Standing a few yards away, Calvin is watching me with a careful look of indifference. He's facing a tall, attractive ginger wearing glasses and clutching an iPad. She's trying to speak to him, her expression determined, but he's clearly not paying attention to her. His hands are stuffed in the front pockets of his jeans, his body language illustrating his boredom. *Typical.* God forbid he has to engage with one of us mere mortals.

"I *said* we're leaving."

*What the frigging hell is his problem??* A blast of humiliation marks my neck.

"Is he always so much fun?" I can tell Justin is keeping it PG because of Sam, who gets off the bench and begins walking toward Calvin.

"I'm sorry, Justin. This has nothing to do with you," I say, chasing after Sam.

His eyes move between Calvin and me. The devious look on young Harper's face makes me pause. "How about I take you to lunch some time?" he shouts loud enough for half the field to witness. It literally stops me in my tracks. Caught between answering and escaping, I choose option B, to escape. Speed walking past Calvin, I take Sam's hand and head toward the exit of the training field.

\* \* \*

On the drive home, we're all silent. Once the Range Rover is parked in the garage, Calvin disappears into the house, not to be seen again. I end up ordering pizza for Sam and me. Sam looks as tired as I feel, so after dinner we go upstairs early and watch television together before bed. My mind is swimming with the events of the day. In the shower, Ethan's words come back to me in a rush. *Calvin's been raving about you. Raving? Yeah, maybe raving mad.* Not even the sweet sensation of the hot water pounding on my head can make that admission sound remotely plausible. I'd have to stretch my imagination pretty thin to believe Calvin had anything better than neutral to say about me.

## WRECKING BALL

By the time the phone rings around eleven and Amber's face pops up on the cell screen, I'm desperate for a distraction. "I'm so excited for you. This is the beginning of great things. I can feel it." She's just booked a national commercial for a major brand of soap and I couldn't be any happier for her. Her gorgeous face will be piped into every household with a television.

"Meh, we'll see," she answers.

"When did you turn into such a cynic?"

"When I found out that Brad and Angelina were getting a divorce."

A tall wall of muscles suddenly appears in my open doorway. *For realz?* He's naked. For all intents and purposes, the man is naked. I'll go on the record once again that I've sworn off men for all eternity, and yet it's impossible for me to pry my eyes off of him. My mouth runs bone dry and heat crawls up my neck as I marvel at his body. I chalk this up to simple biology, to the fact that I'm female and alive. He's staring, those unyielding cool eyes fixed on me over the bowl he's busy eating out of.

"Amber, have to call you back. There's a man darkening my doorway." Before she can answer, I hang up.

He's leaning against the doorframe in nothing but a pair of embarrassingly old and ratty boxer briefs. Those trapezius muscles, my own personal brand of kryptonite, are on full display. I swear I can see everything. *Good grief, how does he even walk with that thing between his legs?*

Without making it too obvious, I sit up in bed and slowly pull the sheet over the white tank top I sleep in. Unlike Mr. Modesty here, I *do* care that my boobs are on full display. The subtle lift of a black, masculine eyebrow tells me he's noticed and finds this amusing.

"Did you at least heat up that pasta?"

"Nope."

"I would've done it for you if you asked."

A shrug. That's what I get, a one-shoulder shrug. My eyes focus below his waist. Technically, it's eye level for me so there's that. And if he doesn't have a problem with the log between his legs practically poking me in the eye, then why do I have to pretend I don't see it? Something about his shameless, close-to-total nudity in front of me, a stranger, irritates the shit out of me. I can't keep my mouth shut for a second longer.

"Do you have an allergy to new cotton?"

"Nope."

"Then why can't you put on underwear that isn't about to disintegrate if a strong wind blows?" *Lordy, did I just use the word 'blow' again?* I'm so cringing inside. He chews his food slowly and continues to stare, his expression not giving a thing away. A half-century later, I'm still waiting for an explanation for this impromptu visit.

"You've been checking out my underwear?" There he goes again with his nonquestion.

"Calvin."

"Hmm."

"What do you want?"

"I'm going furniture shopping tomorrow."

"Congratulations."

"You're coming with me." Standing away from the doorframe, he turns to leave. "Sam, too."

# CHAPTER TEN

"I JUST LOVE THIS PIECE, don't you?"

No, I think it looks like dog shit, but no one is asking me. The decorating consultant, an attractive woman in her early thirties with a perpetual smile on her face that the peacock has hired, doesn't seem to be doing a very good job consulting. I say 'peacock' because today he has another one of his snazzy designer outfits on. A black cashmere hoodie with designer distressed jeans and biker boots that no biker on this planet could ever afford. He stares at the heavy, dark wood coffee table with as close to contempt as I've seen on his face. To her, it probably looks like apathy.

"You don't like it?" she asks with a brittle, nervous smile. She brushes his forearm again, probably for the tenth time today; I stopped counting at eight. He glares at her and she misses the look. I have to lock down the urge to snicker every time. She's either the most incredibly stupid woman I've ever met, or arguably the craftiest.

At the sound of me clearing my throat, Calvin takes an extra long, heavy lidded glance in my direction. Then his eyes move back to the woman who is trying her hardest not to stare at him with serious yearning in her eyes. How does she do this? Allow me to explain, by forcing her eyes wide open. I haven't seen her blink in like three minutes and it's disconcerting, downright creepy actually. Like I said, after he takes a long look at me, he turns to her and says, "No." This is how most of the day has gone. Right now I'm the Emoji with straight lines for eyes and mouth with a gun pointing at it—and I'm not talking the squirt gun. By the time we're leaving the fourth store without anything to show for it, I'm losing my patience and Sam looks bored and annoyed and no one wants to shop with a grumpy eight year old.

"Calvin, if you don't buy something soon we're leaving," I hiss out of earshot of his decorator. "Where did you get her anyway?"

"Barry." My blank stare prompts him to continue. "My agent."

"Whatever—Sam and I are going to grab a snack." For a split second, something resembling worry crosses his face… actually, it looks exactly like worry. "Meet us at Pain Quotidien on the corner when you're done *not* buying anything. God's sake, you're not playing the Patriots, stop making this look difficult."

The last part earns me the filthiest glare. He looks over his shoulder, and I take it as my cue to leave.

"Madison, we're done. My girlfriend and nephew are hungry."

And my steps come to a screeching halt. Girlfriend? *Girlfriend? The fuck?*

Madison looks shocked right out of her Manolo Blahniks. Armed with this new information, her eyes do a much more thorough inspection of my person. The confused look on her face telegraphs that she's found me lacking. I don't blame her. From an objective perspective, even if he wasn't a ridiculously talented professional athlete, his supermodel good looks place him in a completely different league from me, maybe even a different solar system. And this very obvious fact does not bother me in the least. I've never wanted to be in that league. Why would anybody? I like to fly under the radar. I've never had the desire to be famous, or love a man that just about every other female on the planet with a pair of eyes lusts after. No thanks. I mean, Matt was attractive and his charming, playful personality made him even more so, but nowhere near this caliber—and that was just fine by me.

I turn toward Calvin wearing probably the most astonished, confused look on my face *ever*, and all I get in return is a slight narrowing of the eyes, which I know—bizarre that I know this—means not to contradict him. He doesn't wait for Madison to respond. On go his sunglasses, and out the door we go.

The café on the corner serves brunch. We eat at warp speed. When you have one of the most celebrated athletes in the city sitting next to you, you can count on a long line of people crowding the table for an autograph as if they're entitled to it. Pictures are taken. Hands are shook. I'm only beginning to understand what Shaw has to endure every time he steps out the door and a pang of sympathy hits me. Every once in a while, I get a curious look, however, no one is forward enough to ask who I am. Even though he barely has time to take a few bites of his egg white omelet with spinach, Calvin signs each and every one without complaint. I have to give him credit—by the thirtieth, I'm starting to get antsy.

Sam is busy devouring his second chocolate croissant. His eyes have been glued on his uncle the entire time. The awed, worshipful look on his face makes my heart squeeze painfully. If only Calvin could see it. It's become abundantly clear that Calvin is no fan of children. This is a riddle I have yet to solve because for all his grumpiness, Calvin is fundamentally a decent person. This seems out of character, even for him.

As soon as Sam is done with his food, we get ready to

leave. Just as we're about to step out the door, a man approaches Calvin for an autograph. He's having trouble speaking, his hands quivering as he offers up a napkin for Calvin to sign. I don't know what ails this man, what his troubles are. But whatever they are, they are not insignificant. And Calvin? Well, the patience and genuine warmth he handles this man with…yeah, it's pretty much the most amazing thing I've ever witnessed.

As I listen to the two men quietly discuss football strategy, my heart starts to expand inside my chest until the ache is too much to bear. Something inside of me cracks wide open and I have to fight like hell not to let the tears welling in my eyes roll down my face. Up until this moment, I was doing a damn good job tolerating Calvin for Sam's sake. There was a certain comfort in my dislike of him. I know that sounds strange, but not being able to trust my own judgment really screwed me up. And now I have to reassess everything I believe about this man, too.

As we exit, Sam places his small hand in mine. On my other side, I can feel Calvin's eyes drilling a hole in my skull. I brush the dampness away as quickly as possible.

"What's wrong?" Calvin asks. There's nothing remotely consoling about the gruff tone he favors.

"Nothing," I blurt out. Sam can clearly see what I'm doing and keeps my secret. "Why don't you have any furniture?" I ask, hoping to distract him.

"She took it."

"You've been without furniture for two years?"

"Three," he corrects. He walks ahead, head and shoulders above the crowd, and I watch every female and some male heads he passes swiveling to get a better look. On the way back to the waiting Town car, we pass a Restoration Hardware that spans an entire city block. Calvin walks inside and without a glance in my direction, says, "Pick out what we need."

*We?* What we need? I stand there unsure how to react for ten full minutes. My stare goes ignored. His eyes remain glued to his cell phone while he heads straight for a double-wide goose down armchair and plops his big body down.

"Calvin?" Nothing. He continues texting. "Calvin, I don't know what you like," I say more sternly. Without looking up, he says, "Order whatever you want," adding, "and one of these," while he points to the chair he's sitting on. I'm speechless. But then again, he does that to me a lot.

\* \* \*

When we get home, Sam disappears to his playroom to work on a new Lego village he's building, and Calvin heads to the gym. I consider dropping by my parents' house, though before I leave, I know I have to deal with what happened today. With that in mind, I go in search of the man that called me his *girlfriend*. Just the thought has me on the verge of hyperventilating. In the gym, I find him in the middle of his TRX workout. The closer I get, the clearer it becomes that all he's wearing is long, loose shorts. Those frigging traps are like a homing beacon for my eyes.

*Eyes up. Eyes up damn it!* Did he catch me? Of course, he did.

Standing before him, I wait patiently for him to finish a set of bicep curls. Sweat is dripping down his body, muscles are bulging in stark relief from bone and sinew. I have no idea where to put my eyes because everywhere I look there's danger. Finally, I settle on my own nails. Does he stop what he's doing as any other normal, polite human being would? The answer to that is a hard *no*. One minute passes, two, three—by the fifth minute of listening to him grunt through another set, my nerves are on fire. Taking a deep breath, I jump into a conversation I didn't think, not even in my wildest nightmares, I'd ever need to have.

"We need to talk." His sharp gaze flickers to mine, and still he says nothing. I like the strong silent type as much as the next girl but seriously? "Did you hear what I said?"

"Yup."

"Can you stop that for a minute, please?"

Pulling himself up and standing, he places one hand on his hipbone. The unintended consequence of this is that the waistband of his shorts is pushed down and...again, no underwear. Wiping his chest with a hand towel in his other hand, he says, "Talk."

*So charming.* "Why would you call me your...umm... girlfriend?" I almost choke on that word.

"She was touching me."

*Huh?* I'm stumped, I'm completely stumped. Then I think, *there must be some kind of hidden meaning here*, and spend an extra few minutes searching for something I do not find. "Are you a germaphobe?"

"No."

"Do you suffer from some other condition I should know about?" In response to this, I get a triple dose of his signature nasty scowl. "Then what's with this aversion to being touched?"

"I don't like it."

"You. Don't. Like. It. So you announce to the world, 'cause I can guarantee this will get to the tabloids in no time, that I'm your girlfriend without thought to the consequences?"

"What consequences?"

I am *this* close to laughing like a deranged hyena. His face is totally relaxed, like we're discussing the series finale of *Downton Abbey* and not the total and complete destruction of what little is left of my life.

"What consequences? *What consequences?*" I am fully aware that I keep repeating everything like an idiot, but I am steeped in disbelief. Can he really be this self-centered?

"You keep repeating yourself."

"I told you what it's like for me! I'm trying to lay low. The last thing I need is to draw any attention to myself, whatsoever."

"That won't ever happen again if people think you're my girlfriend."

I ignore this ridiculously arrogant statement and plow full steam ahead. "I don't ever, *ever* want to wind up on another newspaper as long as I live. And now you want me to play the pretend girlfriend of the biggest sports star in the country. How is that supposed to help me? How is that staying off the radar?"

I'm getting a panic attack just talking about it. *Breathe in, breathe out, breathe in...*

He scrunches his face up, his head bobs from side to side and says, "Second biggest." I blink repeatedly just to be sure I'm not dreaming this ridiculous conversation. For a second, I'm sidetracked into contemplating who he thinks number one is. "Why are you breathing like that?"

Nope, I'm awake. This shit's real. "Have you heard a word I've said?"

"You can't hide forever."

I don't know what's pissing me off more, the smug look on his face, or the fact that he's dismissing every legitimate concern I have as if it's trivial nonsense. "Thanks Dr. Phil, but that's exactly what I plan to do, hide forever. And what about how this could hurt you? What a PR nightmare this could turn into. Dating the widow of a Ponzi scheme mastermind, whether it's bullshit or not, isn't going to endear you to your fans or the Davis family, for that matter. Your contract expires soon. This could hurt your chances to sign again."

"Camilla—" My name on his lips snaps me out of my rant. There's a serious amount of exasperation implied in the way he pronounces it, like he can't believe he has to labor through an explanation. "Does it look like I give a shit what other people think?" That's the problem. He really doesn't. "It'll be fine."

"For whom??"

"For both of us."

I go for forceful. "Sounds awesome. But again, NO. You better fix this."

"I don't want a relationship and I don't want the hassle of not being in one. I won't get touched anymore, and people won't mess with you. It's real simple. Don't make this more than it is."

*The arrogance.*

"I'm sure you've dated a number of women who would love to be a part of this dog and pony act. Get one of them to do it." There's a long pause and I'm momentarily relieved to think I may have finally scored a point. He seems to be mulling it over.

"No."

Relief erased. I stand there slack faced, marveling at his obstinacy. So it's no surprise that my hands go to the roots of my hair and begin to tug. It's like trying to reason with a brick wall, enough to drive anyone absolutely bat shit crazy. He starts doing those hanging stomach crunches double-time as if I'm not still standing there glowering at him. Up down, up down, his knees pump rapidly. I'm momentarily distracted with a washboard I could do laundry on.

"Anything else?" he grunts out. I throw my hands up and march out the door because what else is there to say?

# WRECKING BALL

After a thirty minute shower, in which I spend the better part of it holding my head under the jet stream trying to soothe the tension headache one gets after a conversation with one pigheaded man, I feel marginally calmer. With this newfound sense of peace and calm, I step out of my bathroom and it all goes to hell.

"Jeeeeezuuuz!" I screech-shout. "What the hell are you doing in my bedroom?!" With absolutely zero shame, he's sitting on the end of my bed, legs spread apart—clearly to accommodate the boulders he has for testicles—lying back on his elbows, in his so-called underwear. Incredulity forces my eyebrows to the top of my head.

His unblinking gray gaze slides up and down my body. "What if I paid you?"

I stand there dumbstruck trying to process what he's just said, until rage hits critical mass and takes over. "Explain to me why you think you have the right to barge in here?" I squeeze out between clenched teeth.

"The door was open."

"For Sam! In case, he needs me."

"I need you." By the look on his face, he's as shocked he said that as I am. "You're the only person that wants a relationship less than I do."

Can someone actually go mute from a surplus of anger? I wonder, because I can't force a single word out of my mouth. Ten minutes later, nostrils flaring, red faced, I say, "Get out."

"Why?"

*He can't be serious.* "You're messing with me, right?"

"No, I really will pay you. I'm not messing around."

"Not about the money! Although that's completely screwy, too. I'm talking about you intruding on my privacy while I'm naked! Boundaries! Ever hear of them??"

"You're not naked. You're wearing a towel."

"Calvin, if you don't get your barely covered ass off my bed and leave right this minute I will throw something at your head." A second later my eyes are searching for an object of substance within reach. Utilizing the two brain cells he does possess, he gets off my bed and stalks to the doorway, hovering just outside of it.

"Think about it. What are you going to do once the three months are up? After taxes, that hundred grand isn't going to last very long." There are so many things wrong with that doozy it would take way too much of my time to correct him. "You don't have an income. What if you can't get another job?"

Walking up to the door, I say, "Thanks for the vote of confidence, *Champ*." Slamming it shut, I lock it. Because I really don't put it past him to come in while I'm sleeping.

# CHAPTER ELEVEN

THE NEXT MORNING, WHILE I'M busy preparing breakfast, elbows deep in eggs, he thunders into the kitchen. There's power to his stride and energy of purpose surrounding him. Basically, he means business and he wants me to know it. His relentless stare is making my hair curl and I can't even get a kink out of it with a hot iron. The only reasonable thing for me to do is to continue stirring the scrambled eggs and pretend he doesn't exist.

"What's it going to take?"

I don't dare look at him. Instead, I shovel some eggs on Sam's plate. "Strawberry or grape jelly?" I ask Sam, who is sitting at the counter.

"Strawberry," is Sam's slow reply because his attention is completely on Calvin, whose attention is completely on me. I spread the jelly on Sam's whole grain toast as slowly as possible.

"I'll have some eggs," the big man looming over me eagerly announces.

When I look up, I don't like what I find—at all. He has his game face on, the one that's won him championships and some shit. Exhaling deeply, I get a plate, push the rest of the scrambled eggs on it, and add a few slices of toast. He has not yet given up on trying to stare me into submission, even as he devours his food.

"Sam, why don't you go brush your teeth and I'll meet you in the playroom after I speak to your uncle." Sam doesn't need to be asked twice. He's up the stairs before I can even finish my sentence. I brace myself for the onslaught of Cal's force of will. Bend not break is my motto today. I am determination with a capital D.

"Okay. Give it your best shot so I can say no and we can go about our business like this never happened."

"Name your price."

"I don't have one."

"Everyone's got one, honey."

*Honey?* "I'm starting to worry. Is this what dementia looks like, or is it just regular garden variety stupidity? You're a gorgeous, famous professional athlete. Walk out the front door and ask the next woman that walks by to do it—or man, whatever tickles your tail. But it won't be me."

"You think I'm gorgeous?"

*Huh? What?* Where do I go from here? How did I even get here? But I'm not given time to respond. Nope. He doesn't even slow down when he sees the expression on my face—an equal amount of anger and frustration.

"Look, I need someone I can trust to keep me from getting molested every time I walk out that door." Hands buried in his sweatpants, he shrugs up his big shoulders and bites the inside of his cheek. "I need you." That's the second time he's used those words, so clearly the first wasn't a slip of the tongue. Had he mentioned the money one more time it would have been so easy, soooo easy to refuse. But having him stand there like a big lump of sorry ass man, looking distressed and asking for my help jolts my cold, dead heart to life. I can hear the crack. I'm starting to break.

"Is that a yes? Your lips are movin' but nothin's coming

# WRECKING BALL

out." The twang is back.

Can you kill someone with a glare? "What exactly is your diabolical master plan?" I say, going with full-on scathing sarcasm.

"You come with me everywhere I go and pretend to be my girlfriend."

"And I get?"

"Money and protection."

"I wasn't aware you'd joined the Cosa Nostra."

His eyes narrow and magically he's back to being his usual arrogant self. "You know what I mean."

So I call his bluff. This should fix him. "It'll cost you. I want to go back to grad school and get a Masters in child development. You can pay for all three years."

"Done." Not a blink. Not a blush. No hesitation whatsoever.

"You said that a little too quickly. Do you have any idea what kind of money we're talking about?"

"'Bout three hundred grand?"

The thrill that chases up my spine at his words really is beneath me, shamefully so. Immediately, the pathetic me makes a pitch for him…

*He did pay you a hundred thousand and put you up in a beautiful room when you had less than fifty bucks to your name. He pays for food and lets you use his car. He asked you nicely.*

My standards have officially hit rock bottom.

"Please," he says in a low, quiet voice. That one softly spoken word is my Achilles heel. My undoing. One look at the vulnerable anticipation on his face kills my resolve, the crack splitting wide open.

"You don't have to pay me," I groan.

"Take the money. I want to pay you."

"I already have a sparkling reputation as a crook by proxy,

I'd rather not add 'paid escort' under my name as well. We'll try it your way, for a while. Who knows, maybe you're right. But if any of this starts to go bad, I expect you to fix it."

"You have my word. I won't let anything bad happen to you."

I look up in the silence and find his expression strangely serious. An ominous foreboding parks itself in my gut. However, I've just given him my word—all I have left of any value—and I intend to keep it. Let the doomsday countdown begin.

\* \* \*

"He's your boyfriend?" my mother screeches.

"Keep it down. I haven't explained it to Sam yet."

Sam is still inside petting my cat, Dozer, and watching a rerun of *Phineas and Ferb*. Or what used to be my cat and is now my mother's. That nasty beast took one look at me, turned tail, and plopped down on Sam's lap, a big grin spreading across the latter's face.

"But he's a Titan," my dear father shouts. Yes, he's shouting. The man that barely made a peep when I explained that my husband had embezzled millions of dollars is close to shouting over an imaginary boyfriend because he plays for the *other* team. Head shaking, he tears his disbelieving gaze from me long enough to flip the burgers on the outdoor grill. Just now I notice that he's wearing an apron. Across it, 'Mr. Hot Stuff' is written in flaming red letters.

"I *said* it's a fake. We're not dating. He's not my boyfriend." I'm almost shouting too now.

"He's a fugazi?"

*Gooood grief.* "Yes, Dad."

"Why would you do this? A fake boyfriend? Why would anyone want a fake boyfriend?" chimes in my mother again.

## WRECKING BALL

*Jesus, Mary and Joseph.* "Nobody *wants* a fake boyfriend and *I* didn't do anything, Mother." Trying to convince my mother of that is going to be tough sledding. "Did you not listen? This was all Calvin's idea...but the plan has merit."

As much as I want to throw Calvin under the bus, I'm not going to. On the drive over, I thought and thought, and even if I still believe it's too much risk for very little reward, for me that is, I have to admit that he's much more media savvy than I am. He's been in the public eye for most of his life. He should know about this stuff, right? Maybe this farce can clean up my image a bit. In other words, and I can't believe I'm saying this, I'm trusting him to know better. *Trust.* Yes, I'm using that word in the same sentence with someone of the male gender. This is a shocking turn of events. However, it's not the gender I'm trusting, it's the man.

"Can I tell the guys at work?" my father has the nerve to ask.

"I'd rather you didn't. We're not advertising it. I just thought you should know in case it got out."

"What do we tell our friends?" My mother is truly at a loss. I almost feel bad for putting her through this, involving her in more of my personal drama. "I'm a very bad liar."

"I know, Ma. If they ask...just tell them...I'm homeschooling his nephew and we're still getting to know each other. It's not serious."

"A fake boyfriend," she grumbles, her shoulders slumping as she walks into the house. "What has this world come to?"

By the time my mother wraps up enough leftovers to feed a small nation, and I tear Sam away from her persistent hug, we get home around nine. The best part of the evening was when my mother's fancy cappuccino machine got clogged and my father decided to take it apart and fix it. Sam was by his shoulder, watching as if it was the coolest thing he'd ever seen.

The kid definitely has a bright future as an engineer if he wants one.

As soon as I park the Yukon, Sam is on his way to get ready for bed. I'm in the kitchen, putting away the leftovers, when a rap on the countertop causes me to glance up. Calvin is sitting on one of the stools, the weight of his stare heavy on me. He's so large and imposing that he actually makes the massive island look regular sized.

"Did you eat?" I ask tentatively. I don't know how to talk to this man. I don't know if I'll get grumpy Shrek, or the guy signing autographs that made me cry. This moment is no different. He shakes his head slowly. "Do you like meatloaf? It's lean, mostly veal. I can warm it up for you." He gives me a brief nod that makes me feel like I just won something.

"Where'd you go?"

*Wow, actual words.* Turning toward the gas stovetop, I get busy warming up his food.

"My parents. They were dying to meet Sam." He nods absently. "Cal...where are his parents?" I place the dish in front of him and wait patiently for his answer. His brow tightens into a scowl and his eyes move to the food he enthusiastically digs into.

"My sister's in rehab. I don't know where his father is. They were never married. He stuck around for a year. We haven't heard from him since." Frustration and anger radiate from his expression, tension rolls off the rigid set of his shoulders.

"Is she going to be okay?"

He meets my eyes and pauses for a beat. "I don't know. She's just like my mother." As the confession leaves his mouth, my heart lurches. We're wading into very personal waters here and I don't want to overstep.

"How?" Curiosity gets the best of me.

## WRECKING BALL

Narrowing, his eyes move off into nothing. I watch his Adam's apple rise and fall. "A drunk." I can tell by his posture and expression how it hurts him, how sensitive he is about it. I'm dying to know more. Although he's being so forthcoming, I'm almost afraid the spell will be broken if I push.

"Is that why I never see you drink?" A small shrug. That's the only answer I get. A teeny, little baby shrug. "They're lucky to have you." The words are out of my mouth before I have time to stop them. His gaze meets mine. Then he gets up and walks to the sink, and I know he's done talking about it. He looks pensive as he washes the dish. "There's a wedding I have to go to next weekend."

I'm too busy thinking about what he's just told me. I'm barely listening, but I catch it, something odd in his voice. *Wedding. Okay. Sure. Whatevs.* Wiping his large hands on a paper towel, he turns and stares me right in the eyes and says, "You're coming as my date."

\* \* \*

"I'm going as his date," I say past a mouthful of maraschino cherries I snagged from the bar well. I waited all night to tell Amber. Yes, I'm a coward. And I didn't even consider telling her about his quarter million dollar offer.

She slips her arms into her jean jacket and simply stares. Amber speechless is a rare thing. "Da fuck??" she finally screeches.

"I know, I know, I know. I had it out with him the other day, but he's convinced it can benefit both of us." I grab my purse and we begin to walk out the back door. It's like someone pushed the button on spring, the weather getting remarkably warmer overnight.

"I can't wait to hear more about this stinking pile of bullshit."

"He doesn't want women hanging all over him, and he seems to think that his superstar, king of New York status can whitewash my tarnished reputation."

"I don't know, Cam—" she offers, her skepticism coming through loud and clear.

"I know. I'm hoping it can distract people long enough to forget about Matt." What I don't say, though we both know, is that it's impossible for me to say *no* to someone who asks for my help. Impossible.

"If he hurts you, so help me God they'll find him floating on the Hudson in five separate coolers." That's Amber for you. Girlfriend always has my back.

"I admire your creativity, but let's hope it doesn't come to that."

We spot the Range Rover waiting at the curb at the same time. Hanging out the window, he's signing autographs for two young dudes who look like they can't believe their luck.

"Your chariot awaits," Amber drawls.

"You want a ride?"

"It's warm out. I'm hoofing it." Calvin glances up and when he catches us standing there, his eyes hold mine. "Too bad you can't use him for sex. He's hot as fudge."

"I believe the expression is 'hot as fuck'."

"Why is that a thing? There must be a lot of optimistic virgins out there using this verbiage because at best the odds are fifty/ fifty when in reality it's closer to seventy/thirty in favor of it not being hot at all—" There's no stopping her once she's on a rant. "Where as fudge is almost *always* hot."

"Duly noted. Hot or not, he's the last person on the planet I would use for sex. Even if that was even remotely on my mind, which it isn't."

"It will eventually. You're too young to be alone."

"Doesn't matter. Everything south of the border is dead.

My cooch is broken."

Snorting, Amber replies, "Your cooch is not broken. It's just...taking a refreshing nap, waiting for a hot as fudge babymaker to come along."

"No thanks. Any kids that man manages to spawn will be mini Shreks."

"Grumpy and cute?"

"Yup."

"I like Shrek."

With a huff, I grumble, "So do I."

Before heading off, Amber narrows her eyes at Calvin, lifts a finger to her neck, and ever so slowly drags it across her throat. I have to give him credit—Calvin doesn't so much as bat a thick black lash.

# CHAPTER TWELVE

THE NEXT MORNING WE LEAVE for the Hamptons bright and early. I'm elated to learn that Sam is coming with us. Both the bride and groom have a couple of kids from prior marriages, as well as the ones they share, which means there will be plenty of kids in attendance for him to play with. Sam seems to have a hard time communicating with other kids, something I noticed at the playground, and frankly it's been bothering me for a while.

When I asked Calvin what the dress code for the wedding was, he magically produced a number of garment bags from Barneys and handed them to me without a word of explanation. There are so many things wrong with that I don't know where to begin, however, I wasn't going to spend money I don't have to dress the part of a *fugazi* girlfriend. Hence, I accepted the clothes without complaint.

The weather is unusually temperate for early May, the road to the Hamptons clogged with traffic. While Sam is busy watching *Minions* in the back seat, my gaze strays to the make believe boyfriend sitting in the driver's seat. A long, muscular arm is extended, his wrist sitting on the wheel while his large mitt hangs down. His sleeves are rolled up and I spot the intricate scroll of a tattoo on the inside of his arm. I'd noticed it a while ago, and even though I'm insanely curious, I'm still not brave enough to ask about it. He got a haircut. Hallelujah. It's not too short or long, and I determine this suits him.

"What are you staring at?"

"Your haircut looks good." I inspect some more. "What happened? Did you run out of razors?" The bottom of his face is covered with scruff, though at least it's neat. For this, I get a grunt. Then my eyes skim over the pale, lavender shirt he's wearing—clearly no issue with his masculinity—and designer jeans. I just can't help snickering. Personally, I like his clothes, but I'd rather pull all my teeth out with a monkey wrench than admit that to him.

"You got a problem with something?" The inquiry is delivered with a bit of an edge to his voice, his eyes trained on the road ahead.

"Seriously, what's with the clothes? When I met you, you looked like someone scraped you off the bottom of a moonshine barrel and now you're Derek Zoolander?"

After a long, *long* pause, he says, "I like clothes."

"You don't say."

Another decade's worth of silence, and he adds, "I never had any growin' up…other than what we got from church." His twang is more pronounced than ever. *Lord have mercy.* Why didn't he just kick me in the teeth? It would've hurt less. My poor, poor bleeding heart can't take it. I'm a pathetic sucker for a hard luck story and his are beginning to pile up.

"And what is the deal with the beard," I question, desperately trying to lighten the mood.

"People don't recognize me."

"You mean women."

He shrugs, his face as still as death. It's so easy for me to read him now, to make his gorgeous ass squirm…like fishing with dynamite. When did that happen?

"Yes, what a hardship it is to be a sex symbol." He shifts

uncomfortably in his seat, a semi-disgusted look on his face. "Maybe posing naked on the cover of the ESPN magazine body issue wasn't the best idea, Champ." The tortured look on his face is so precious I wish I could get a picture of it.

"That wasn't my idea," he snaps.

"Oh really? Whose was it then?"

He grumbles something in a super low voice that sounds like, "My ex." *Hmm. Interesting.* His eyes dart from the road to me. "You saw that?"

I didn't. Amber mentioned it. However, I'm having too much fun to stop now.

"Who didn't? You were on the cover—*naked*. Did they grease you up for that picture? You looked shiny." He looks like he wants to melt into the floorboard of the car. I have to turn my head away from him and bite my lower lip to stop the laughter from busting loose. "What's so horrible about women finding you attractive anyway? Present company excluded of course." At this I get a slow turn of his head, a narrowing of eyes, and a small twitch of his plump lips.

"This may be the last contract I sign. I don't need the complication…besides, I like being alone." He says it so earnestly I can't bring myself to tease him anymore. We descend into silence that eats up time, the mood suddenly grave.

"How do you do it?"

"Do what?"

"Keep going when the world is against you? I remember people calling for your head two season ago. But you bounced right back." For the next few minutes, I watch and wait for his answer.

"I don't listen when they're cheering, and I don't listen when they curse me to hell." Large pale orbs peer at me thoughtfully. "I know what I want, and I'll do whatever it

## WRECKING BALL

takes to get it—nothing gets in the way of that."

If only I had a tenth of his strength and determination. The single mindedness it must've taken him, the force of will—especially since I know he didn't grow up under the best of circumstances. I take those words inside of me and tuck them somewhere safe. So that next time, when things seem bleakest, they might light the way.

*　*　*

Calvin decides to stop by the groom's house before we head to the hotel. The house is a sprawling Nantucket style beach home covered in pale blue shingles with white rose bushes surrounding it. A lawn as tidy as a putting green extends for acres all around, backing right up to a deserted beach. *Real people live here? It's a fairytale house, for goodness sake.*

Barry Marshall, Calvin's agent, an attractive black man in his late fifties I estimate by the look of his short silver hair, greets us at the door with an easy smile. After a lot of bro hugging and back slapping, he directs those pearly whites at me.

"Pleasure to meet you, Camilla. Calvin's told me so much about you."

*Huh?* I sneak a peek at Calvin and find his attention trained on Barry. "Some of it good, I hope?" I follow that up with a strained laugh.

"Come in, come in," he prods, ushering us into the kitchen. Through a wall of windows that overlooks the back of the house, I notice a swarm of people busy setting up the backyard for the wedding. "I'll show you to your rooms."

*What?*

"We got a room in town, Barry. We don't want to impose," Calvin pipes up. *Thank the good Lord.*

"Knock it off. Leslie may leave me at the altar if she finds out I let you stay in a hotel. Besides, the kids are all here. Sam has his own room, and you guys are just down the hall from him."

*Did he just say room? As in singular?* I'm not sure I heard him correctly. What's worrying me more, however, is that Calvin isn't arguing with him. A man that lives to argue is presently *not* arguing.

"Alright."

*Excuse me?* I turn to glare at him and get nothing but mild amusement in return.

"Is that a good idea? I mean—you have a wedding to set up for," I manage.

"It's fine," Barry continues. "Calvin's family."

Two minutes later, we're being shown to a large guest bedroom one door down from Sam's room. After Barry leaves us to get settled, I'm off to Sam's room to make sure he's okay. Cracking the door open, I hear two small voices drifting out from the room. A beautiful girl with long, light brown corkscrew curls and cocoa colored skin is holding a tiny bunny rabbit while Sam is petting it gently on its head. She's older than Sam. I'm guessing around ten years old.

"What's his name?" Sam asks.

"Velvet," answers the girl…and I suddenly feel like a party crasher. Swallowing the lump of cuteness overload stuck in my throat, I back away and walk reluctantly back to my room to deal with the change of plans.

Inside *our* room, that being half the problem, I find the cause of my annoyance sprawled out on the bed with one hand tucked behind his head, and the other flipping through channels. And surprise surprise, he's in his underwear and a t-shirt. Without context, I sometimes forget how big he is—until I see him taking up most of the king size bed I'm supposed to be sharing with him.

"Umm, this is—inappropriate," I say, my tone broadcasting my incredulity. I didn't grow up with brothers. My dorm in college was sex segregated. I've been with one man my entire life! This is NOT OKAY.

With a completely straight face he says, "Why?"

"How about you put some clothes on."

"I have clothes on." The fact that he's completely earnest when he says this would've had me doubled over in laughter if I wasn't so put off. Should I tell him that I have a great view of his balls and pubes from this angle?

"Again, does Barneys not sell underwear? What you're wearing is *not* underwear. It's considered a scrap of cloth—barely."

A deep v carves itself on his brow. "I don't like underwear. And you've seen me in these before."

The hint of sarcasm insinuating that I'm the one being unreasonable burrows under my skin. "Yeah, and I didn't care for it then, either."

Without pausing, he boldly continues, "I'm wearing a t-shirt," and then adds, "for you." Heavy emphasis on the last two words.

*Jesus, Mary, and Joseph.* I press my index finger and thumb to the bridge of my nose, trying to stave off the dull ache growing larger by the second. "You said I would have my own room."

"Change of plans. Roll with it."

*Roll with it?* I can feel the heat *rolling* up my neck. "I thought this was an asinine idea to begin with, but I deferred to you because I thought *just maybe* your judgment wasn't as impaired as I had originally thought. I'm not *rolling* with jack shit. I work for you. I'm the *help*, remember? We're not besties. I didn't pinky swear to share a bunk at summer camp. I don't owe you any favors."

His deep exhale lasts a good five minutes. Then I get a blink, another blink, then more silence. "I'm sorry I said you were the help. I didn't mean anything by it." His voice is low…remorseful. "I'll go tell Barry that we're not staying." He sits up, his legs swinging over the side of the bed. "I'll put some clothes on," he mumbles. I might as well be sticking hot needles under his nails. *Just when I think my life can't get any stranger.* Inexplicably, I'm gripped by an overwhelming urge to laugh.

"So I look like the villain?"

"I'll tell him we need—privacy."

It's my turn to exhale deeply. I'm such a frigging pushover it's disgusting. "Forget it. I'm not troubling them on their wedding day." He turns and stares, his gaze expectant. "But you're putting pants on." A quick nod and he's up, rummaging through his large duffel bag. He pulls out a pair of threadbare bottoms and shoves them on.

"What time do we have to be ready by?"

"Four."

That gives me two hours to try and sleep the headache away. "I'm going to take a nap. If Sam needs me wake me up, but I think he'll be busy with his new girlfriend."

"Girlfriend?"

"Cute girl with long, curly hair."

"Phoebe. Barry and Leslie's daughter."

Grabbing my lounge pants and t-shirt, I walk into the bathroom to change as any normal person would when sharing a room with a man they are *not* routinely sharing bodily fluids with. Upon my return, Calvin is in the same spot I left him in, lounging back on the bed like he's the Sultan of Brunei waitin' on his harem. I watch his eyes work their way down the length of my body and chalk this up to him being male, and therefore, simple.

# WRECKING BALL

"This is the line you do not cross under any circumstance," I state, drawing an imaginary line down the center of the bed. He says nothing, though I notice a subtle twitch of his lips. Lying down with my back to him, I set the alarm on my phone and fall quickly asleep.

*  *  *

*Why is my cat scratching my head?*
"Dooozzzer, get de fud off," I mumble, drifting in and out of consciousness. The scratching sensation on my head persists. *Frigging cat.* Then I catch a whiff of laundry detergent and…man. This piques my interest. Prying my eyes open one at a time, I realize I am not, in fact, on my pillow, nor is my cat even in the general vicinity. It's a beard scratching my head.
*Oh shit, oh shit, oh shit.* I peel my face off a hard, t-shirt covered chest, my cheek sweaty, a little spittle on the side of my mouth, and look up. *Damn.* He's staring down at me, his expression relaxed. As if it's perfectly normal for me to be sleeping with my entire body wrapped around him like I'm a baby orangutan clutching its mother with my arm thrown over his waist and my leg straddling his…
*Is that a woody against my thigh?*
I want to die a thousand deaths at the moment, a thousand frigging deaths. Slowly, ever so slowly, I pull all my appendages away from his body and roll over onto my back.
"Sorry." What the hell else is there to say? When he doesn't answer right away, I brave a sideways glance.
"It's fine."
"Why didn't you wake me…push me off?" *Punch me in the face*—it would've been less humiliating.
"You were comfortable."
Without meeting his eyes again, I scurry into the bathroom with my tail tucked. "Taking a quick shower."

Twenty minutes later, after a long shower, I've mostly recovered from my bout of shame. It's so strange sharing a room with a man again. It reminds me of Matt, the first time I've given him a thought in the last three weeks. I guess this is just one more step in the grieving process. Maybe I should thank Calvin for helping me with it, because I can't imagine ever doing this willingly with another man.

I step out of the bathroom wearing a large robe I found on the back of the door, and find Calvin in the process of stripping out of his t-shirt like he gets paid to do it. I'm instantly rooted to the spot on the carpet. Do I turn around and go back into the bathroom? Do I say something? He lifts it over his head and a wall of cobbled muscles swiftly kicks me in the organs that make babies. Not like I haven't seen them before, but I was never allowed to stare. I'm staring now.

The words "breeding stock" come to mind—no doubt they thought of him when they coined the term. I might have sworn off men for all eternity, but I still have all my reproductive parts intact and they are presently rousing from deep hibernation. I can almost hear them sputtering on in the same manner my grandmother's forty year old Lincoln Continental used to every Sunday when she drove it to church. Not five minutes after I've stepped out of a shower, my pits are sweating heavily.

His head pops up, and I quickly look away.

"Bathroom's all yours," I mumble. Taking his stuff, he shuts the door behind him. *Thank frigging heaven.*

Inside the Barneys garment bag is one of the most beautiful dresses I've ever seen. A pink, gauzy Valentino creation that I'm scared to touch because I'm certain it costs a small fortune. I'm convinced it won't fit. And yet as I zip it up, I'm shocked to learn that it fits perfectly. How Zoolander even got my size right is beyond me. Also, I'm pretty sure I don't want to know.

Without fanfare, I pull my long hair back, slap on some mascara, and apply lipgloss. I'm ready to go to Sam's room when Cal steps out of the bathroom wearing only a towel wrapped around his waist. I give myself major props for managing to keep my eyes fixed firmly on his face.

"I don't know how you got my size right—and I'm pretty sure I don't want to know—however, thank you for the dress. Playing your pretend girlfriend isn't such a hardship in this," I say, glancing down at the pink gauzy silk swishing around my legs. My eyes lift and I realize he's scowling. "It's a joke, Cal." Still scowling. "Obviously, a poor one—I'm thanking you for the dress. It's very generous of you." I get one of his signature short nods and he walks off to get dressed. "I'll go get Sam," I say over my shoulder. Well, that was weird.

# CHAPTER THIRTEEN

SAM IS ONE HANDSOME YOUNG man dressed in his gray dress pants and blue dress shirt. He hands me his tie and I make quick work of it. After he slips on his loafers, we go in search of Calvin. Guests have been steadily arriving. The din emanating from the backyard reaches well into the large house. Calvin steps out of the bedroom just as we're passing. He's wearing a three-piece, dark gray suit with a pearl gray shirt and black tie. If this football thing doesn't work out, he definitely has a future as a fashion model.

"Ready?" I ask. A short nod later and I'm taking Sam's hand again.

In the backyard, a who's who of professional athletes in a variety of sports, a couple of team owners, and other industry professionals mingle like they all know each other well. You can smell the money wafting off these people. The thought makes my steps falter. Right about now I'm feeling like a real *fugazi*. Cal's observant eyes catch the reticent look on my face. Scowling, he takes my hand, and pulls me and Sam through the crowd.

A stunning trellis covered in hanging wisteria, along with rows and rows of white chairs, sets the scene for the service. Acres of green lawn back right up to a deserted beach. Soft jazz plays in the background. Not only does every detail scream money and class, but worse yet, full blown romance. And not of the over the top kind. The kind that every female, even the cynical ones, melts over.

As we walk through the crowd, Calvin's expression is tight, vigilant…well, tighter than usual. He seems to be growing progressively more stressed by the minute.

"Are you okay?" I dare to ask. His eyes, glacial as they play off the color of his shirt, snap to me in irritation. *Okay… I'm sorry I asked.* Then he spots someone in the crowd and the muscles of his neck pop in relief, his jaw pulsing. I'm actually afraid he may shatter a molar.

"What is it?" My gaze follows his and lands on a tall brunette. She's elegant, very pretty, not eye popping gorgeous though definitely noticeable. She's also older than me. Around late thirties, I estimate. Not that she has a single line on her face, but she has a certain confidence about her that comes with age. Her wide smile is all for the tall, attractive man with salt and pepper hair standing next to her. I study them surreptitiously. They seem very much in love and I determine they suit each other. My gaze shifts back to Cal. He's still watching them. And then it dawns on me.

"Is that your ex?"

"Let's get a drink."

Suspicion confirmed. He walks away before I can utter another word. *His ex?* And now I know why he wanted me here. Sam puts his hand in mine and we follow Calvin to the bar. While we're waiting for our soft drinks, Phoebe comes to fetch Sam. There's a glimmer of excitement and curiosity in his big gray eyes I haven't seen before.

"Hi, I'm Phoebe," she announces without a shred of timidity. She's so cute in her pale blue flower dress it's no wonder why Sam is so taken with her.

"Hi Phoebe."

"Can Sam come play with us over there?" she says, turning to point to a bouncy castle off to the side of the house.

"Sure, you don't mind if I tag along, do you?" Without a reply, she takes Sam's hand and leads him away.

Glancing up, I find Calvin staring out in space. I know what loss looks like and it's written all over his face. Something about that look pricks at my conscious. However, this isn't the time, nor the place to explore what's going on in his head. I murmur to Calvin that I'm going with Sam, and distractedly he gives me a curt nod in reply. While I'm standing near the bouncy castle, with two other nannies in attendance, I notice a friendly face approaching.

"Has your ear recovered?"

"No. Can you kiss it and make it better?"

"Didn't I warn you to save that stinky ass cheese for my mother?"

Vaughn's smile is wide and ultra white. One hand is tucked in the pants pocket of a navy suit, the other cradling a drink. He's absurdly handsome. Though now that I've gotten over the initial shock of all that handsomeness, I notice it the same way I would notice if someone was wearing two different shoes—as an interesting and peculiar novelty.

"On the run from your fan club?"

My eyes are still on Sam, who looks like he's having the time of his life. He's holding both of Phoebe's hands as they bounce up and down out of synch, both of them giggling and screeching hysterically.

"My ego needed a boost so I thought to come find you."

Surveying the growing crowd, I ask, "Have you seen Calvin?"

"Talking to Hendricks." He looks over his shoulder, and motions to the twin towers near the bar. One, dark and brooding. The other, light and sunny.

# WRECKING BALL

"How long have you known him? It seems to be more than a working relationship."

"We've been friends since Florida State." Lids at half-mast, lashes throwing shade, he peers at me thoughtfully with deep brown eyes. "How did you convince him to come?"

"Get him to come? Are you joking? I can't even get him to wear underwear—" My words come to a stuttering stop when Ethan's eyebrows climb up his forehead. "Strike that from the record, counselor. You should know your client well enough by now to know that he does whatever he wants. He asked me—strike that, too. He didn't ask, he *informed* me that I was to attend as his date."

Ethan's mouth hooks up briefly. "That sounds about right."

Before the silence has a chance to grow awkward, he adds, "He pretty much hasn't been out of the house for the last three years—besides practice and games." His intense eyes remain on me like a spotlight, measuring my reaction. *Three years? Wait...what?*

"His ex is here," he adds.

"We saw her with a date."

He nods. "Yeah—her husband is the new GM of the NY Gladiators. That's another reason I'm glad he came with you. Now it won't be so fucking awkward when we see her at team functions."

I can do nothing to hide my surprise. "Why would he see her at team functions?"

"She's Director of Player Personnel for the Titans."

*Wow, didn't see that coming.* "So he has to see her all the time?"

"All the time," Ethan repeats with an exasperated sigh.

"I've been looking all over for you," growls a low voice I've come to know well. By the time I glance over my shoulder, he's right behind me. I turn and take him in. If I didn't know any better, I would think he was completely chill. But I *do* know better and the ticking of his jaw muscle is a dead giveaway.

"I told you," I explain very softly, "that I was going with Sam, and you nodded."

This new information takes a few seconds to process. I see the wheels spinning and know when he recalls it because his chin tips up and jaw relaxes. Looking away, he mutters, "I didn't hear you."

In my peripheral vision, I notice Ethan watching Calvin closely, a question in his eyes—though he doesn't voice it.

"Do you need me? Because I can get Sam out. I'm not leaving him in that thing unattended." Calvin's pointed gaze moves to the two nannies talking and not paying any attention to what's going on around them. "I'm not leaving him," I repeat and get one of his nods.

"I'm going to need another one of these if I have to last another couple of hours," Ethan deadpans, rattling the ice in his now empty tumbler.

"Later, counselor. Try not to cause a stampede of single ladies." Ethan walks away after giving me one of his slaying grins. I glance up and catch Calvin frowning, his lips tight. He doesn't seem to find my humor amusing, or anything else for that matter. "Didn't your mother ever tell you that your face is going to freeze that way?"

"My mother was too concerned with getting wasted than what my face looked like."

I'm speechless. It takes me an eternity to recover from that stunner. Mouth hanging open, words caught in my throat, all I manage is a feeble, "Cal..."

His troubled gray stare moves over my shoulder, his full lips pinch. "I shouldn't have said that. I'm sorry." He blows

## WRECKING BALL

out a deep breath and rakes his fingers through his hair. My gaze remains on him, willing him to look at me—but he won't.

"Let me get Sam."

At the bouncy castle, Sam and Phoebe are getting out. His face is all sweaty, his hair sticking to his forehead, his shirttails falling out of his pants. There's a wild, excited look in his big eyes I haven't seen before. "Let's get you cleaned up before the service starts," I say, taking his hand. Calvin follows us as we make our way through the crowd, toward the bathroom.

Fifteen minutes later, we take our seats as the wedding begins. It's beautiful. The couple is surrounded by a passel of children, some from a prior marriage, some they share. They make quite the stunning pair. Both tall and fit. Him, dark and solemn. Her, pale and bubbly. Their love for each other and their kids permeates everything around them, extending over the crowd like a blanket of warm fuzzies that has me on the verge of shedding tears. The whole day has brought back memories and feelings I was doing a good job keeping at bay.

Calvin's brooding silence continues throughout the service and dinner. Our table is mostly Titans players and their wives and girlfriends. He doesn't socialize unless someone approaches him—even though he seems to know everybody. While he continues to ignore the world at large, I watch the bride and groom slow dance like no one else exists and it makes me sad as shit.

Phoebe comes to collect Sam shortly after the meal is over. He leaves Cal and me without a backward glance. Tempting as it is, I resist the urge to give him a standing ovation as I watch them walk away hand in hand. I guess he just needed the right person to come along and change his mind about keeping to himself.

I'm waiting in line at the dessert buffet, ready to drown my gloom in a triple scoop ice cream sundae, when someone taps me on the shoulder.

"How about a dance, darlin'?" Justin is standing behind me, uncharacteristically subdued and wearing a suit.

"What are you up to, Dimples?" I drawl suspiciously.

"Come on. You look like you could use a dance." Before I can object he takes my hand and drags me onto the dance floor.

I've never been much of a dancer. Actually, I suck at it. But if I don't distract myself at this point, my spirits will hit rock bottom very soon.

Justin clutches my hand like I'm his eighty year old grangran and places his other one respectfully high up my back. Then we proceed to do the white man shuffle, rocking back and forth from foot to foot.

Still sitting at our table, Calvin is staring out at some indefinable point in the distance that seems to have somehow offended him. By the look on his face, *not* getting his attention would be the best course of action. In this mood, he's liable to do anything.

"You're doing this just to piss him off."

"He's an asshole."

I snicker at how simple things seem at his age. "Not usually," I find myself answering truthfully. "You're going to need him to throw you the ball, Dimples. Not antagonizing him would be a good idea."

My eyes meet Calvin's and the amusement falls away from my face. Putting it mildly, he looks like he's about to commit bloody murder. It certainly looks like he's daydreaming about it. Suddenly, to his left, I spot trouble in the form of a stunning blonde in a painted on cocktail dress. She wraps her claws around Calvin's forearm as he's rising from his chair. His expression instantly transforms to a frozen look of dread and just as quickly, an odd streak of protectiveness raises my hackles.

"Thanks for the dance, Justin, but I gotta go rescue my… um…boyfriend." I mutter the last word under my breath.

"Boyfriend?"

The question hangs between us, which I don't bother to explain. Instead, I ditch the dance floor and march over to the table where the aggressive blonde has made herself at home in my seat. Without preamble, I do my best impression of a possessive girlfriend. Might as well have some fun, I figure.

"Boobear—" Placing my hands on my hips, I go with an over the top whine. "You promised me the next dance."

Every conversation at the table comes to a screeching halt, a curious look on all their faces. Both the blonde and Calvin glance up. The blonde releases her grip while her eyes travel over me. I know she's calculating her chances of stealing him away and see exactly when she's determined that I'm an unworthy rival.

The embalmed expression Calvin's wearing lifts for a moment. He murmurs something to the blonde and shoots out of his chair. As we make our way to the dance floor, he leans down and whispers in my ear, "Boobear?"

The feel of his wide palm on my lower back makes my breath catch. So foreign, and yet so familiar, comfortable…*huh*.

"You wanted me to block bitches for you. Consider her blocked." In the silence, I look up. I'm almost positive I can see a smile in his eyes…maybe. The eye contact makes me edgy so I redirect my gaze to his shoulder.

Taking my hand in his, he wraps the other securely around my waist and we start moving slowly across the dance floor. Just as a Sinatra song comes to an end, Etta James' *At Last* comes on. Cue the eye roll. Could there be a more sickeningly romantic song? That's a hard no. I'm suddenly flushed and embarrassed, unsteady, where as Cal's hold on me is determined. The man expertly takes charge. He isn't at all awkward about it like I am. I don't even have the stones to look up at him again. Every single place his body touches mine feels scalded. My boobs are smashed up against a wall of granite wrapped in silky wool. And the heat…good golly, the heat coming off of him is nuclear. My thighs are starting to sweat. I can feel the dampness accumulating between my bare thighs. *This is not good.* He's a great dancer. I don't even bother pretending to know what I'm doing; I just follow his lead. And I can say without a doubt that this is not the white man shuffle. This is like…well, it's like good foreplay.

"I'm a shitty dancer."

"I know."

At his absent reply, I glance up and find his mouth curving up ever so slightly. "Don't spare my feelings, really."

"You'd rather I lie to you?"

Those words hit me hard and fast. "No," I say, shaking my head. "Whatever happens, please don't ever lie to me. It's the one thing I can't handle." The look on my face must've broadcast my panic because concern just as quickly alters his.

"I won't ever lie to you, Cam. I promise." Guileless and open, I can see it in his eyes that he means it. His promise reaches inside my heart and makes itself at home.

"Calvin," calls a smooth feminine voice. We both stop moving. His ex-wife stands before us with a soft smile, her expression serene. "I wanted to say hello." She extends a slim fingered hand at me. "Kim Holtzman."

She's elegant, self-assured from something that has nothing to do with her looks. Next to me, Calvin seems to have moved. He's standing even closer—and as tense as he would be for a rectal exam. I shake her hand without hesitation, "Camilla DeSantis."

Her focus shifts to Cal and my eyes follow hers. "I didn't

expect to see you here." She smiles affectionately. "Then again you've always had a knack for surprising me."

"I have a good reason to get out more." Nobody fails to get the implication. My gaze drops to avoid her scrutiny, afraid that she may see the guilty look on my face.

"Well, you look good," she states. And for some absurd reason, the way she checks him out bothers me.

Without thought, I lace my fingers through his and say, "We should find Sam."

Calvin nods and smiles at me. Yes, smiles. No teeth, but it's definitely a smile. It's like a sighting of Bigfoot. I'm momentarily stunned. Did I really just witness it? Am I losing my mind? Probably a little of both. Recovering quickly, I say, "Nice to meet you, Kim. I'm sure we'll have occasion to speak again," and pull Calvin away.

\* \* \*

The young man in question is busy playing a video game with four other children of various ages. After determining that the game isn't too mature, I allow him to play a little longer. It's so wonderful to see him smiling and laughing like all the other kids that I don't want to do anything to diminish his joy.

Back in our room, I strip and hang the dress back up. I can't imagine when I'll ever have the opportunity to wear it again. Merely entertaining that thought for a moment sinks my mood further into the mud.

As soon as I'm tucked in, Cal enters dragging his feet and tugging on his tie. He's quiet—what else is new. No thought to privacy whatsoever, he starts undressing in front of me as casually as if he's done it a million times. God only knows how many women he's gotten naked with. I don't wait for him to notice the disapproving frown on my face because, more than likely, he won't care anyway. Instead, I scramble out of bed as soon as he begins to unbuckle his belt, and take it as my cue to go check on Sam. Like my hair is on fire, I throw on a hoodie and head out the door.

Sam's already tucked himself in and turned off the lights. It seems like he's been taking care of himself for a while; he's too self-sufficient for a boy his age. Not for the first time, I wonder if his parents know what an amazing kid they have, how unbelievably lucky they are. By the looks of it, I'd have to say no. Which, of course, pisses me off beyond measure.

After counting to ten, I enter our room again. Calvin's sprawled out on top of the covers, no t-shirt, barely any underwear—no surprise. *Oh brother, he's staring at the ceiling.* By the look on his face, I know this is not a good time to argue the merits of pajamas so I remove my hoody and climb into bed. Waves of angst are rolling off his big body. I could pretend I don't feel them suffocating me…I could. I probably should…but I don't.

"You want to talk about it?" I get absolutely nothing in response. "I'm a great listener…and let's not forget I signed an NDA." Still nothing. "I think it'll help if you talk about it." An eternity later, I give it one last try. "Are you still in love with her?"

"No."

Why is it that one word can make me feel like I just won the lottery? Pathetic, I'm completely pathetic. I turn on my side and tuck a hand under my face. He's still staring blankly at the ceiling.

"Does it bother you that she's happy?"

"No."

I believe him. Calvin is many things, a liar is not one of them. "What happened between you two?"

"She cheated. Then she left me for the person she cheated with." I can only imagine what that did to a man as proud as

## WRECKING BALL

Calvin.

"How did you find out?"

"She got pregnant."

"They have a baby?" I confirm, my voice just above a whisper.

"Hmm."

"Did she tell you? That it wasn't yours."

"She insisted on a paternity test...but I couldn't have gotten her pregnant."

I can't stop the eye roll at his gullibility. "A lot of women lie about birth control, Cal. Not to mention a shit ton of reasons why it fails."

His eyes catch mine in a sideways glance, measuring me, considering his words. The silence stretches on and on. I yawn. I'm about to give up and go to sleep.

"The first thing I did after the draft was get a vasectomy."

*Huh. Say what?* His dark head does a slow turn in my direction, his eyes searching for a reaction. Shock. That's my reaction. Total. Frigging. Shock.

"Did you say va–sec–to–my?"

"Yup."

"*Why?*" A teeny, tiny bit of outrage on behalf of womankind makes me sound a tad shrilly.

"Because I don't want kids," he spits out sharp and fast. Processing his words takes an inordinate amount of time. My mind goes down alley after alley of every conceivable reason and still hits dead ends.

"There has to be more to it than that."

Resignation rings loudly in his deep exhale. "I'm the oldest of eight. I've changed more diapers and heated more bottles than any one person ever should. I don't want any part of that ever again, as long as I live." His twang is back with a vengeance. And now I have about a million more questions wanting to burst out of me.

"What about your parents?"

"More concerned with getting wasted than with the kids they kept spittin' out like jackrabbits."

*Jeeezuuuz.* The bottom drops out of my stomach. Gray meets brown and I'm hit by the conviction burning in his eyes, blown away by it. This is what determination looks like. I sympathize, I do. And yet as a woman who wants children, it hits me on a personal level.

"But...but...but..." He's reduced me to a stammering idiot. "Didn't your wife want kids?"

"Not when we got married. She was all gun-ho about her career. I explained it to her a thousand times and she promised she understood. But then I was only twenty-two, she's five years older, so she probably thought she could change my mind."

"How did she feel about the vasectomy?" His cool gaze bores into mine. "Holy shit, she didn't know?"

"I told her I wasn't having kids." His full lips are set in a tight line, his dark scruff covered jaw locked.

Hiding my shock is out of the question. *Face-palm. How to handle this?* I understand his point, but to omit a bombshell of this magnitude? Talk about a matter of trust.

"Calvin," I say über gently. "I completely sympathize with your plight, I do, but you can't believe that a marriage based on an omission that important could survive the aftermath."

Unapologetically, his heavy-lidded gray gaze holds mine. Sometimes I really do admire his arrogance, how self contained he is. If only a microscopic piece of it would rub off on me, maybe I could start to put my life back together. I can see the wheels turning in his eyes, past hurts and old argument coming to the surface and retreating. He bites the inside of his cheek, a clear sign of his discomfort.

## WRECKING BALL

"I was young. If I were to do it over again...I don't know."

"I give you more credit than that. I think you would tell her. As a matter of fact, I think it would lighten that yoke you carry around your neck if you told her that you regret it."

"Not happening."

"Suit yourself," I reply with a shrug and close my eyes.

An age later, I hear him say, "Why?"

I crack open my eyes one at a time to find another lovely scowl doctoring his face—although it looks more like frustration this time. "Why do I give you credit?" He answers my query with a quick nod. "Because I've learned the hard way to judge a man's character by his actions, not his words." He holds the eye contact longer than I find comfortable. I turn my back to him and pull the blanket up to my neck. "Now stop chewing my ear off and let me get some sleep."

The next morning I wake up with the sweet scent of clean man filling my lungs and soft puffs of air hitting my temple. After wallowing in confusion for a few seconds, it dawns on me that I'm snuggled in the nook between Calvin's throat and armpit. Right before mortification can set in, I catch a soft snore. I can't resist the temptation to listen for a while, the feeling bittersweet. The sound wraps around my heart and squeezes painfully. Tears pool in the corners of my eyes. The memory of what I had and what I lost, the knowledge that I may never have it again, hits me like a freight train. That's the thing with grief. It's fickle and selfish. It doesn't follow any rules, and shows up when you least expect it. One limb at a time, I slowly peel myself away, retreat to the bathroom, and shed my tears in private.

*** * ***

On the drive back home, Calvin remains in quiet contemplation for most of the ride. I determine this must be the result of all the disclosures of the night before. Maybe he regrets telling me. Maybe he's had second thoughts about whether I can be trusted with such personal information. Whatever the reason, I feel this pressing need to clear the air between us. I would hate for him to worry that I'm someone he needs to protect himself from. Though, in the end, I can't muster the courage to broach the subject.

By the time we pull into the garage, close to nightfall, we're all dog-tired. I slide out of the Rover and go to grab my bags but he beats me to it.

"It's okay. I've got it."

"Let me," he mumbles, directing the words at some unseen point in the distance. As he reaches the door, he stops and turns, his shuttered eyes meeting mine squarely. "Thanks for coming."

The words 'what are friends for' are on the tip of my tongue but they die on my lips. We're not friends. We're just two people thrown together by circumstance. Before I can do something really stupid like persuade him into talking about what's bothering him, I remind myself that in two months time I'll be gone and his life will continue as if we've never met.

"No sweat," I answer. After which, I watch him disappear inside, taking his heavy thoughts and somber mood with him.

# CHAPTER FOURTEEN

"Hmm," says the man sitting across from me. I look up from picking at the nail bed of my thumb and meet his thoughtful gaze.

Four months ago, out of some insane unfounded optimism, I sent my resume to a bunch of schools that had teaching positions available. One of them actually called to set up an interview. The cherry on top was that I received the call while Calvin was busy digging into the egg white omelet with mixed vegetables I'd made for him. Such sweet delight. I won't lie, I spoke loud enough for the entire block to hear. Okay, so it isn't the greatest. Located in one of the worst sections of the Bronx, the commute to New Jersey is awful—and dangerous if I have to stay late for meetings. Regardless, I can really make an impact on the lives of the kids living in that neighborhood so the risk is worth it…and let's face it, not like I stood a chance landing any of the primo jobs in Manhattan and Westchester.

"Are you currently employed, Ms. DeSantis?" Mr. Rodriguez, the Principal and head of the hiring committee asks with a warm, sincere smile. The groves fanning out from his dark eyes and the bristly gray hair lend him an appealing gravitas. I perk up at his query and nod enthusiastically. "I am. I'm currently homeschooling an eight year old boy."

"You didn't list that on your resume."

"Ah, that's because his uncle, the man who hired me, is a… uhh…public figure. I signed a nondisclosure agreement."

Principal Rodriguez's curiosity is piqued. I notice his eyes grow a touch wider. He reclines in his chair and places his hands behind his head, a silent debate clearly being fought somewhere inside his skull. "Well, Ms. DeSantis, as much as I'd like to say it doesn't make a difference that you have no references, I'm afraid I can't. Do you think your employer would be willing to write you one?"

Just the thought of asking Calvin for a favor sets my teeth on edge. "He takes his privacy very seriously," I explain, dejected beyond measure. His blank stare prods me to continue. "I can try." The corners of my mouth creep up in a forced smile.

"Great," the principal answers as if it's all settled.

"Great," I mirror, stiffly reaching out to shake his hand. All that's left for me to do now is to give up the microscopic particle of dignity I have left.

It takes me an excruciating four hours to get back to Calvin's, an accident on the Cross Bronx Expressway turning it into a parking lot. I'm in the kitchen, making myself tea before heading off to bed, when Cal walks in. His intense gaze takes in my rounded shoulders and the mood I'm wearing. Walking past me, he grabs a bottle of water from the fridge and takes a seat at the counter.

"How'd it go?"

"Good."

"You think you'll get it?" he murmurs in between sips of water, his scrutiny a palpable thing.

"Not sure."

A lengthy pause ensues. "Do you need a personal reference?"

## WRECKING BALL

I thought I was immune to surprises. I thought Matt had cured me of those. I was wrong. It takes me a full minute to dig my voice out under all the disbelief. I turn to take in his face. Which is a bit difficult when you have a mostly naked Adonis before you. I may not be cured of surprises, but he'll never be cured of parading around nude.

"You'd do that?" I say, my voice overly bright with excitement. And then he surprises me again by frowning.

"What do you take me for, Cam?" There's a wounded look on his face that makes me feel like garbage. *Jezuz, I hurt his feelings*. I don't ever want to hurt anyone's feelings, least of all his. He stands, looking…shit, he looks disappointed. "I'll have it for you tomorrow."

Without waiting for me to respond he walks out of the kitchen, leaving me to deal with the fact that I suddenly really care about what he thinks, that I'll do anything to avoid seeing that look of disappointment in his eyes ever again.

\* \* \*

We spend the rest of next week treating each other with polite indifference, falling into a routine of sorts. As promised, Cal wrote a glowing letter of recommendation—which only made me feel worse. And to add insult to injury, when I called Principal Rodriguez to inform him I was emailing it over, he in turn informed me that they had already hired a more qualified applicant.

Without me extending an invitation or him voicing a preference, we all eat breakfast together. Not much is said. Then Calvin goes off and does whatever he does. Training most days. Sometimes at home, sometimes with his trainer while Sam and I complete our lessons. When lunch rolls around, Calvin magically appears again. Not much is said at lunch. Once we're done he goes to his bat cave, I mean his office and Sam and I usually head to the park. Which is exactly what happened today.

After a solid hour of playing basketball, Sam and I go food shopping. It's already late afternoon by the time we pull into the garage. We're in the process of unloading grocery bags and carrying them to the mudroom that leads to the kitchen when I hear shouting. The noise descends into a sort of groan. Sam and I look at each other, drop the bags, and hurry from the garage to the kitchen.

"Camilla!"

Without sparing another second, we run to the gym where we find Calvin sprawled face down on the mats.

"What happened?!" Cal turns his head to face me and I drop to my knees.

"Pulled a muscle in my back," he groans.

"Sam, go get the cold packs in the freezer," I order. Sam doesn't hesitate, sprinting out of the room.

"Where's Mercedes?"

"Needed the day off."

"How long have you been lying here?"

"Maybe an hour."

Instinctively, I start running my hands down his back to check for heat and swelling and find it on the left side of his lower back.

"Tell me if you feel any pain," I say while I palpate the area.

His breath catches. I can feel him holding it. "A little… right there."

"It doesn't seem serious. Most likely a strain. I'll ice it and get you some ibuprofen. Do you want me to call the team trainer?"

"No."

"What about that blonde? The one that comes over to give

you massages?"

"Natalie? Hmm, better not."

"Why?"

He mumbles something that vaguely sounds like 'can't deal with her hitting on me right now', and I have to bite my lower lip to school the grin spreading on my face. Very gently, I massage the area, the heel of my hand pressing and stretching the hot skin of his lower back.

"Ughhh—keep doing that." Short, breathless moans break the sentence apart. "You seem to know what you're doing."

"Played softball 'til my senior year in college."

"Really?" He sounds genuinely confused.

"I think I should be offended."

"No, no, please. I just…"

"Don't worry about it, Champ," I interrupt, taking mercy on him.

Sam returns with the ice packs and hands them to me. His eyes are wide and anxious.

"It's nothing serious, Sam." That seems to calm him a little.

"I'll be fine, Sam," Cal adds gruffly. *Yeah, very reassuring.* However, I cut him some slack since he's in pain.

"Sam, I'll take care of this. Why don't you go start that book we got yesterday." At my suggestion, Sam leaves skid marks. I'm pretty sure he's still not entirely comfortable around Cal.

"You've really been pushing it lately."

"Have to be ready for minicamp."

My eyes do a slow dance over his perfect butt. "You're more than ready. I'd say give it a rest, but your body just did it for me." After he responds with some incoherent grumblings, I continue with, "I don't think we should move you. Maybe I'll just turn the television on while I alternate icing and massaging."

"Okay." That one word does what nothing has ever done before—make him sound vulnerable. My poor, weak heart spasms. After I get him the painkillers and order Chinese take-out for dinner, I start icing and massaging.

"You don't have to stay with me if you don't want to." Something in the tone he uses belies his words, although I could be imagining it—not like I can trust my judgment any longer. "Yeah, right there," he groans.

"If you don't want me to stay, just say so."

"Stay if you want to," he says, hurriedly.

I pick up a remote complicated enough to operate a military drone, and spend the next few minutes fumbling with it. When I have zero success turning on the television, Calvin patiently walks me through it, after which, I resume my tender ministrations. Last season's conference championship game pops up on the flat screen.

"You're a split second late on your release. You didn't trust your receiver—the defensive back read it perfectly." The words leave my mouth before I have a chance to stop them. The moment I finish the sentence I know I shouldn't have.

Palms flat on the mat, his cheek resting on them, he lifts his face slightly to look at me. It's tight—and not from pain.

"Stewart wasn't where he was supposed to be. That's why he got traded."

It's plain as day to me. Cal was a fraction of a second late pulling the trigger and it cost them the championship. "Why aren't you saying anything," he spits out. He's pissed. I hear it loud and clear even though he's trying hard to hide it.

"Because I disagree. You didn't trust him. Watch the film from three years ago. You had the quickest release I've ever seen." We both fall silent for the rest of the game. By the time it ends, he's in 'deep brooding' mode.

## WRECKING BALL

"Do you think you can make it up the stairs?"

"No. I'll sleep on the couch," he mumbles without glancing my way. The rest of the furniture we ordered arrived earlier in the week. The extra oversized down couch is wide enough to sleep two people comfortably.

Slowly, I help him get up, throwing my entire body against his to support his weight, his arm hanging over my shoulder. The scent of deodorant and soap hits me in the strangest way. I recognize it as Calvin's scent. One that's become familiar in the same way that Matt's once was.

That realization spirals out of control. My throat begins to close up and the dampness in my eyes threatens to turn into full on tears. Biting the inside of my cheek, I try desperately to keep that from happening. While Cal stretches out on the couch, I run upstairs to grab his pillow and blanket, and take the time to collect myself.

I'm momentarily stunned when I step into his bedroom for the very first time ever. It's pristine. Everything is either white or beige, the furniture expensive, sheets that look like the King of England would sleep on are ironed perfectly. I grab a pillow and a cashmere blanket off the bed—yes, cashmere—and run downstairs.

"I got your fancy shmancy blanket and a pillow."

After I place the pillow behind his head and hand him the blanket, I glance his way and notice the very serious expression he's wearing.

"The first time I ever slept on a mattress off the ground was in college." His tone is unmistakably defensive...and now I feel like a complete and total jerk for teasing him. Good grief. If he keeps offering hard luck stories, I'm going to have to start a collection plate for him.

"I'm sorry...I didn't mean—I was just being a smart ass. I like your fancy schmancy blanket."

Those gray orbs are still peering intently. I stand there awkwardly for what feels like an eternity, waiting for him to say something, anything. He's so handsome it's a frigging crime against womankind. I can say that as a matter of fact. Talk about hitting the DNA Powerball. It seems inconceivable that someone could be this beautiful and ridiculously talented as well.

"Thank you," he says super seriously.

"You're welcome."

He keeps staring as if he wants to say something else… until it starts to get weird.

"Good night."

The expectant look in his eyes dissipates. "Night."

\* \* \*

When I step into the living room the next morning, I find him watching the same game tape we'd watched together. He turns to look at me and the expression I find does not bode well.

"You're right," he mutters. Then his gaze returns to the television. For the sake of peace, I bite back the urge to say 'I know.'

"How's your back?"

"Better."

"I suggest you relax today. Can I bring you some stuff to keep you busy? Books or anything?"

"Na, I'm good," he grumbles like a sullen teenager.

"Veggie omelet?"

Tearing his eyes away from the game footage one more time, he pins me with an intense gaze. I have no clue what this means and I'm pretty sure I don't want to know. I give him a 'well?' look and he nods.

In between my lessons with Sam, I spend the better part of the day shuttling back and forth from the living room, to the kitchen where Sam and I work on reading comprehension, addition and subtraction. Cal seems to get progressively grumpier as the day wears on. I had no idea how many different ways my name could be yelled until this very moment. Mercedes wanders into the kitchen around lunchtime. I give her my most pitiful look, which goes nowhere. "Don't look at me. He's calling you," she bluntly states, no sympathy for my plight.

As soon as I'm done with Sam, I walk into the living room to see if he needs anything and find him on the carpeted floor stretching.

"How does it feel?"

"Much better."

"Yeah, well, you need to take it easy for the next two days. Are you going to get an MRI to see if there's a tear?"

"Made an appointment already." I get another indecipherable look.

"Turn around and I'll massage it."

I don't have to ask twice. I almost laugh at how quickly he gets into place. Lifting his shirt, I palpate the area. And after I determine that there's no heat, which tells me he should be on the mend in no time, I grab the heating pad and apply it. He lets out a deep sigh as I begin to work the balm into his skin. His eyes flutter shut, his long black lashes sitting on high cheekbones.

"Lower," he orders. "Pull my pants down."

"Excuse me?" I chuckle.

"What's the big deal?" he grunts out.

"I get it that you like getting nude in front of strangers, however, I'm not one of your many admirers. Believe it or not, I can live my whole life without seeing your bare ass and be just fine." As I say this, I yank the elastic of his track pants down to his crack (no underwear, obvs) exposing two back dimples...I think they just winked at me.

An army of red ants is suddenly crawling up my neck, which irritates the crap out of me. Next, I start to feel everything south of my waist grow suspiciously warm. *What the*...I avert my eyes from those pesky dimples and work the muscle next to one.

"I grew up sharing a two bedroom trailer with ten people. I had no idea what privacy was until I bought my first house. You get over being shy real quick." The last few words are colored by a twang.

Aaand I just got double barrel kicked in the sternum. Ouch. This is starting to become a habit. I don't even know what to say to that, so I keep my fat mouth shut.

"How long did you play softball?" he continues in that panty melting deep voice of his.

"Until my senior year at Boston College."

"What position?"

"Pitcher."

At this, his eyes crack open and study me closely. "You must've been really good."

"Hmm. I had an ERA of 1.82 and 237 strikeouts." Softball had always been easy for me.

"That makes you one of the best in the league. Why'd you give it up?"

For the first time in years, I'm tempted to tell the truth, the truth that I can barely admit to myself, let alone out loud. And yet for some reason, it feels like if anyone would understand without judgment, it's this man.

"The official answer is chronic shoulder pain."

He scans my face, his sharp, intelligent eyes reading every nuance. "And the unofficial?"

"I didn't have the heart for it anymore. I'm not a competitor like you. The time spent practicing and traveling, the dedication it takes. You know—" At this, he gives me a commiserative nod. "I played because I was good at it with very little effort, but I never had a passion for it."

He's now staring at me like he wants to say something and doesn't know how to begin. After too much time spent in silence, I add, "And if you ever repeat that, I'll get Amber to murder you in your sleep."

At the mention of Amber, he groans. Just then, Sam shuffles awkwardly into the room and mumbles something about his new Lego set.

"Sam—do you know how to play Madden?" Calvin asks him. Sam nods vigorously. "Wanna play a little with me?"

Hiding my shock is out of the question. Calvin has never actually asked Sam anything, let alone to play a game. The smile this produces on my face is just plain silly. I point it directly at the big man lying on his stomach and he kindly answers with an eye roll and a headshake.

Two hours later, I'm groaning, "Can't you just let him win once in a while? Sam? Are you listening?" Both of them ignore me. Sam is as relaxed as I've ever seen him while Calvin looks like he's about to smash the television into a thousand pieces.

"How can you suck this badly?" This question is directed at Calvin in genuine bewilderment. "And how the hell did they pick you for the cover? Do they know how bad you are?"

In response, I get a look intended to melt the skin off my body. "I'm not that bad. It's him!" he says stabbing his index finger at his eight year old nephew.

"Have you played this game a lot?" I ask Sam.

"Yeah."

"With your friends at home?"

"By myself."

My stomach clenches as I realize the subtext; he's hinted at how lonely he is at home on more than one occasion.

"You have this game at home?" Calvin adds.

"You got it for me."

A detail that Calvin seems to have forgotten because his gaze swings back to Sam in surprise. Then Cal's eyes meet mine. In them I see regret and embarrassment.

"If I would've known you were gonna beat my butt like this, I woulda sent you another Lego set."

A huge, white grin spreads across Sam's face. Be still my beating heart.

# CHAPTER FIFTEEN

"It was so much easier to hate him."

It's a busy night at the lounge and since I only have one table left, I'm helping Amber clean the back bar while she serves the stragglers. Amber's face goes unnaturally still. I don't like it one bit. It's the same face she gave me when we were in junior high and I had a crazy crush on Sonny Lynch and she found the doodles in my binder I had drawn of our initials. Yeah, she never let me live that one down.

"You like him, you like him," she sing songs.

"I don't like him. I respect him—which is far worse." She raises a blonde brow. "Okay, maybe I like him a little."

"He's a man. He'll do something real shitty in no time and you'll be back to hating him."

"And I wonder why you're still single."

"'Cause I'm smart, that's why."

"Don't you think it's time to let Parker go, Ambs," I say as gently as possible.

"Is he picking you up?" She's back to staring at the sink she's cleaning. That's what happens every time I bring up the subject of her scumbag ex-fiancé. It's been two years though—and officially time to worry.

"It's impossible to get him to stop. Trust me, I've tried."

I walk to the end of the bar to clean up the well area when, out of nowhere, the flash of a cellphone blinds me. I rub the floating orbs out of my eyes to see a middle-aged woman—with a raging Botox addiction by the waxy texture of her face—giving me a sly, tight-lipped smile.

"Star News. Would you like to comment on the rumors that Calvin Shaw is impotent?"

"What?!" I shout in outrage. "He's not impotent!"

That's my first mistake.

"So you *are* sleeping with him. Does he know who you are? Who your husband was? Are you after his money?" She pelts me with questions so fast I don't have time to do anything other than stand there frozen. The flash of her second photo snaps me out of a deep freeze. I search for Amber and find her busy mixing drinks for a fresh set of customers. I have to get out of there, away from the prying eyes of this woman before I break down in front of her. Ducking out from behind the bar, I march double time toward the kitchen with the reporter hot on my heels.

"Mrs. Blake? Mrs. Blake one more question—" The urge to refute whatever she hurls at me gets the better of me. My steps slow.

That's my second mistake.

"Does Calvin Shaw know your husband killed himself to protect you?"

As the words hit me, the ground beneath my feet seems to fall away. The oxygen is sucked out of my lungs and my heart beats so hard inside my chest I'm pretty sure it's about to implode into a black hole.

*Breathe in, breathe out, breathe in, breathe out.*

But it's too late. The panic attack sets in before I can head it off. On noodle legs, I somehow manage to stumble to the employee lounge and lock myself in the bathroom. Splashing water on my face doesn't help. No matter what I do I can't catch my breath. Sucking in gulps of air that never seem to be enough, I lean against the bathroom wall as long as I can. My knees buckle and my body does a slow slide down. Struggling for every tiny breath of air, it gets too much to fight against. I'm tired beyond measure, so goddamn tired. I just want to sleep for a thousand years. Until all of this fades away. Until I fade away. I don't have the energy to fight it any longer. Resting my forehead on my knees, I close my eyes and let go.

\* \* \*

"You selfish, fucking prick!"

Amber's voice jolts me out of the dark numbness I'm drifting in. Her ladylike shout is followed closely by a *bang, bang, bang*. The door rattles on its hinges. I'm actually surprised it doesn't splinter into a million pieces. *Where am I?* Oh yeah, I'm huddled on the floor of the bathroom, arms wrapped around my knees, forehead resting on said knees. I have absolutely no concept of time. As in what time it is, or how long I've been sitting here.

"If something's happened to her, I swear on all that's holy, they won't find a single tooth of yours to identify, not a goddamn filling."

*Who the heck is she screaming at?* The banging persists. Then I hear the click of the lock. The door is pushed open and a large man crams inside the small space. *Calvin? What the hell is he doing here?* Suddenly he's on his knees in front of me, scowling fiercely. *What's his problem? Because I can't take any more crap tonight. I just can't.* He grips my arms way too tightly.

"Ouch." That startles him. His grip immediately relaxes.

"Let go of her, you pig." Amber is trying with zero success to push the big man out of the way.

"Are you okay?" Calvin's worry is palpable, his face tight. "What happened?"

'Your husband killed himself'…the memory comes crashing back.

"I had a panic attack," I mumble. My eyes flicker between the fury on Amber's face and the concern on Calvin's.

"This is all your fault," she growls at Calvin, who continues to act like she's not standing there ready to murder his ass. He runs his extra large and very warm hands up and down the length of my arms. God it feels *so* good.

"Is this the first time?" he asks softly. Shame robs me of the ability to speak. I shake my head, my eyes moving away from his perceptive gaze. I should be stronger. I should be able to control this. "Can you tell me what happened?"

After exhaling deeply, I start to form actual words. "Reporter from Star News was here…asking about us."

He looks so completely stricken with guilt I almost regret telling him.

"Motherfucker!" shouts the skinny blonde with the foul mouth.

Calvin levels a slightly annoyed glare at Amber. "Give us a minute?"

"No."

His expression softens when it returns to me. "Can you stand?" At my nod, he wraps a muscular arm around my shoulders and lifts me up, securing me to his side. Essentially, I'm under his big wing like he's a mama duck, and I'm the puffy, ruddy faced duckling. Amber's eyes skip back and forth between us. She doesn't budge from her spot in the bathroom doorway. Next to me, I can feel mama duck growing tense, his muscles assuming a certain rigidity.

"Amber—" At my weak prompt, she turns and walks away, grumbling something under her breath—more charming pet names for Calvin, no doubt. While Amber grabs my jacket and purse, Calvin walks me out the employee entrance.

"You're staying with me tonight," she announces once we're in the alleyway behind One Maple.

"No, she's not. She's coming home with me." Amber responds with a filthy glare, which Cal pretends he doesn't see. "Stop flapping those lips and make yourself useful by getting in the car."

I'm surprised Amber doesn't gut him then and there. By the look on her face, she's definitely slow cooking him in a vat of acid in her mind...or skinning him alive with a dull and rusty paring knife.

"Amber, please get in the car." I'm ready to beg on my knees if it will get her compliance. All I want to do is get into bed, hide under the covers, and never come out again. The clear exhaustion in my voice quells her fury for a moment.

"Fine," she grumbles through gritted teeth and jumps into the Range Rover without further argument. Wearing a carefully neutral expression, Calvin helps me into the back and buckles my seatbelt. I'm letting him manage me. I know I am. And yet I can't muster the requisite energy to care. Truth: he's being so considerate it's easier to let him, pride be damned.

Amber wraps me in her slender arms. On the drive to Greenwich Village, to Amber's apartment, Calvin repeatedly glances in the rear view mirror at me.

"How long was I in there?"

"We couldn't find you anywhere. You scared the shit out of us," Amber tells me.

"You didn't answer my question."

"It's two thirty. We've been looking for you for over an hour." Calvin's voice is low, underscored with a hint of anxiety I'm not too far gone to miss. I don't let the thought linger, however, because I *am* too far gone to care.

Not another word is spoken until we reach Amber's

building. It takes another fifteen minutes for me to convince her that it's best I go home with Calvin. As much as I love Amber, I've always licked my wounds in private—that's just how I'm wired—and right now I feel the need to be alone. I can do the postmortem with her tomorrow.

Killed himself? No. No way. Matt's death was an accident. The police ruled it an accident. The roads were icy that night. Was he stressed in the weeks leading up to it? Yes. Depressed? No.

We wait for Amber to enter her building safely before Calvin drives away, on a tear back home. I can feel him watching me.

"I'm fine. Stop looking at me that way," I manage weakly.

His pointed gaze holds mine in the rearview mirror. "You're not fine," he insists, his full lips set in a grim line. "We'll discuss it tomorrow."

"Thanks, Champ, but I already have a daddy."

His eyes instantly turn into two shards of steel, hard and intractable. Whatevs. I'm not sorry. His sudden concern is a bitter pill. He hadn't given two figs about what was good for me not so long ago, and now he thinks discussing it will magically make me feel better?

The Rover moves swiftly up the West Side Highway and over the George Washington Bridge, I close my eyes and stop fighting the sleep pulling me under.

\* \* \*

When I wake the next morning, my head throbs from an emotional hangover like I've been on an all night bender. Minus the fun, of course. I'm in bed, fully clothed with a blanket thrown over me...*hmmm*. I don't even recall getting home last night—and thank my maker it's Saturday because I'm positive I would've been useless to Sam today. A shower

# WRECKING BALL

will have to wait for later since it's already eight and he's probably wondering where his breakfast is.

Throwing on a white button down and skinny jeans, I dash downstairs…and come to an abrupt halt when I spy two Shaw men sitting at the recently delivered kitchen table. Sam is busy digging into a large stack of misshapen pancakes while Calvin eats the last bite of his eggs.

"Who cooked breakfast?" I ask in open surprise. I take a seat at the table and load my plate with food. Sam glances at Calvin, who's watching me with alarming focus.

"Are these pancakes *square*?" All I get is a short nod. "Please stop looking at me that way."

"How often does it happen?"

"May I be excused?" Sam cuts in.

"I thought since it's raining we could go to the New York Aquarium today? What do you say?" Sam nods quickly. "Go on and get ready." I barely finish my sentence and he's already bolting out of his seat with a big smile on his face. His adorableness almost too much.

Turning my attention back onto the pancakes, I say, "Often enough." I can't look at him. I'm hanging onto the edge of control with only a bare grasp on my emotions, what that woman said about Matt hovering over me like a black cloud.

"What did she say to you?"

After a long, long pause, in which I decide I'm too beaten down to verbally spar with him, I go with the truth. "She asked if you were impotent."

The coffee comes flying out of his nose and lands right between my breasts. Hacking and coughing, he stands so quickly the chair topples backward. I get up and pound on his back. Then he tries to dab my white button down with his napkin and I have to swat his hand away from my breast. He actually scowls at me for that.

"What did you say," he wheezes.

"I told her you weren't."

That starts a whole new coughing fit. "You did?"

"A: she took me by surprise," I indicate with my thumb. "And B: what did you want me to say? 'I haven't given him a prostate exam yet but I'll let you know.'"

"Jaysus," he half chuckles.

"Everyone will believe I'm your girlfriend now."

His wheels are spinning, his mind jumping from one possible scenario to another. It's all over his face, and in the way he studies mine.

"You okay with that?"

"I guess. We'll have to see though, won't we?" I say, resigned to my fate.

The silence feels like we're standing on the precipice of something important, a turning point in our relationship that could go either way.

"I won't make you regret it." His expression is so open and earnest that I almost forget that I should be worried. "You can't work there anymore." There's no thrill of victory in his voice. On the contrary, it's comforting and kind.

"I need that job," I say, shaking my head.

"I'm paying you for lost wages. Besides, you're saving me a fortune in what I was paying for those specially prepared meals."

Still too bruised and demoralized by last night's revelations, I don't have the will to argue. "You win."

Except by the look on his face, I'd say he lost as well.

# CHAPTER SIXTEEN

SURPRISES, I NEVER CARED FOR them. There's nothing I hate more than the rush of adrenaline. And after having been woken in the middle of the night to be told that my husband had drowned, I hate them with a passion. So you can imagine how I feel when I'm at Whole Foods shopping, and get a text from my mother telling me to meet her at the hospital because my father had to be rushed to the emergency room. I abandon the full cart in the cereal aisle, grab Sam's hand, and dash to the car.

Ten minutes later I pull up to the valet at the hospital, throw the keys to the attendant, and drag Sam to the ER. The nurse that checks me in directs me to examination room two after I tell her that I'm his daughter and Sam is his grandson—wink, wink. Outside the examination room, I shoot Calvin a text. He's at team facilities, meeting with his trainer, and will be gone for most of the day. I don't want him to worry about Sam when he gets back to an empty house.

"Sam, just sit here for a moment, okay? I'll be right back," I say, pointing to the chair right outside the room my parents are in. I have no idea what to expect and if things get ugly, I don't want him to witness it. Eyes burdened with worry, he gives me a brief nod. It's unquantifiable how much I love this kid.

Peeling back the curtain, I find my father sitting up in bed, hooked up to a bunch of machines. Most importantly, a heart monitor. My mother's face looks drawn, weary. And my chest wants to go ahead and collapse in on itself.

"Dad?" The adrenaline that's busy burning through my veins turns me into a jittery mess, though I do my very best to keep it together.

"I'm okay, Punkin'."

"He fainted," my mother shrills in accusation.

"I got light headed," my father responds.

"The client found him on the floor of her bathroom—passed out."

"I was replacing the bathroom sink."

"Thank God, she called 911 immediately."

"I didn't have breakfast."

And back and forth they go.

"They're checking his heart for a valve leak. I told him two weeks ago to see his doctor." Then my mother turns her full attention on the man in question. "I told you two weeks ago to see your doctor, but did you listen?"

Time to jump into the fray. "When are they doing the tests?"

"Any minute now," my father answers. Over which, my mother adds, "That means we'll be here all night."

A large man is suddenly standing in the doorway. He's dressed in black track pants and a white t-shirt and he's sweaty—like he ran here. "I got here as fast as I could." His gray eyes move from me, to my father, to my mother. None of us move a muscle, or say a thing. We all just stare.

There are moments in life where you don't get a do-over, where the true nature of your character is revealed. You either step up to the plate or lose your chance forever. These moments shape a life. These moments earn you the right to say

# WRECKING BALL

to yourself 'at least I got the important stuff right'. The man standing in the doorway might not consider me a friend, but in this moment he has earned my eternal devotion. "Calvin?" is all I say, stunned and on a level that I don't want to examine too closely, happy as shit.

He steps further into the room and holds a hand out to my mother. "Calvin Shaw, pleasure to meet you ma'am."

My mother looks as dazed as I feel. Then her face cracks into a huge smile as she takes his hand. "It's so nice to finally meet you," she coos. *Good grief.* "We've heard such wonderful things about you. It's a shame it has to be under these circumstances."

Calvin's attention shifts to my father's equally stunned expression. "Sir." The two men shake. "How are you feeling?"

When my father remains mute, my mother interrupts with, "Tom."

"I'm okay...thank you for asking," Tom finally answers.

Who knew my parents were such groupies.

"Can I speak to you for a minute," I say with eyes wide and point to the door. He follows me out to where Sam is still sitting patiently.

"Is Mr. D okay?" Sam asks.

I nod and answer, "Go ahead and say hello if you want." He gets up and leaves Cal and me standing in the hallway. Just then, over his massive shoulder, I realize we are not alone. A large group of nurses and orderlies are now loitering near the nurse's station where there were none before. I can feel the frown forming on my face.

"Are you here to take Sam home?" I ask the big man.

His hands are on his hips. He's peering down at me thoughtfully from his lofty height. He doesn't answer right away, still in the middle of his thorough examination of my person. I start to get a little nervous for reasons I can't explain.

"Do you want me to?"

"I think that would be best. I'm sorry I dragged you two into this. I had no idea what to expect when I got here."

"Don't apologize. I'm just glad he's okay." He stares at me some more. "I'll come back later. Mercedes can watch Sam."

"No, no," I say shaking my head. "It's going to be a long night. You guys need to eat dinner."

"Let me get you something before I go. Coffee?"

I'm about to answer when a pretty, young nurse approaches us. Expecting an update on the schedule for my father's tests, we both turn toward her.

"Mr. Shaw, I'm like, your *biggest* fan," she gushes. *Sure you are, honey—of his face, you mean.* "Can I get your autograph?"

Calvin's expression transforms before my eyes. His brows lower, lower again. His eyes narrow into cool gray slits and his jaw hardens. I want to take a step back and that look isn't even directed at me.

"This isn't a social call. I'm here because my *girlfriend's* father has been admitted for a heart issue. Unless you have some information regarding Mr. DeSantis I suggest you leave us alone."

Heavy emphasis on the g word—heavy frigging emphasis. My stomach is busy doing a flippy thing while the poor girl blanches. Her jaw works in an attempt to respond but nothing comes out. That's when I rush into this, "What Mr. Shaw means to say is that we're all a little concerned at the moment—maybe later."

"Oh…okay," she stammers out, turns on her heels, and flees the scene of the crime.

"Why'd you do that?" Cal practically growls.

"You have a contract to renegotiate, Champ. Bad press isn't going to help your cause."

His sullen expression says everything he doesn't say out

loud. "Coffee?" he grumbles.

"Lots of milk and two Splendas."

"I know."

Before I have a chance to ask how, his broad back is already disappearing down the corridor.

* * *

Sam and Calvin leave shortly afterward. We wait an eternity for the nurse to come fetch my father for his tests. In the meantime, my mother and I hang in the cafeteria.

"He seems like a nice man."

I glance up from my emails to find my mother's attention still buried in a paperback she always carries in her purse.

"Who—Calvin?" She arches a dark, well-groomed eyebrow in a 'don't be stupid' look I know all too well. "Yeah, he is."

"How do you feel about him?"

"I don't feel anything. He's my boss. For the next month and a half at least." That thought sits in my gut like bad fish.

"Hmm," she says, her eyes returning to her book.

"What's that supposed to mean?"

"Camilla, you're a young woman. What happened to you was a tragedy. But at some point you need to move on with your life."

"What does that have to do with Calvin?" I say sharply. Okay so I sound a little defensive.

She takes a long, hard look at me and says, "Nothing."

"And at what point is that?" I push on. "Who gets to determine what a sufficient amount of time is to grieve?"

"So sarcastic," she chides, her short hair bouncing as she shakes her head. "I'm not saying it'll be easy...Matt would agree."

At this, my anger boils over. I have always suspected that my mother was not a fan of Matt so for her to bring his name into this irks me beyond measure.

"Don't bring Matt in to this. And let's stop pretending—you never really approved of him."

"I had nothing against Matt."

"Oh really?"

"You could have done so much more with your life. You're smart, you're talented. You gave up on softball. You gave up on getting your Masters. For what? To make his dreams come true. And look what happened."

Finally—the truth comes out.

"Ma, Matt didn't make me do anything. It was all my choice. Even if the choices were wrong, they were mine to make." The truth of those words crash down on me all at once. I had enabled Matt's behavior. The thorn that has been needling me for the last three years is so obvious now.

"All I'm saying is don't let a good thing get away. Matt's gone. Don't waste your youth grieving for him."

Tears prick my eyes. Part of me knows she's right. The rest of me, however, wants to yell and scream and rail against the world. Why is it that everyone has the answers when they aren't the ones in pain?

My mother glances around at the two other people in the cafeteria. "This isn't the time or place to discuss this." I can't say another word, lost in the knowledge that I may have been just as much to blame as Matt was, that I may have sanctioned his behavior.

*　*　*

Shortly afterward, my father is admitted and moved to a room in the cardiac unit. When my mother informs the nurses that she has no intention of leaving, they set up a cot for her. More for my own sake than theirs, I decide to hang around a little longer, until they both start to nod off. A hot ball of fear large enough to choke a water buffalo gets stuck in my throat as I watch my father sleep. It's so hard to see a man I have only thought of as indomitable, suddenly look so vulnerable.

Fighting back tears, I walk out and find the lounge area down the hall. The clock on the cable box nailed to the wall flashes midnight. For the first time all day, I have a chance to stop and think and realize that, in spite of the bone deep fear I felt when I got the text, I didn't have a panic attack. I guess that's something to celebrate out of this mess. I'm so lost in thought, basking in the relief of this newfound discovery, that I barely grasp what the nurses standing just outside the door in the hallway are saying.

"He's soooo hot," murmurs nurse number one.

"Is he married?" nurse number two tosses up for discussion.

"Divorced, no kids."

"I'll give him some babies, some pretty, cocoa colored babies," joins in nurse number three, followed by a peal of feminine laughter.

"Shhh. He's coming this way." The laughing immediately ceases.

"Can you tell me which room Tom DeSantis is in?" says a man in a smooth baritone.

"Calvin?" I call out in a strangely high voice.

His head pops into the lounge and his alert eyes meet my curious ones. For a fleeting moment, a burst of pure joy steals over me. This is *so* not good. I have absolutely no business feeling anything about him. Taking the seat next to mine, he extends his long ass legs straight and crosses them at the ankles. He has nice ankles, of course. This definitely warrants an eye roll. He drums his thumbs on the armrest of the chair while his eyes travel over the dingy room.

Maybe it's because I'm exhausted and my defenses are down, maybe it's because I'm a shallow, superficial creature at heart...all I know is that I can't stop myself from drinking in the sight of him like he's an oasis and I've been wandering the desert for thirty days.

His hair is still damp from a recent shower, nearly pitch black. And those lashes...gawd, those lashes are cruel. How does a dude get lashes like that when the rest of us are forced to wear mascara? Lit by the overhead light, they throw shadows on his model worthy cheekbones. He hasn't shaved in a couple of days. The scruff covering his lower face, heavy and dark, frames his full pink lips. I think he knows I'm looking at him. And the funny thing is—I think he's letting me.

In a spell, I murmur, "What are you doing here?"

"When you didn't come home, I thought I'd check to see how your father was doing." Perfectly relaxed, his attention returns to the television on the wall, on which a rerun of *The Golden Girls* is playing. "How is he?"

"They ran the tests. We won't know anything until we speak to the doctor tomorrow." I exhale heavily, concern weighing on me. "He's sleeping now." At this, he nods. "Are your parents still in Florida?" The words are out of my mouth before I can stop them. I know how closely he guards his privacy but I can't resist. I want to know more about what makes him tick. I want to know so much more.

He turns to look at me. A long pause ensues. "They both passed away. My mother when I was at Florida State, and my father a few years ago."

"I'm sorry...do you mind if I ask how?"

"My mother had cirrhosis of the liver. My father car accident...I'm surprised he lasted as long as he did." An overwhelming urge to grip his hand and comfort him comes over me. Obviously that's out of the question, so I tuck both hands under my thighs. I literally have to sit on my hands to stop from embarrassing myself. "Ready to go home?"

At my nod, he stands and holds out a hand. As soon as I place mine in his, warmth spreads all the way up my arm. Pulling me up, I feel a brief squeeze before he drops it.

"What about the Yukon?" I mention as we're exiting the building.

"I'll drop you off tomorrow morning."

"You don't have to do that. I'll take Uber."

"The hell you will." He opens the passenger door of the Range Rover and waits as I slide in.

"Excuse me?" On his face, I find a decidedly recalcitrant expression. *Hmm.* I wiggle my brows at him. Anything to throw off his game because that look does not bode well for me; God forbid Calvin Shaw sets his mind on something. For my efforts, I get nothing. Not even a twitch of his lips.

"I'm not having a total stranger drive you."

*He's not having it?* That's…I don't even know what that is. "How is that different from a cab driver?"

"I'm dropping you off." He starts the car and taps on his playlist. George Strait starts to sing *Give It All We Got Tonight*. End of discussion. Might as well save my breath.

# CHAPTER SEVENTEEN

THE NEXT MORNING, I HAVE every intention of calling Uber and sneaking out. Until I step into the kitchen and my plans are smashed to bits by the very determined man standing in the kitchen drinking a green smoothie.

"Ready?" he asks with a slight lift of his lips.

"As soon as you wipe the smug look off your face, Champ."

Twenty minutes later, we pull up to the hospital entrance. I turn to speak but he beats me to it. "Don't worry about Sam. Mercedes and I will take care of him today," he says, rubbing his big hand on his thigh. He's not done surprising me though. "Call me as soon as you have some news."

A hot chunk of emotion clogs my throat. I don't know why I have a sudden urge to cry. I'm not a crier by nature. You would think all the shit that's happened to me lately would cure me of it. Battling the dampness welling in the corners of my eyes, I stare ahead and say, "I can't thank you enough."

"Don't," he cuts in. His hands, on the outskirts of my vision, tighten on the steering wheel. I know I'm making him uncomfortable, but if I don't get this out now, I'll regret it forever. And I'm done with regrets—all stocked up here.

"I just want you to know how much I appreciate everything you've done for me, okay. These last three years have been horrible. Sometimes it feels like the whole world is against me. And you..." The words get caught in my throat. I can't look at him, I'll erupt if I do. "I've learned the hard way not to put off saying stuff...that I might not get another chance." With that, I rip open the door and get out without a backward glance.

By the time I reach my father's room, the doctor has already paid them a visit. I find my mother sipping coffee in the armchair next to his bed, and my father wearing a sullen expression I've never quite seen on him before.

"It's his blood pressure. The doctor said he has to take it easy."

"He said slow down," my father corrects. "How are you doin', Punkin'?"

"I'm worried. But at least, now we know what it is."

"How'd you get here?" Tom casually asks. Who's he trying to fool? We all know this is a well planned hunting expedition.

"Cal brought me." Silence falls like a lead balloon.

"Angel, I could really use a freshly squeezed orange juice."

My mother gets out of her seat. "Anything else, Dear?"

"A rib eye steak and fries."

"I'll be right back with the orange juice. Cami, you want anything?"

"No, I'm good, Ma, thanks."

My mother grabs her purse and exits. We both watch her go, a soft affectionate smile lingering on my father's face. "God, I love your mother."

"I know, Dad." My entire life, that's never been in question. Growing up with these two lovebirds was mortifying when I was a kid. As an adult, I've always envied them.

He looks at me pointedly. "You know how your mother and I fell in love."

At this, I'm ready to poke my eyes out. "Not again, Dad, please. I've heard the story a million times."

"No, you haven't." At the serious inflection in his voice, my eyes snap to his. "We never told you about Liz Infantini."

"Who the heck is Liz Infantini?"

"The reason your mother and I fell in love."

"Huh?"

"Liz was the girl every guy in the neighborhood wanted."

"Am I going to hate this story?"

"Patience. Now where was I...Liz, right. Young. Old. It didn't matter. One look at Liz and they all fell like dominos." I sit on the end of his bed, so taken by the story my knees turn weak. "Guys went at her hard. Flowers, expensive gifts. Tony Bartorelli offered her a ten day all expense paid trip to Jamaica. Liz wouldn't have any of them. Me, I liked Liz, really liked her. I mean...five ten, a body like Sophia Loren, auburn hair like Rita Hayworth—"

"Alright, Dad. Stay on topic."

"Anyway, I was a good lookin' kid. You're beautiful and I had something to do with that." Tom isn't exaggerating. I've seen enough pictures. Blunt and even masculine features coupled with large dark eyes and a blinding white grin. My dad was handsome.

"But I was shy. I didn't know how to talk to her, so I didn't...until she talked to me." Dad takes a deep breath. "It lasted a year. I was crazy about her. Then, right after graduation, she dumped me for Eddy Wachoski. I enlisted in the Navy and that was that."

"You're going somewhere with this, right?"

"Patience. We docked in New York for two days. My mood was still in the dumps. My buddies insisted I hit the bars with them. I said I would, but first I wanted a really good slice of pizza, so we headed to Little Italy to get a bite to eat before

## WRECKING BALL

we made the rounds. That's when I spotted your mother… beautiful, not in the same way Liz was, in her own way. She reminded me of an angel." The dreamy look my father gets on his face makes me smile. "The line for the pizza joint wrapped around the block. We were all in line, waiting to be served, when my buddy started speaking to her friend.

"The first thing I said to your mother was that I just broke up with my girlfriend and I wasn't ready to start something new. She said she understood. We waited in that line for forty minutes. We talked the whole time. And after we ate, she scribbled her address on a paper napkin and said—to my dying day I'll never forget this— 'I know your heart is broken, but a man that can love that deeply is a man worth having as a friend. If you ever get lonely, write me a letter and I'll write you back.'"

The wet glaze in my father's eyes is almost too much for me to bear, my throat closing up.

"That's how the letters began?" I say, shocked out of my Converse All-Stars.

Nodding, a soft smile gracing his lips, Dad says, "That's how the letters began. I was nowhere ready in my head to fall in love again. But something in my gut told me to take that paper napkin. Take it and keep it. I listened to my gut instinct. I didn't let my head talk me out of it…I would've lost the best thing to ever happen to me if I had."

I fight the tears trying to sneak out of the corners of my eyes. "What are you getting at, Dad?"

"You might not be ready now. But don't let your head talk you out of anything your gut tells you."

* * *

Two days later spring explodes onto the scene. It's well in the seventies so Sam and I decide to go to the park. On our way out, I grab the basketball. New discovery: Sam is surprisingly good at it. I've been working on getting him to open up, to engage the other boys at the park. Unfortunately, I've made very little progress and it's been bothering me.

The parking lot is full when we get there—obvs, everyone else had the same idea. There's nothing I love more than the boisterous shouts and giggles of kids playing, and there's plenty of that going on. Glancing sideways, I can tell Sam is quietly retreating into his shell. We walk up to one of the less crowded basketball courts and I start stretching while Sam begins to dribble. Over on the next court, a skinny blonde kid, who appears to be around Sam's age, attempts to shoot. I say attempts because the cutie is excruciatingly uncoordinated. I glance at Sam, who's doing great with the dribbling exercises we worked on last week, and see that he's noticed the boy as well.

"Derrick, bend your knees a little," a gravelly masculine voice gently instructs from the edge of the court. My gaze swings in that direction and finds its owner. He's attractive. Like really attractive. Tall, fit, square jaw—your typical smoking hot, all-American blonde. He glances my way and our eyes lock. After a beat, his hard expression lifts and he smiles crookedly at me. I turn beet red because there's no mistaking the interest in his baby blue eyes. I return a tight smile and walk over to Sam, who is in the process of sinking a shot. I catch the ball on the rebound, and for the next twenty minutes, we have a great time playing. It's impossible not to notice that 'Derrick' is seriously struggling while the man I assume is his dad does his best to coach him.

"Sam, what do you say we ask Derrick to play with us?"

Sam glances at poor Derrick and nods his head.

"Derrick, would you like to play with us?" Derrick glances at his dad, who smiles and nods. Showcasing a wide grin, Mr. All American walks up to me and holds out a hand.

# WRECKING BALL

"Jason Miller, and this is my son Derrick."

"Camilla DeSantis," I say, extending a hand that gets swallowed up by his. He holds it a second longer than I deem necessary. The skin on my neck starts to prickle. I can't hold his direct gaze. To me, this is indisputable evidence that I will never be comfortable dating.

"This is Sam, my student." In a sweet gesture, Jason shakes Sam's hand as well. A short while later Sam starts dribbling the ball and passing it to Derrick. While the boys play, Jason Miller leans in.

"Thank you for that. I keep trying to get him to play with the other kids. He's just so shy and…well, I don't want to push him too hard." Jason looks genuinely concerned for his son. I feel for him, I really do. I can imagine how hard it is for any parent to watch their child struggle.

"I'm homeschooling Sam while his mother is away and I've been dealing with the same issue. You're doing fine… you're patient with him. That's the most important part," I reply, doing my best to reassure him.

"I don't know what else to do. Both my ex and I are athletic." I almost laugh out loud at the strategic info drop.

*Men, smh.*

We turn to watch the boys take a couple of shots and miss. They seem to be talking, which is kind of amazing in and of itself. Jason approaches them, and for the next twenty minutes the boys play while Jason helps them work on technique. As the afternoon gives way to early evening, we say our goodbyes.

"Can I get your number?" At my blank stare, Jason backpedals. "I mean so we can meet for the boys. They seem to be getting on well."

"Oh yeah, we'd love that."

Shortly afterward, Sam and I head to the supermarket.

We're in line to pay when I spot it—a picture of Cal and me walking out of the furniture store in the city. The caption over it reads, 'Off the Market'. As much as I feared this happening, I'm not as stressed about it as I thought I would be. In that moment, I realize that I do trust Cal. He won't let anything bad happen to me. I know he won't. And anyway, it was bound to happen. I mean, he's a celebrity for goodness sake. Funny how easily I tend to forget that. To me, he's just Calvin, pigheaded, bossy, though mostly great. Because he is—great, that is. However, to everyone else he's a public figure. And now that the news has gone viral, we'll know soon enough what the consequences will be.

As soon as we get home, I go in search of the great guy in question. The shouting coming from his office gets my full attention. Calvin does not shout, ever. Outside his door, I wait and listen.

"You listen to me, Phil. Have I ever tested positive for PEDs? Have you had to deal with me sending pictures of my dick to questionable women? No. That's fucking correct, the answer is *no*. So whom I date, or don't date is no concern to the *organization*. Am I making myself clear? She's an incredible person…fuck the PR department. I'm lucky to have her…. I don't give a single shit about the optics. If I hear one disparaging word being said about her at team events then we're going to have a problem…You *will* be seeing a lot of her. I'm calm, I'm calm…speak to Ethan and Barry about that. Oh and Phil, I can name at least five teams that are going to be lookin' for a starting quarterback next year. Yeah, that's exactly what I'm sayin'…uh huh yeah, I'm cool…just as long as we don't have to have this discussion again…yeah, see you in a week."

That's a lot of f-bombs in one conversation. I've never heard him swear. Well, except for that one time…cowgate comes to mind. My heart is suddenly a jackhammer pounding against my poor bruised chest. I step into the doorway of his office and he glances up from his computer screen. The stern look he gives me doesn't bother me as it used to. His gaze glides over me like hands making sure I'm in one piece.

"What's wrong?" he says brusquely, which only confirms my prior sentiment.

"I heard your conversation," I confess, dissembling at the moment is beyond me. "Was that the GM?" He answers with a slow nod. "I was coming to tell you that we're in the tabloids."

His eyes do a slow perusal of my face, reading every single nuance. "You look weird."

"I don't look *weird*," I argue, the corners of my lips curving up at the absurdity of the situation. "I'm just…I can't believe you spoke like that to the GM. Aren't you concerned about your contract?"

His gaze drifts away for a while, his expression pensive. Then it swings back to me purposefully. "Not anymore."

Waiting for him to elaborate ends in vain. Silence ensues. I spend most of it rocking back and forth on my heels and dissecting into a million pieces what he just admitted and all I can come up with is this, "That was very nice of you."

His eyes lock with mine, narrowed, sparking with irritation. "No, it wasn't," he grumbles and looks away again. "It's the least I can do."

"It was very chivalrous of you—to come to my rescue like that."

His face twists into a semi-disgusted look, a deep v doctoring his brow. "I'm not *chivalrous*." Still not looking my way. I just can't resist…shooting fish in a barrel.

"You're much too good to me."

The look of utter confusion on his face is priceless. "I'm not good to you at all. I got you into this." It comes out all rushed and surly.

"Are you sure about that?" I tease some more.

"Yeah. I know what I want, and I know how to get it," he says absently. Like I never stood a chance against the power of his will. He's partly right about that. He's kind of irresistible when he's being sweet.

"What do we do now?"

"We're not hiding, that's for dang sure." His twang popped up sometime during the shouting match on the phone and has hung around since. Then his eyes slam into mine, sharp, cunning. He's a man with a goal in mind. "You wanna go on a date?"

I don't answer. Because we both know I don't really have a choice.

# CHAPTER EIGHTEEN

WHEN CAL INFORMS ME THAT we're going to a Yankees game, I lose my shit—to put it mildly. I almost vibrate off the planet is more like it. Adding to my excitement, they're playing Boston. I'm squirming in my seat all the way to the stadium. Even Sam, who Cal thought to include without me needing to suggest it thank goodness, is looking at me funny.

I was positive that Calvin would've gotten seats in a suite. I'm more of a 'brave the elements' kind of fan. I mean, if you're going to go to a stadium then what the frig are you doing watching it inside on a screen, right? Anyway, he astounds me once again when I'm informed that we have MVP field seats low down on the left side of the field. Not in this lifetime will I ever be able to afford such great seats on my own. Those seats are reserved for legacy season ticket holders and such. At this point, I'm almost in hysterics.

Even though it's a night game, Calvin pulls a Yankees cap out of his back pocket and puts it on, keeping it pulled down low and his eyes trained on me while we look for our seats.

"Are you always like this at games?" he asks as we make our way down the aisle. I have a ridiculous smile splitting my face that hasn't budged since we've stepped into the ballpark. I nod vigorously, and he adds, "Make sure you wear a hat when you come to mine."

It takes me a minute to grasp what he's just said. I squirm in my seat and brave a sideways glance. He's staring straight ahead...like he hasn't just lobbed a hand grenade at me. *Go to his games?* It's June. That won't be for another two months. By then, Sam will be back home with his mom. And I'll be... somewhere else. All of a sudden, I have an upset stomach. Except I haven't eaten anything in hours. I'm definitely not wearing a smile anymore.

"What's wrong?" My attention jerks back to Cal.

"Nothing."

"Bullshit."

"I just..." I look into his patient eyes and my stomach flips. *I'm going to miss him.* How the heck did this happen? "I was just thinking about where I'll be in two months."

I can only hold his gaze for a fraction of a minute, scared that he may notice that it makes me sad to think I won't be seeing him and Sam ever again. I've lost so much already. People I love, my career, friends—or rather people I thought were friends until the scandal. And now I'm going to be losing two more. Two of the best people I've ever had the luck of meeting.

He's staring intently, in a way that's become familiar, as if he has something to say but doesn't know how to broach the subject.

"You want some popcorn?"

*Huh?* Okay, maybe not so important. "Uhh, yeah, sure," I answer distractedly, thrown off by the change in gears.

"Great, get me some too, and whatever else you guys want. And a light beer, bottle, or draft is fine." He hands me a hundred dollar bill.

Chuckling, I stare at the bill in my hand. "You always this charming on dates?"

The expression he returns is oddly serious. He shrugs. "I

# WRECKING BALL

haven't been on a date in eleven years."

*Huh?* The twists and turns of this conversation are making me stupid. I'm completely at a loss. And then it dawns on me. Briefly checking that Sam is not within earshot, I say quietly, "Really? I didn't picture you for the midnight booty call type."

"Booty call?"

"Fuckbuddy—whatever you guys call chicks you sleep with. Personally, I never cared for that term. I mean, who treats their buddy like that? I know I don't."

"What? What are you talking about?" Judging by the look on his face, we're both confused now.

"Hold that thought. I'm going to get nourishment," I say, standing, and turning to my left, add, "Sam—you coming?"

He tears his eyes away from the game long enough to nod and we both climb out of our seats and head to the refreshment stands. When Sam and I return, the Yankees are down two scores, bases loaded, and Chase Headley is up at bat. Calvin leans in and murmurs in my ear, "Keep an eye out for the paps. Don't hide and don't forget to smile." He's so close I can see a ring of dark, steel gray on the edge of his irises. I stare at this discovery for an inappropriate amount of time. I know this because he frowns at me.

As anticipated, everyone in the general vicinity has been surreptitiously turning to stare at Cal since we sat down. Then they take a long, measured look at me. It's one thing letting people assume we're together, flaunting it someplace as public as a Yankees game, however, is a completely different beast. My paranoia reaches an all time high that someone will recognize me and start hurling insults. So far, I've managed to not let it spiral into a panic attack. God knows how because two rows down from us a trophy brunette keeps turning around and staring like she can't quite place how she knows me.

"Hey!" A grating female voice shouts. Definitely trophy wife. "I know you. You're that bitch that's married to that guy—" she snaps her fingers "Blake. The Ponzi scheme in Stamford, Connecticut." The brunette is standing, her voice getting louder and louder while I'm progressively getting smaller and smaller, trying to disappear under my seat. I feel Calvin's body go stiff next to me. My grouchy knight in black armor starts to rise out of his seat.

"Cameras are on us. She's not worth it." I'm hanging onto his arm, trying to hold him back. My hands instinctively go to cup his face, to keep his attention on me. His eyes, narrowed and cold, find me and soften. Then his gaze drops to my lips. Every part of me goes very still. I can smell his scent, soap and something else, something good. Small puffs of air hit my cheeks. *Oh crap, that feels good.* His gaze holds mine, the atmosphere between us crackling with tension.

Just then, by the grace of God, the ballpark erupts in cheers as Headley hits a line drive that produces two scores and ties the game up. The spell is broken and my hands drop. I watch trophy's husband grab her arm and yank her down. He's whisper shouting at her something to the effect of "blah blah blah, Calvin Shaw, blah blah you're wrong."

*Uh huh, yeah, little does he know.* Three innings later and the Yankees are up by two and Boston has bases loaded.

"Where would you go?" I vaguely hear Cal say. My eyes are glued to the game in progress, which is why the question takes me by surprise.

"Pardon?" I say with a sideways glance. He's looking straight at me, his focus ultra intense.

"You said you'll be somewhere else…where?"

The game interrupts for commercial break, and on the jumbotron directly in front of us, the kiss cam comes on. I love the kiss cam. There—I said it. A couple of octogenarians flash on screen. She pecks him chastely on the lips and everyone joins in on the *oohhh* and *ahhh* moment. In the privacy of my mind, I'm making up stories for them. That they were teenage lovers separated by cruel parents. That they later found each other after the war in some over the top romantic, star-crossed lovers way. Which war? I have no idea, but I let my mind run away with me.

"Cam?"

"I don't know. Probably back at my parents' place." I shrug apathetically. "Hopefully, I can find a job teaching. It's all I've ever wanted to do." The note of longing in my voice could be heard in Alaska. A young white couple flashes on screen. The man waves and kisses his pregnant wife, who looks more excited about being on camera than she is about getting kissed.

"You could stay."

It takes me a while to register what he's said because, again, I'm not paying attention to him. I'm way too busy ogling the loving couples on the massive screen. I used to be part of a loving couple. I used to be frigging happy—*used to be* being the operative words.

And then they point the camera at us.

On the jumbotron, my eyes go saucer big, actually bigger, like monster truck tire big. Calvin is a completely blank slate. Before I know what's what, he slips that big paw of his around my neck, pulls me closer—and kisses me. I'm in shock. I am in *shock*. Of course I am. That's why I don't move a hair. I don't even breathe. He cups my face gently and slants his soft lips. *Damn, they're soft.* One, two, three brushes.

"Kiss me back," he whispers.

His eyes are cool and smoky at the same time, smoldering dry ice. That must be an oxymoron. I'm in a trance, wrapped up in solving this enigma, so it's no surprise that all I can manage to stutter out is something incredibly stupid like, "What?"

And as I do, his tongue slips into my mouth and makes love to mine. Just the taste of him has my lonely soul begging for more. I press closer and he deepens the kiss, giving and giving. Lush, seductive, sweet. And so gentle for a big man. I can't get enough of him. I'm greedy as all get out for more. I thread my fingers through his thick, short hair. His hat falls off. And I take, and take, and take. I don't ever want it to end.

The crowd goes wild. Mind blown. Game over.

* * *

Two weeks have passed since *The Kiss* starring him and me, and neither one of us has brought it up. Not a word. We just go about our day as if it never happened. Which is nearly an impossible feat because A: it happened. I know this because I dream about it every frigging night. And B: it was the most intense, earth shatteringly good experience I've had since... well, in a very long time. His kiss was not at all what I expected. Then again, nothing about this man ever is. It was soft and teasing, and generous...like him. *Awwww crap.*

"Cam?" His voice jerks me out of my wayward musings. I stare at the gorgeous man sitting across from me at the dinner table. *Jezus, did I just say 'gorgeous'?*

"Yeah?"

His lips twitch in amusement. "Did you hear a word I said?" At my blank stare, the corners of those ridiculously soft and tempting lips hook up. "I asked if you have plans for the Fourth?"

I say nothing, completely and stupidly taken by those pink lips. His brow quirks. I'm pretty sure he just caught me staring at them. Great. "Ahhh, yeah, my parents always have a big barbecue and invite all their friends. Sam's coming with me." At this, it's his turn to stare back blankly. "How about you?"

# WRECKING BALL

He shakes his head and resumes cutting his steak into very precise pieces, trimming the fat off with the dexterity of a neurosurgeon. He seems disappointed somehow, like something took the air out of him, but for the life of me I can't figure out why.

"I just assumed you have plans."

His head snaps up and his eyes meet mine. "No plans."

A strange silence hangs between us. If I didn't know better, I would almost say he looks hurt that he wasn't included. That sounds hilarious even inside my head. Therefore, just to prove to myself how wrong I am, I throw out this, "Do you want to come with—"

"Yes."

"—us." *Okay, now what?* I chose a different strategy. "I need to warn you that you're going to be subjected to hours of incessant fawning."

"I don't mind."

*Huh...*it never once crossed my mind that he would willingly want to hang out. However, I don't have time to examine this with the level of attention it deserves because my cell phone vibrates with an incoming text. It's from Jason Miller.

"Sam, Mr. Miller wants to know if we want to meet Derrick at the courts tomorrow?"

"Cool," Sam answers enthusiastically. I watch Calvin's eyes move between Sam and me, his brow doctored with confusion. I type back my response and put the phone away.

"Who's Mr. Miller?" says the big dude who's been taking up a lot of space in my head lately. His tone, I don't fail to note, is a tad suspicious.

"Derrick's dad. Derrick's my new friend and his dad is real nice and he's helping us play better," Sam answers in one long breath. Calvin places his fork down and crosses his arms.

This new information displeases him. Before his mood can get traction, I cut in.

"I'd love for you to come." My breath comes to a screeching halt when I realize I just used the word 'love'. The serious expression Calvin was wearing a second ago disappears, replaced by...he looks happy. He looks happy and I get happy, too. *This is really bad.*

* * *

By the time we reach the park the next day, Jason and Derrick Miller are already waiting for us. Standing on the basketball court, stretching, Jason Miller beams a thousand watt smile at me that gives me pause. I sincerely hope he's not getting any amorous ideas because I am definitely not interested. He's a great guy and all, but there's another great guy that has been haunting my dreams every single night, and I need to deal with excising him from my head before I can even consider how I feel about dating again.

"Wanna play two on two today?" Jason asks with a mischievous twinkle in his eyes. Groan. That better not be what I think it is...blatant male sexual interest.

I glance at Sam, who nods. "Sure," I answer with a tight lipped smile. I'm warming up when I hear the bling of an incoming text.

**Cal: Where are you?**

Why do people forget simple manners when they're texting? I text back.

**Me: At the park. Oh hey, how are you? Having a good day, Shrek?**

A second later.

**Cal: Shrek? What park?**

*Hmm.* My fingers fly across the screen.

**Me: The one off Hillside Ave.**

Ten minutes later, I spot the Range Rover pulling into the

parking lot.

*Da heck...*

Rendered mute by the sight of the big guy jogging toward us in his workout gear, all I can do is stare. As usual, he draws all the attention; everybody at the busy park is suddenly elbowing the person next to them and gawking. Calvin stops less than a foot from me, his expression neutral. I don't have a clue what to expect. His gaze moves between my lips and eyes, and a prickle of discomfort crawls over my skin. It's clear we are an item of intense interest and it sets me on edge. Then he turns to Jason, who's staring back at us in total confusion, and says, "Sup," accompanied by a short nod.

*Sup?* "What are you doing here?" I do my best to contain the smile that's threatening to spread across my face. And then the s-h-i-t hits the fan because he swoops down and smacks a kiss on my lips. *Huh?* I might as well have stepped in front of a freight train because, at present, it definitely feels like I just got hit by one. Stiff as a corpse, I don't move a muscle while Calvin extends a hand at Jason and hooks a heavy arm around my shoulders like it's been living there its whole life.

"Calvin Shaw, Sam's uncle." It takes Jason a second to snap out of his confusion but who can blame him—it'll take me a heck of a lot longer. I glance briefly at Sam and find him grinning at me, *grinning.*

"Jason Miller, Derrick's dad."

*Jesus, Mary, and Joseph.* Now Jason is fangirling. Calvin shakes Derrick's hand and Derrick gives him a shy little smile in return.

"Do you like football, Derrick?"

Although he keeps smiling, Derrick's timid gaze falls to the rock he's nudging with his toe.

"Whata ya say, Derrick," Jason gently prods.

Derrick nods, and Calvin adds, "Would you like to come

to a home game this season as my guest?"

Oh Jeez, the bright excited look on Derrick's face feels like a punch to the sternum. I rub the ache.

"I have your jersey," Derrick softly says and Calvin smiles. *Slay me now.*

Thirty minutes later, Calvin is exchanging numbers with Special Agent Jason Miller of the Federal Bureau of Investigation's New York office, some serious man love developing between him and the dude that kissed me. The four males ended up playing while I bit my lip and wrung my hands in a state of high anxiety that one of them would end up in the emergency room. Calvin drapes his arm over my shoulder while he says his goodbyes and Jason's gaze goes straight to the hand hanging loosely over my breast. Instantly, my face goes up in flames. All this touching is making me crazy. I'm constantly wavering between turned on, craving it, and complete embarrassment. On the way back to the cars, I decide to get to the bottom of this strange new behavior.

"What's with the moves, Don Juan?" I whisper.

"Doing my part to sell this thing. Don't look so disgusted."

"I'm not disgusted!" I'm shouting. I'm *shouting*, emphatically disputing that his kisses do not gross me out. The smile flirting at the corners of Cal's lips tells me I am a class A sucker. Time for a change of topic.

"You could've hurt yourself. Can't you just take it easy for once?"

"I don't *do* losing."

"Ever? Even if it's for your own good?"

"Even if it kills me."

\* \* \*

"Cam?" Sam yawns loudly. It's late but he wanted to read one more chapter of *Harry Potter,* and I didn't have the heart to say no.

"Yeah?" I say, reaching to turn off Sam's bedside lamp.
"Are you going to marry my uncle?"
"Why would you ask that?"
"I saw you kissing."
Umm, this is awkward.
"Not everybody that kisses gets married, Sam."
"'Cause if you do, maybe I can live with you guys."
"What do you mean?"
"I can live here…for good."
"What about your Mom? She'd really miss you."
"No—she wouldn't."

I take a moment to decide how to handle this very delicate situation. "Sam, your Mom is sick. You know that, right?"

"Uh huh, she says she can't help it. Why can't she help it?"

"I'm not an expert, but I know that your grandmother had the same sickness."

"Does that mean I'll get it, too?"

"No. Your uncle doesn't have it. But I'm not a doctor so maybe we can find one to explain it to us. Would you like that?" He nods vigorously. "Okay, tomorrow we'll talk to your uncle about it."

# CHAPTER NINETEEN

OF ALL THE HOLIDAYS, THE Fourth of July has always been my favorite. Hot summer nights, sparkly fireworks, a sense of togetherness, of common ground. Have you ever heard anyone say 'I hate the Fourth of July'? No, you haven't. Know why? Because nothing bad ever happens on the Fourth. Everybody's too busy having fun.

It's still early afternoon when we head over to my parents' house. I glance at the man sitting in the driver's seat. He's wearing a simple white polo and long khaki shorts. His hair is getting longish again. Sam is in the backseat wearing the Beats headphones that Cal brought home for him the other day, watching *The Secret Life of Pets* and giggling every two seconds. It all looks so domestic. Like we're a regular family going to a barbecue. My spirits sink to the bottom of the shitter when I realize Amanda will be here any day now to pick up Sam and I'll be…who the hell knows where I'll be.

"Why do you look like that?" His voice is gentle, concerned.

"I'm going to miss you."

Just like that, it comes flying out of my mouth. I watch his nostrils flare and his pouty mouth pinch. *Great—I've embarrassed him.* He doesn't know how to respond to my mopey confession. The silence grows excruciatingly uncomfortable. Though, thankfully, I don't have to bear it for too long since we're only a block away. He parks the Range Rover on the street and we head over, walking around the side of the small saltbox house I grew up in. In contrast, my parents' back yard is quite large, the first reason why they always host the Fourth. The second reason is that we get a perfect view of the fireworks celebration the town holds every year, and the third is my father's green thumb.

"Wow," Calvin offers when we step into the backyard. My father could give Martha Stewart a run for her money. The landscaping is meticulously cultivated, every flower imaginable in full bloom. I notice this year all the flowers are white. And then I stop noticing the flowers because every head in the area, from my estimation fifty or so, swivels in our direction. My face goes up in flames while the man standing next to me remains one cool customer.

Cal drapes an extra muscular arm over my shoulders, pulling me closer, and my color goes from hot pink to tomato red in seconds. And that arm...sweet Jezuz that arm. It wraps around me like a security blanket, the heat of it sinking all the way to my bones. I want to lean in so badly it hurts. I want to wrap my arms around his waist, tuck into his big hard body, and bask in the comfort. But I don't. I can't. Because I'm a *fugazi* girlfriend. I don't have a right to lean, touch, think, consider, or have any kind of feelings for him. That truth needs to get straight in my head.

Standing with my father and a passel of other males I don't recognize—some young, some old—is Amber. Her face goes from joy to surprise to confusion in a span of seconds. Then it spirals down to suspicion. Her refined features contort into a really cute scowl. She raises her Amstel bottle at us in salutation.

My mother approaches us beaming, and I mean *beaming*.

"Camilla Ava Maria you didn't tell me you were bringing your…" This is priceless. Ange looks momentarily perplexed as to how to address Calvin.

"Boyfriend," he adds, coming to her rescue with a smile. Yes, an honest to goodness smile, a real one. And as I stare at it, my heart does strange things inside my chest that it's not supposed to. Ange gives him her toothiest grin in return. Gawd, I can practically hear her drawing up the wedding list in her head.

"Let me get you something to drink. What can I offer you Calvin?" she says ushering us further into the backyard.

"That's alright, Mrs. DeSantis. We'll help ourselves," Prince Charming replies.

*Da hell?* Who is this guy? I turn and give him 'the look'. The look that says, 'What the hell are you doing?' Having seen it often enough by now, he knows what it means.

"There are beers in the first cooler and soft drinks in the other. Let Tom know what you feel like eating and how you want it cooked."

"We got it, Ma, thanks," I say interrupting. I push Calvin in the direction of the grill and watch his six. I'm afraid that if I leave him alone with Angelina for a single second, she may start measuring him for a tux. The crowd congregated around the grill goes completely silent as we walk up. Yup, Tom is wearing his *Mr. Hot Stuff* apron again.

"Well if it isn't Persephone and her date," Amber drawls with a smirk.

My eyebrows nearly reach my hairline. "Amber," I mutter. I have to give Calvin credit, all he does is raise a black eyebrow and smile.

"How do you feel, Dad?"

"Your mother replaced my french fries with kale chips. How do you think I feel?"

## WRECKING BALL

"Sir," he says, extending a hand at my father.

Tom wipes his hand before reaching for Cal's. "Good to see you again. What can I offer you? Sirloin? Hamburgers? These are my friends by the way." An explosion of voices erupts as they all come forward at once to shake Cal's hand. Up until now all the males around us were silently gawking, now they're flat out fangirling.

Twenty minutes later, Tom has somehow wrangled Cal into manning the grill while they argue the merits of the new *unsportsmanlike conduct* rule. The men congregating around them hang on Cal's every word as if they've just witnessed the second coming.

"You're falling in love with him." It's not a question, it's a statement of fact. Or at least, Amber seems to think so. Raising a beer bottle to her lips, she takes a sip and skewers me with her x-ray vision. I meet her gaze head on (can't show any fear with Amber). Then we both turn to watch the man in question from our perch on the deck.

"Don't be ridiculous. I'm not in love with him."

"Then what is it? Mad cow disease? Pharmaceuticals? Because you have that vacant, blissed out look on your face every time your eyes land on him."

"Really?" At this, Amber gives me an exaggerated eye roll. I cringe in return. "Do you think he's noticed?"

Shrugging, she says, "Probably. He's not stupid."

*No, he's not, damn it.* "At most, it's a teeny tiny nothing little crush. I'll get over it."

"Hmm."

"He kissed me"

"Did he?" she drawls with a haughty arch of a blond brow.

"He's a face holder."

"Shit, I love that."

"Me, too."

"He's looking this way. He's smiling—don't smile back." Amber's hazel eyes furtively check me out. "I said *don't* smile back."

"Too late." Calvin's warm gaze holds mine and I can't look away. I can't stop the warmth spreading inside my chest that tugs the corner's of my lips up.

Her defeated sigh gets my attention. "What are you going to do?"

"Enjoy it while I can. I won't be seeing him anymore in a couple of weeks anyway."

She nods.

"You want us to drive you back to the city?" I offer.

"Na, I called Uber." Her gaze falls on the label she's busy picking at. Then she glances sideways and adds, "Got a date."

My eyes slam into hers. She looks away first. This is the first time in years Amber's been on a date. Joy explodes in my chest. "Wanna tell me about it?"

"Not yet…I'll let you know if there's a second one."

"Okay," I say curling my lips around my teeth. The force of the smile threatening to grow could seriously break my face in two.

"Ugh, don't look so damn happy. It's one date."

She gets up and pours out what's left of her beer. Grabbing my face, she smacks a kiss on my cheek. "See ya. Gotta go say goodbye to Ange and Tom."

"Have fun!" I sound downright giddy. In return, she gives me her surliest look.

Calvin is still talking to the guys around him. Heads above everyone else, it's impossible to miss him. I cannot be developing a crush on a man that is using me as a safeguard against other women. To distract myself, I start cleaning up the deck. I need to keep busy. But more importantly, I need to

## WRECKING BALL

keep my eyes off the incredibly hot guy I live with.

An hour later, night has fallen and the fireworks set to begin shortly. Did I mention I love fireworks? Was there ever a more romantic scene on film than Heath Ledger silently pining for the love of his life—one very sexy rodeo cowboy—while fireworks go off in the background? That's a rhetorical question, there isn't. Back to me, though.

At the perimeter of the yard, away from everyone else, I park myself in an empty lawn chair and watch my Dad play a game of bocce with Sam. They're both laughing at something, the huge grin Sam's wearing on his adorable face is so infectious it makes me smile too.

"Hey." My attention turns to one very tall man loping in my direction. "Hiding?" Conjuring full sentences is becoming difficult when the object of my fascination is this close, so I resort to a head shake. Hands in his pockets, his stride is as relaxed as his expression. The smile I see on those lips that I know are soft and sweet makes me sick. Yes, you heard it right. I said sick. Because I crave it. I want it all for myself, and that isn't going to happen.

"I think Tom made some cash tonight. How many autographs did you have to sign?"

An honest to goodness smile spreads across his face. He's been doing a lot of that lately. "He cut them off at thirty."

"He definitely pimped you out."

Shrugging, Calvin says, "I don't mind. Two were season ticket holders." Then he throws that championship winning body down in the nylon chair next to me. It's a miracle it doesn't split in two—although the chair does protest with a loud groan.

As luck would have it, it's clear tonight, the sky a perfect blank canvas for the show that's about to begin. A minute later, everything goes dark and suddenly my senses are on steroids. I can feel the bead of sweat crawling down between my breasts. I can smell the sweet scent of the honeysuckle hedge right behind us. I can even hear each relaxed breath the large man sitting next to me takes. The first candle is lit. A red ball of sparkles explodes over us. Glancing sideways, I catch his profile illuminated by the red glow in the night sky. He's beautiful…there's no arguing that. What's even better is that he's wonderful.

"You're a good man." The words come tumbling out of my mouth. *Good grief, I'm turning into a love struck teenager.* Calvin turns to look at me, his expression neutral, his thoughts unreadable. "Don't ever believe otherwise."

His hand covers mine on the armrest of the chair. When my gaze falls on it, I expect him to remove it but he doesn't. He holds it 'til the sky turns smoky from the tail end of the fireworks. And I can't help but think that this, *this* is the most romantic scene I've ever witnessed.

* * *

"So that went better than expected," I mention while the three of us walk around the side of the house, headed for the car. "Bob only managed to cop a single feel this time."

Calvin's head whips around, his expression a mix of surprise and anger. "You better be joking."

"Camilla."

The smile I was wearing a second ago melts right off my face. Standing a few feet to my left, walking up my parents' driveway, is Barbara Blake—Matt's mother. She's holding a manila envelope. Her bright blue eyes narrow a touch as her gaze settles on Calvin. My body goes stone cold. The perceptive man standing next to me doesn't miss a thing. His strong, warm fingers lace through mine, the feeling so unbelievably good that for a second I forget I should be nervous.

## WRECKING BALL

"I need to talk to you."

Barbara and I never had the warmest of relationships, but it was never hostile. Like many mothers, she had impossibly high standards for the woman who would be her precious son's wife. For Matt's sake, though, she usually kept things civil. And it's not like we saw her all the time—one of the reasons I didn't mind moving to Connecticut. After Matt died, we completely lost touch. Unfortunately, by the look on her face, I'm not sure civil is what she has in mind right now.

"Sam, why don't you and your uncle go ahead. I'll meet you at the car in five minutes." Calvin doesn't budge. A sidelong glance reveals that…oh crap, he has his game face on. Nudging him only earns me a hard look. "I'll be there in a minute," I murmur. He wants to argue—it's all over his face—though thankfully, he doesn't. After a meaningful pause, he places his hand on Sam's shoulder and reluctantly ushers him down the driveway while stealing backward glances at me.

"I didn't believe it," Barbara announces, her eyes glued to Calvin's broad back. "Not when I read it on the front pages of those trashy magazine at the supermarket. Not even when I saw it on tv," she adds, her tone reeking of disapproval.

Her words are arrows that hit their intended mark. A momentary pang of shame hits me. The look of contempt on her face makes me sweat and cower. Except I'm no longer the woman she knew three years ago. There's no denying that the shit ton of hardship I've endured has toughened me up. There's your silver lining, I guess.

Having to justify myself to her, of all people, makes me furious. Not once did she come to see me, or call, or email a single word in support. Not once did she apologize for the hell her son put me through. Somehow, in her twisted mind, he remains the white knight wrongfully accused of a felony. And now I'm the harlot he married? No. No way.

"Matthew's been dead for three years, Barbara. Did you think I was going to throw myself onto his funeral pyre? Would a blood sacrifice make you happy? Or maybe I should've gone to jail for the crime Matt committed."

"He was wrongfully accused."

"Not according to the U.S. federal government."

"I didn't come here to argue with you. I came here to give you this." She holds out the manila envelope, and I take it gingerly, as if it came right out of the bowels of hell. "I thought to spare you the pain, but you might as well know the truth."

The impact of what she's insinuating knocks the wind out of me. The Range Rover pulls up right in front of us and Calvin steps out, his concerned gaze roams over me. When I make no effort to move, he walks up to us and wraps his big heavy arm around my shoulders, his comfort jolting me out of my catatonic state.

"We're leaving," he announces and follows that up with a pointed glare at Barbara. Neither she nor I say our goodbyes.

# CHAPTER TWENTY

THE ATMOSPHERE IN THE CAR ride home is as thick as mud, and the mood just as dark. No one says a word. I'm so lost in my panic attack inducing thoughts that I don't notice that Calvin has taken my hand, placed it on his thigh, and covered it with his own—that's how anxiety stricken I am. I only realize it when he parks the car and I can't jump out because he has a hold of it. My vacant gaze meets his, which seems to be alternating between concern, affection, and anger. How did I ever think he was cold? At the moment, his eyes are two smoldering blue flames.

"You okay?"

"No...can you help Sam get ready for bed?" I murmur. "I just..." I can't even finish the sentence I'm so tired, so bloody tired I just want to crawl under the covers and sleep for a hundred years.

"I'll handle it. Don't worry."

I take my hand back and get out of the Range Rover. As soon as I'm in my bedroom, I lock the door, move to the far side of the bed, and sink to the carpeted floor clutching the manila envelope close to my heart. With my back resting against the side of the bed for support, I slowly peel it open.

For months after Matt's death, I had a sneaking suspicion that at some point I would receive a letter...a suicide letter.

The feeling only grew stronger when the investigation into his business affairs started. The idea just kept festering inside of me like an abscess. Only, I never did. During the year I was being investigated, I thought more than once about how Matt would've handled it. I was never formerly charged, but Matt definitely would have been—had he lived. With his volatile moods, I just don't see how he would've survived an extended prison sentence. Emotionally fragile is what Barbara called it. I called it insecure. To myself, never to him.

I slide another envelope out of the manila one, my name scribbled across it in Matt's chicken scratch. Immediately, tears begin to gush out of my eyes. In spite of it all, I loved him. With all his faults…I really loved him. Then again, I loved the man I thought he was. I never expected my marriage to be perfect. I never aspired to perfection. I've always been too aware of my own shortcomings to expect it from others. But I did expect honesty. I don't think that was too much to ask for.

The envelope is sealed. Gingerly, I peel it open and wipe the tears running down my cheeks away with the back of my hand. Not fast enough, though, as some splash onto the letter, blurring the word 'love'. I lick the salt off my lips, which seem to have blown up to the size of pontoons, and begin reading.

*Babe,*

*If you're reading this then I'm no longer here. I gave this letter to my mother's lawyer because you were always too nosy for your own good and it wouldn't have done anyone any good for you to find it until after my passing. I'm twenty-eight now so you could be thirty or eighty. God, I hope you're not twenty-four, that would mean I don't live much longer. A little gallows humor there.*

*You're probably wondering what this letter is about, so here goes. I need you to hear it from me. I owe you the truth.*

*If I'm gone then at some point you'll know what I've done. I'm not proud of it, but you should know that I didn't start out trying to*

## WRECKING BALL

deceive or hurt anyone, most of all you. I was trying to fix a hole I was in and it got out of hand. I had, or have so many plans for us, for our family, plans that would've been impossible if I didn't take drastic measures to stop the losses. I want you to know that I did it for us.

I hope you're reading this when you're old and gray and we've spent our lives together. I hope we had five kids. I hope that somehow I managed to right all the wrongs. I hope you were there to hold my hand when I left this planet. And if all those things didn't happen. I hope you forgive me. And I hope you find someone to love. Because if you love him, then I'll love him too.

Your Loving Husband,
Matthew Edward Blake

\* \* \*

"Camilla...Camilla, open the door."

I don't have the strength, or the will to answer. I've been crying hysterically for an hour and I have nothing left. No fight, no words, no ability to form thoughts.

"Go away."

"Open the door, or I'll break it down.

I lift my head off the tear soaked pillow and stare at the door because I don't put anything past this man. "Please, *please* go away, Cal."

"I don't want to...let me in for a minute and I'll leave you alone."

My face looks like I saw the business end of a two by four. I'm an ugly crier, always have been. I get really swollen while my skin turns the color of raw meat. The last thing I want to do is open that door.

"I'm not decent." A moment of silence and I think I may have won this time.

"You're crying naked?"

*Oh for heaven's sake.* I get up and unlock the door. I don't dare look at him. No way—I am not that brave. I turn right around and fall face first on my bed, hiding my swollen punching bag of a face into the pillow. The mattress dips. He's sitting right next to my hip. A wide, warm palm gently covers my shoulder, which triggers another round of sobs. I can't handle him being nice to me right now. I just can't.

"Who's the letter from?" I don't answer because it'll just start the tears all over again. "Your husband?"

A nod is all I can manage. His hand starts moving, traveling between my shoulder blades in a slow soothing circle. The weight and warmth of him seeps into my skin and trickles all the way to my bones. Pain and stiffness gives way to comfort. I've never felt more grateful for the power of touch. Of *his* touch. That launches me into another fit of hysterics.

"Can you please turn around and look at me?"

"No."

"Why not?"

"Because I look like I just went ten rounds with Rhonda Rousey."

He snorts. "I don't care what you look like. Turn around."

Of course, he doesn't. Why would he? *Fuck this shit.* I flip onto my back, warts and all in plain sight. I don't have the balls to look at him, though.

"There. Happy?"

He gently pushes a few strands of hair off my face, and I have to bite my bottom lip to stop it from trembling.

"Why are you crying?"

"Because…"

"What did the letter say?"

Aaaaand there go the tears again. My face crumbles into ruin, and my body convulses like it's being jumpstarted with electric cables. I'm wrecked. Laid open. I cover my face with my hands in a poor attempt to hide. And he helps me—he helps me hide. He picks me up off the bed as if I'm a rag doll and holds me close. I wrap my arms around his neck in a death grip and empty every ounce of liquid in my body onto his t-shirt clad shoulder—shoulders that have been carrying a heavy burden since he was a boy.

His big mitt rubs up and down my back and I press harder against him, my breasts crushed against his chest. "Matt didn't kill himself." His hand stops moving, every muscle he possesses suddenly still.

"You thought he had?" The deep baritone murmuring in my ear is cashmere socks on cold toes, it's cashing your very first earned paycheck, it's watching a flamingo pink sunset at the beach. It's one of the best things in life. Something you never forget, and never tire of experiencing.

"I wasn't sure...then the reporter said he did." The rubbing starts up again. He exhales heavily.

"I'm sorry. It's my fault."

"No...no. It's not," I grumble and crawl completely onto his lap. "Barbara said as much tonight."

"But he didn't?"

"The police said they found a dead deer a hundred feet away. The damage to Matt's car was consistent with the injuries on the deer. He turned into the river instead of away... it really was an accident."

"And the letter?" I feel a brief brush of his lips on my neck. Probably a mistake. Probably. I ignore the thrill that chases up my spine.

"A goodbye letter." My eyes fall shut in exhaustion. I breathe out a tired sigh. He pats my back twice.

"Get under the covers. You need sleep."

Reluctantly, I unwrap myself from his big warm body and immediately shiver from the loss of body heat. I slide under the sheets without meeting his eyes once because I'm way too vulnerable to defend myself from his searching gaze. If he were to look into my eyes now, he would read every thought I own.

That I'm lonely.

That I'm so grateful for him.

That I'm in serious danger of falling in love…God help me.

Just when I think he's all done surprising me, he gets on the bed, above the covers, and curls his body around mine. A muscular arm shoves under my pillow, my head resting on top of it. His legs neatly tuck against mine.

I don't move a hair. Nor do I say a word. With my back pressed up against his broad chest, I can feel the flow of his relaxed intake of breath. It lulls me into a sense of peace I haven't felt since the time I had my wisdom teeth pulled and had to take Vicodin. Except this is better. He's better than narcotics.

He wraps his other arm around me and I catch a glimpse of the black ink of his tattoo. Most of the delicate artwork is on the inside of his bicep. The vine-like black scroll reaches around the back of his arm and down to his elbow. I can't read the inscription from this angle. As I trace the vine with my finger, he shivers, goosebumps popping up on his skin.

"What does it say?"

After a beat, he says, "Know thyself."

"Isn't that a Greek proverb?"

"Plato…from the Suda's definition which says 'pay no attention to the opinions of the multitude'."

"Why do you know so much about whatever this Suda is?"

"I was a history major. I like history."

"Why history?" I say in a disgusted tone. I'd like to forget my past entirely.

# WRECKING BALL

"Hmm…because it reminds us how far we've come. What we've accomplished."

"No wonder, you've accomplished so much."

"Not enough."

"You kind of awe me."

"I'll remind you of that next time you get that look on your face like you want to punch my lights out."

I can't help but giggle. Between his voice and his presence, I feel drugged. He's stripped every inhibition I have away.

"How did you manage to play football and take care of your little brothers and sister?" Behind me, I feel his whole body tense.

"You didn't Google me?"

"No. Why? You Googled me?"

"Of course, I did."

"Creeper." On second thought, I get a little nervous of what he may have read about me. God knows most of the stuff on the internet isn't flattering. "Don't believe anything you read." He shifts his big body, pressing closer, and I do my best to resist the urge to press back.

"I don't," he murmurs in my ear and I melt a little more. "I didn't play football in high school."

"You've lost me, Champ."

"There was no money, or time."

"How'd you get to college then?"

"Academic scholarship."

I'm way too stunned to say a word for a good long time, and even then I'm at a loss. "Wut? I don't understand…how?"

"I was a walk-on."

"You were a walk-on try out—at Florida State?"

"It's been done before."

*I can't. I just can't…this man.* I turn around and face him with my mouth still hanging open in shock. He places his finger under my chin, and shuts it for me.

"You, Calvin Shaw, are a remarkable man."

And then I watch it happen—he turns as red as a Roma tomato. The flush remains on his high cheekbones, his expression frozen as we continue to stare at each other. He licks his lips. His Adam's apple rises and falls. The small space separating us is suddenly filled with tension.

"It's late. You need to rest."

I turn around and shut my eyes. Fifteen minutes later, I hear a soft snore. The puffs of warm air that hit the side of my neck make me smile. He went down hard and fast. I lay awake for another ten minutes thinking about Matt's letter. The words 'I forgive you' are a silent mantra playing on a loop inside my head until I drift off as well.

\* \* \*

"No…Mandy. I start training camp in four days…that's not the point. Now is not the time for you to be *finding yourself*. I don't give a…no, you listen to me, you need to focus on your son. He needs you…we'll fly down…me and the woman I hired to take care of him…Sam loves her. She's amazing with him."

*Amazing?* I can feel the flush start at my toes and travel all the way to my hairline. We've been treating each other with kid gloves in the ten days since *The Sleepover* starring us. I don't see much of Cal during the day. He's training with someone new, focusing on stretching muscles for better recovery and less injury. He always seems to be home in time for dinner, though. I know Sam appreciates it. Me? I guess I can officially call myself a masochist. Every time he walks through the door, I become a giddy mess inside.

The change in Sam is breathtaking to witness. Sometimes I can't believe it's the same kid that hardly spoke and wouldn't look anyone in the eyes. I can't say I'm looking forward to meeting his mom. Mostly because I don't know what that will do to Sam. The thought of him retreating back into his shell makes me sick to my stomach.

"You can ask him yourself when you see him….no don't… Mandy, don't hang up. Amanda Shaw don't you dare… goddamn it!"

The crashing sound kicks me into action. I step into the open doorway of Calvin's office and find him gripping the roots of his hair. The stuff that was on his desk is, at present, covering the floor.

"Calvin?" His head jerks in my direction and his cool gray eyes slam into mine. I wait patiently for him to explain. He exhales deeply and falls into his chair.

"My sister has decided that a drive would be *therapeutic*. She wants to clear her head before she picks up her son." His head drops back onto the headrest of the chair, his gaze fixed on the ceiling. Without invitation, I walk in and sit in the chair facing the desk.

"Where is she?"

"Betty Ford—Rancho Mirage, California," he answers after a long pause.

"That'll take at least a week."

"Could be up to a month, knowing her."

"Has she spoken to Sam? Did she tell him?"

"Nope."

"What can I do?" He points the power of those crystal clear eyes on me. There's anticipation in that stare—along with a large dose of uncertainty.

"You can stay."

Something passes between us. Something I don't want to examine at the moment because it feels a lot like…umm, affection and I *cannot* be feeling that for him.

"For you, Champ, anything."

He smiles then. It reaches his eyes and makes them all warm and sparkly.

*Sparkly? What the…*

My heart flops around inside my chest like it's a fish out of water. Crap. Things just went from bad to worse.

# CHAPTER TWENTY-ONE

AMBER LANDED A MAJOR PART in a minor play. Like way way waaaay off Broadway. But it's something to put on her resume, so I'm headed to the city for her opening night performance. I've had this nude colored, silk dress I've wanted to wear forever and had nowhere to wear it to. Now that I'm sporting a sweet tan, it's time to bust it out. I slap on some mascara, lip gloss, shake out my hair and head downstairs to the den where Sam and Mercedes are watching the new *Star Wars* movie. I walk in and both their heads swivel in my direction.

"You look wonderful," Mercedes announces. "What do you think, Sam?"

He gives me a thumbs up and a shy smile. God, I love this kid.

"Nothing is covering your back," says a grumpy voice right behind me. While the front of the dress is covered, the back is open down to the base of my spine except for a thin strap for the built in bra.

"Yeah, Champ, it's the style all the cool kids are wearing."

Glancing over my shoulder, I find Calvin inspecting me closely. No smile to be found anywhere. By the look on his face, he's displeased. He also must've just stepped out of the shower because his black hair is slick and his long lashes beaded with moisture. He's wearing sweatpants. Thank heaven for small favors because the rest of him isn't covered. The testosterone spewing off of him kicks me in the babymaker...and I'm suddenly warm all over. I'm pretty certain the man could reverse menopause. Each minute I'm around him it gets harder and harder to hide this seriously inconvenient attraction. I've got to get out of here before it becomes obvious.

His eyes do a slow perusal of my bare feet and legs. Climbing higher, they glide over my dress. By the time they reach my flushed face, his frown has deepened into a stormy scowl.

"You're gonna get cold."

"Hmmm. It's only eighty five with a hundred percent humidity, but I'll risk it." I slip on the Jimmy Choo silver sandals he bought me to go to the wedding, and say my goodbyes to Sam and Mercedes. Without waiting for more of Cal's 'fashion tips', I head for the front door, pretending I don't hear him hot on my heels.

"How are you getting there?"

"I'm taking Uber, Dad. And don't worry, I won't break curfew."

"Hell no. I'll drive you."

"This again? Come on, Champ. It's fine. Millions of people all over the globe use Uber daily. I think I'll be okay."

"I'm coming with you."

I stop and turn to face him. "Calvin—what's wrong? You have training camp early tomorrow. The last thing you need is to schlep downtown and sit through what will probably be a mediocre play at best," I say in my most gentle voice. He looks...upset? Torn? I can't put my finger on it. The machinations of this man's mind are a total mystery to me.

"Give me five minutes to get dressed."

Insert eye roll. But he doesn't see it because he's already

taking the stairs three at a time. Fifteen minutes later, Cal, who by the way looks like sex on a stick in a closely tailored pale gray suit that has Tom Ford written all over it, is driving us into the city. I'm about to tease him for his unmanly love of fashion, until I catch the dark circles under his eyes and a protective streak I usually reserve for the people I love rears up and makes a fuss.

"I'm sorry you got dragged into this. We can leave at intermission if it's bad."

"If you really didn't want me coming with you, you shouda just said so."

"That's not it, at all," I say, more emphatically than I intended. "Of course, I want you to come with me. I'm glad you did but—"

"You are?" he interrupts.

"You're my friend. Everything's better when you're around. And I'm *not* sorry if that makes you uncomfortable. Man up."

At the silence, I glance his way again and find Calvin watching me. A silly smile spreads across my face and he smiles back. Before I know what's what, he takes my hand, places it on his thigh, and covers it with his own. I spend the rest of the ride wavering between confused disbelief and elation.

* * *

It's a busy Thursday night, the downtown sidewalks congested with people. Naturally, we do not go unnoticed. It seems like every pair of eyes we pass follows us. Or more specifically, follow the gorgeous specimen of manhood walking next to me.

Calvin's been holding my hand since we got out of the car. I don't know what to think. Are we still playing a part? Am I still a *fugazi*? It feels like more than that…it's starting to feel real.

No surprise, photographers are stationed at the entrance of the theater. Which is not as off, off Broadway as I had initially thought. They see fresh meat and start snapping wildly. Cal hangs his arm around my neck as if he's been doing it all his life and pulls me closer. The brush of his soft lips on mine triggers a tsunami of feels while the wild flashing lights from the bulbs nearly blinds me permanently—no seriously, I almost walk straight into the glass door of the theater.

By the time we get inside, the play is about to start. I'm surprised to find that, not only is it not small, it's also packed. For a big man, he's insanely coordinated. He nimbly squeezes past a wall of bodies standing to let us get to our seats. Duh, his accuracy throwing a ball fifty feet plus downfield is legendary, why would this be any different.

One hour into the play, a modern retelling of *Little Red Riding Hood* set in Aleppo, Syria—no, I'm not making this up— I glance at the man sitting next to me and my heart squeezes painfully. Eyelids heavy, he's fighting tooth and nail to stay awake. My gaze travels down to his lap, where my hand has been since he took it hostage an hour ago. When I pat his thigh, he blinks and looks at me.

"That's it, we're leaving."

"I'm fine."

"No you're not. Move it, or I'll carry you out."

At my threat, his mouth kicks up on one side and my stomach does backflips. *Goddamit!* This is extremely inconvenient. The lights blink on. Saved by the bell.

It took only five minutes to convince him to let me drive. That's when I grasped how tired he really was. Two minutes after that he was asleep in the car. He didn't stir once until we were home and I opened the passenger side door.

# WRECKING BALL

"Let's go, Champ. I can't carry you to bed."

Without hesitation, he swings his arm around my neck and leans on me. Together we walk into the house and up the stairs. By the time I drop him on his bed, I'm feeling mighty uncomfortable. This feels very intimate. I don't get how he can be so casual about this. But that's men for you. He's sitting on his bed, not making any move to undress. His eyes flutter shut.

"Champ, you should probably undress and go to sleep.

"Help me." Then he looks up...and for the life of me, I can't look away.

"You're serious?"

"Okay, don't." He falls onto his back, his eyes shut, his Tom Ford suit in danger of becoming a casualty of my inability to touch him without spontaneously combusting.

*How? How is this my life?* I'm trying my hardest not to crash into love with this man because God knows it won't end well for me—he's made it abundantly clear he's not interested in a relationship—and yet life keeps having a good chuckle at my expense.

"Okay," I grumble as I reach for his hand. I try to pull him up into a sitting position, but it's useless. Might as well try to lift Mt. Rushmore. "Cal? Can you sit up please?" Eyes closed, he pulls himself up by my arms. Thank heavens he took his shoes off downstairs. I can just picture it. Me crouching down to take his shoes off, eye level with his crotch...no, just no.

I push his jacket off his broad shoulders and he sighs. I unbutton his shirt and pull it out of his pants and he lets out a relaxed breath. Meanwhile, I'm frigging sweating bullets. *Sweating bullets.* Every delicious square inch of skin I reveal makes me warmer and warmer. It feels like I'm being slow roasted over a spit of hot ass man. When I take his shirt off, his eyes slow blink open. There's no heat in his gaze. Just... gratitude.

*Jezuz, I'm an idiot.* He really isn't attracted to me. He's tired and I'm his friend, someone he trusts not to maul him. And here I am getting all hot and bothered.

"Thanks, Cam. I can handle the rest," he mumbles.

Of course, he can. Because this attraction is a one way street. More importantly, a dead end street.

\* \* \*

The slow rock of the hammock and the canopy of stars blinking brightly in the clear night sky all make for a ridiculously romantic scene—minus the romance, of course. My thoughts drift to Matt and I'm surprised to find that I don't feel the familiar pang of pain that usually grips my chest, only a slight soreness. The letter has definitely moved things into a different space, both in my head and my heart. One step closer to closure.

"What are you doing out here?"

"Agghh! You scared the shit out of me!" I jerk up and the hammock almost dumps me on the ground.

Out of the darkness, I watch him saunter up to the second hammock dressed only in a pair of shorts...with nothing underneath, I suspect—though I keep that to myself because what difference would it make at this point. He throws himself down in it, the wood creaking loudly.

"It's a wonder how that oak hasn't come down yet," I say, glancing up at the massive tree.

For this, I get one of his lazy smiles. Then he tucks his hands behind his head and his biceps pop out. He's so damn handsome it's a crime against every straight woman that lays eyes on him and isn't allowed to touch. And I'm suddenly afraid that I may do or say something wildly inappropriate, so I don't let that thought settle for long.

"Shouldn't you be asleep?"

Why did I mention sleep? Because I'm an idiot, that's why.

## WRECKING BALL

My mind instantly conjures images of us tangled up in my bed, his nose buried in my hair, his groin smashed up against my rear end...and now I'm sweating. It's cool out and I'm sweating bullets.

*Note to self: invest in clinical strength deodorant.*

"I'm only playing a couple of snaps tomorrow. What are you still doing up?" He inspects my face closely. "The letter?"

"That and the fact that I need to come up with a plan for the rest of my life...Amanda will be here soon."

He watches me thoughtfully. The silence stretches on. We both rock back and forth, the creaking of the wood soothing my nerves. This easy comfort between us is addicting. I can't relax into it. I can't because I'm drawn to it like a fly to shit. And if I'm not vigilant, if I let my guard down, it could get out of hand real quick.

"You're still in love with him?"

I almost fall out of the hammock. Wow. He's just dropped the bomb on me, the million dollar question that not even Amber has the courage to ask. *Am I still in love with Matt?* I'm surprised at how quickly the answer pops into my head. I've done my best not to think about it much. Mostly because for so long I couldn't think about him without letting all the extenuating circumstances taint my feelings. And yet it's true what they say about time and distance lending perspective. For the first time since the police knocked on my door, the thought of Matt isn't clouded by the pain of his betrayal.

"Not anymore," I say to the man brave enough to ask. The Christmas lights wrapped around the oak offer only the dimmest of light. Even so, I can see his alert gaze is on me. Sometimes it feels like those eyes could pry every truth out of me if he were to set his mind to it. "I'm different...and I've had enough time to come to terms with the fact that he wasn't the man I thought he was. The man I loved didn't exist...it's not all his fault, though. I chose to ignore the parts of him that didn't suit my narrative." He nods in understanding. He, more than anyone, knows what I mean. "Do you miss it? Being married?"

His scrutiny moves away from me. "I'm fine by myself."

"You don't say." I don't even bother to hide the eye roll.

"What about you?"

"Yeah…I want kids. I want a family. But I want something different next time. And I'll definitely have my own money." His face screws up into the most ridiculous scowl. "What's that about?" I say, half laughing at his weird reaction.

"Any man worth marrying will share everything he has with you."

His words reach into my soul, hitting me in a spot so tender and vulnerable it scares the living daylights out of me. I want to believe that, I really do. And yet, I'm almost one hundred percent certain that I've lost the ability to trust without reserve.

"Amber says every woman should have 'fuck you' money."

Cal arches a black brow. "The only thing Amber is qualified to advise on is how to shrivel a man's nuts."

I watch him rock back and forth, a long, *long* muscular thigh draped over the side of the hammock. This handsome man that I'm grateful to call my friend. Not too proud to admit his mistakes. Taking on other people's responsibilities without a word of complaint. He really is a good egg.

"I don't think I can trust a man like that again," I mutter. I get no reply to this. He holds his silence, and as it stretches on, we both relax into it.

"You trust me, don't you?"

His query catches me off guard. Turning, I find him watching me closely. As if my answer means something to him. Or maybe the rollercoaster I've been on for the past three years has finally sent me over the edge of madness. I could be making all this up in my head...I don't know what to believe anymore. The fact that I can't trust my own judgment anymore is incredibly depressing.

"With my life," I say without hesitation. "That's different, though—we're friends."

His eyes hold mine for a second too long, long enough that we're entering the weird zone. Goosebumps crawl up my arms.

"You consider me your friend?" There's an indecipherable look on his face.

"Sure, I do...I don't know if that look on your face means you don't want me, but tough noogies, Champ, you've got me. So deal with it."

"I want you," he finally says, his tone hushed.

I'm incapable of looking away. Aaaaand we're back in the weird zone. With the way he's watching me, I'm petrified he can see what I'm thinking. And what I'm thinking, I'm mortified to admit, is that Amber may be right. This feels like more than friendly affection. This feels like the little crush I was harboring is growing into a monster. One I have no control over.

Ughhhh. A crush on my friend, one that's been good to me, one of less than a handful of friends I have left and who isn't the least bit interested in a relationship. Or anything else for that matter because, quite frankly, I haven't seen him look in a woman's direction once since the day we met. So he's not exaggerating in the least when he says he likes being alone.

"What do you miss most?" His voice cuts into my idiotic inner monologue.

"About what?"

"Being married."

My inside voice immediately starts screaming, *Sex! Seeeeeexxxxxx!* A flame of shame burns right up my neck and over my face. He grabs onto my hammock and we both stop rocking. His pale eyes narrow, bright with a little mischief and a lot curiosity.

"You don't have to be married for that."

The thought of having casual sex with a stranger makes me nervous as all get out. I let my imagination run wild regularly, sure I do, who doesn't. However, they're fantasies—that's all. I know I don't possess whatever it is that allows a person to disconnects emotions from sex. Maybe it's my history, the fact that I've always been in love when I've had it. Maybe it's because I've only ever had sex with one person. The bottom line is, I can't imagine sharing myself with someone I don't care about.

"Don't judge, but I don't *do* casual sex. And falling in love again is a long shot at best, which pretty much eliminates sex with another person."

He's back to staring very intently. I feel the full brunt of it and it kind of freaks me out a little.

"I don't judge you." His voice is low and soft and does strange things to my body. Suddenly, my heart is pounding fiercely and my nether region is achy and empty. I watch his tongue dart out and lick his lower lip and *oh my God* if I'm not immediately picturing myself sucking on that tongue. I have to put a stop to this before I end up embarrassing myself.

"Are you…uh," I mumble semi-coherently. I can't take my eyes off his mouth. *Shit!* This is my friend, my good friend, and I'm eye fucking his mouth. "Are you…uhh…ready to date? What about that chick in the PR department?"

"No."

"Why not?"

He lets go of my hammock and I'm back to swinging.

"Not my type." His gaze returns to the stars above, neatly avoiding mine.

"Attractive and sweet isn't your type?"

"She just isn't," he repeats.

"Fine, be mysterious."

His lips quiver and I know we're back on safe ground. Time to make a graceful exit before I jump him. I get up to go back to my room.

"You're coming to the game tomorrow?" The nonquestion makes me snicker.

"Stop begging. It's so unbecoming for a man of your stature." The small smile I get out of him makes me feel like I just won a gold medal.

"I'll leave the clubhouse passes and tickets on my desk." As soon as the words are out of his mouth, I freeze. He scans my face, his expression hyper-alert. "Why do you look weird?"

"I don't look weird."

"Yeah, you do. Whenever something bothers you, you get that look—like you're sucking on a lemon."

"I do?"

"Hmm."

"I'm worried some of the wives or girlfriends won't want me there—and I know I sound like I'm in junior high, it's just that I've been through this before."

His expression alters lighting quick. His face crystalizes into a mask of pure malice. "No one is going to do, or say shit to you. I promise."

He looks like he's about to go mental. Probably not a good time to argue this point. "Whatever you say, Champ."

"It'll be fine," he announces brusquely. Then his gaze swings back to meet mine squarely. "You'll see."

# CHAPTER TWENTY-TWO

IT'S THE FIRST PRESEASON GAME, and although Calvin is only playing a couple of snaps, I'm buzzing with nervous energy. As soon as we step into the stadium, I can feel it. The excitement of the new season is palpable. Both Sam and I are wearing jerseys Calvin left for us in the office along with the tickets. Just to mess with him, I almost wore my 'Brady' jersey, but thought better of it since I didn't want to get jumped in the stadium parking lot. Do I need to explain how bloodthirsty Titans' fans get at the mere mention of number 12?

We're supposed to meet Ethan in the field level club, the section where the players' families sit. I have to admit I'm nervous. News that we're "dating" is everywhere. On tv, in magazines. The picture of us kissing at the Yankee game has been shared a million times. At least, that's what Calvin's PR people told him. I don't know how I'll be received by the wives. Sadly, I can only hope that having Sam with me will shield me from any overt insults.

The first thing Amber insisted I do when the investigation into Matt's business began is to disconnect all my social media accounts. Best decision I ever made. It's been three years since someone's told me to go kill myself, or prayed that I contract AIDS and die a slow and painful death—and those were the PG rated insults. It got much worse. After living in blissful ignorance since then, I'm now convinced that social media is the root of all evil.

"Hello, Team Shaw." Ethan walks up wearing jeans and a vintage Titans t-shirt, looking…young. I've never seen him wear anything other than a suit so it's a bit of a surprise.

"Hello yourself, counselor."

He looks down at his t-shirt. "Just plain, old Ethan today."

"There is nothing plain, or old about you, Ethan." The compliment has him smiling shyly.

"You guys want to get something to eat before we go in?" Sam and I nod, and we make our way over to one of the food kiosks. We're standing in line, bodies of fans streaming around us, when Ethan notices my fingers drumming nervously against my denim covered thigh. "Too much caffeine?" He delivers this with a curve of his pretty lips.

"I don't know how it's going to go in there and I'm nervous," I murmur in a low voice. "Maybe I shouldn't have come. But I really *did* want to come. And I don't want to regret coming, but now that I'm here, I kinda do…" My voice trails off when Ethan's expression alters.

"I talked to Cal. There's nothing to worry about." I've never seen Ethan be anything other than totally affable, and seeing the scowl on his face almost makes me laugh; he couldn't even scare my grandma with it.

"I don't understand. Is that supposed to be your mean face?"

He assesses me thoughtfully. "You should sit in when I negotiate Cal's next contract."

"I thought Barry did that?"

"Barry's happy to let me do it." The sly smile he gives me and the casual way he throws that out has me rethinking my prior judgment of affable Ethan Vaughn. Maybe the house cat is a tiger in disguise.

Minutes later, we walk into the clubhouse and every head swivels in our direction. All conversation ceases. "Get your game face on, counselor," I murmur quietly to the handsome man standing next to me. On my other side, Sam takes my hand. Surprised, I glance down and am met by a pair of determined gray eyes. My sweet protector…be still my beating heart.

We find our seats and pull out the hotdogs we grabbed at the stand. While we're quietly eating, I glance down at the field. My eyes find him immediately. It's odd how familiar everything about him has become. The way he moves with stealthy, feline coordination, the way he stands, the set of his shoulders, how he stretches his neck from side to side when he readies for battle. When the hell did that happen?

He's warming up, throwing to, of all people, Justin "Dimples" Harper. Even from a distance, I can see it—the intensely focused look on his face, that force of will that awes me. In my dirty stinking mind, I picture him as a gladiator in ancient Rome and my body heats up hotter than the sun. A sideways glance reveals that no one has noticed the filthy wandering of my mind so I return to ogling. He's wearing those undercover shirts and leggings made for athletes that band across and supports muscles. And they're tight. *Reeeaaal* tight. What devil thought those up? Every muscle, every curve of that mouthwatering body is on full display.

*Okay, enough.*

I tear my gaze away before I do something super stupid like pant. That's when I notice the peculiar look on Ethan's face. I take a sip of my diet soda and wait him out.

"You know he hasn't dated anyone since Kim left."

My brows inch up my forehead. "And you're telling me this because…"

Ethan's alert gaze narrows. "Because I think you two

would be good for each other."

Furtively, I check to see if Sam is listening and find that he isn't, thank God. He's busy playing *Minecraft* on the new iPod touch Cal brought home for him the other day. The look on his face when he opened the box had me biting the inside of my cheek in an effort to stave off the tears welling in my eyes. Ever since the day Sam destroyed Calvin on Madden, the two of them have been getting along really well. Calvin is making a serious effort with Sam, which has not gone unnoticed by yours truly.

"No," I say, shaking my head. "No, he doesn't want a relationship. He's told me repeatedly. He's into booty calls, nothing serious. And trust me, I'm the least likely candidate for a booty call."

"Booty calls? Where did you get that idea?"

*Huh.* The befuddled look on Ethan's face gives me pause.

"He basically said so." I scroll through my mental diary. "When we were at the Yankee game."

Not only does this not clear up any confusion, Ethan looks utterly shocked. "He said that? He said he's looking for *booty calls?*" The last word is spoken with a laughing inflection, his brown eyes wide in anticipation of my answer. I get the sneaking suspicion that I'm missing something.

"Well, he didn't *technically* say it."

The expression on Ethan's face clears. "Calvin has never—to my knowledge and I've known him since we lived together our freshman year at State—been with a woman he wasn't dating."

*No booty calls? Why didn't I see this before?* He hasn't had a woman over since I've known him. But I thought that was out of concern for Sam…*huh.*

"Okay, so he dates a lot. Why are we even discussing this? He's still not interested in a serious relationship. And I'm not either...looking for anything, that is...neither a booty call, nor a relationship."

"Camilla—" Ethan says, followed by an exasperated exhale. As if he's trying to explain algebra to a two year old.

"What?"

"The only person Calvin's ever dated is Kim."

He said he hadn't been on a date in eleven years. *Holy shit...that's what he meant.* The only person he ever dated...he married the only person he ever dated. Ethan waits patiently for me to wrap my mind around this newfound information. Meanwhile, the stadium roars and everyone comes to their feet. Titans' players charge through the tunnel and fireworks erupt. I snap out of my trance just as Calvin takes the field for the coin toss. My eyes start at his broad, padded shoulders and work their way down to the swells of his perfect ass. I mean... Lord have mercy. No one, and I mean no one has ever looked better in a pair of tight, shiny pants. *He married the only person he ever dated?* My mind keeps returning to this incongruity, and chewing on it.

The camera pans to Calvin's face. It's on every screen in the clubhouse and around the stadium. His expression stoic, his scruff covered jaw tight. His eyes are twin icebergs resembling the one that sunk the Titanic. I can't see the pretty features anymore. All I see is a man that has been a true friend in my hour, strike that, hours of need, my confidant...my protector.

*Crapola, this is bad, this is really bad.*

The L.A. Rams won the coin toss and have elected to receive. Calvin marches onto the field, relaxed, in command, a general rallying his troops. The game starts and all goes well. Cal makes a couple of easy completions. The atmosphere in the clubhouse is much more relaxed because my dear friend is marching the troops steadily downfield.

# WRECKING BALL

On a third and ten, he connects with Justin on a slant route that turns into a thirty yard sprint into the end zone. The crowd goes nuts. I'm jumping up and down while Sam and Ethan smile at me. I catch the eyes of a couple of the wives and they smile back. All is right in the world.

After the Rams go three and out, Cal is back on for one more series. The first down, Calvin hands off the ball to the running back and they squeak out three yards. On the next snap, they go into a spread formation.

*Spread formation?*

That puts Cal open to a nasty pass rush. I don't like the call, but it's preseason. No one is going to go full out. *I'm not worried,* I tell myself…until the center snaps the ball.

The number one pick for the Rams, a rookie linebacker, comes flying off the edge and hits Cal in the back just as he's releasing the ball. I gasp, my hands go flying to my mouth, the stadium goes as quiet as church while Cal writhes on the ground, clutching his lower back. Two of his offensive linemen start pushing and shoving players of the opposing team. A fight almost breaks out.

I look around frantically, and the dark sympathetic eyes of a very pretty black woman holding a baby tangle with mine. "He'll be okay, honey," she murmurs. Her quiet assurance does nothing to dispel my anxiety because Cal is still down, a number of players kneeling and praying now.

*Fuuuck!* I glance at Sam, then Ethan. Both standing, their focus is on the field. The team staff is crowded around Cal, who hasn't moved. If the flat bed comes out, I will lose my frigging mind.

Just then, the team trainers help Calvin to his feet and the crowd goes wild. He's walking gingerly, his face twisted in pain as they escort him off the field. Toes tapping, thumb drumming on my thigh, I manage to sit there for a full ten minutes before I pop up on my feet. On the clubhouse screen, they show Cal getting escorted to the locker room.

"Let's go, counselor. You have to get me access to see him."

Ethan's wearing a smug smile and a wicked gleam in his eyes. "I was wondering how long it would take you."

"He's my employer. I'm concerned as any human being with half a heart would be."

"Uh huh."

"Fine. He's a friend. Okay? Satisfied? He's my employer and my friend. It would make me inhuman if I wasn't concerned."

"Mmmm."

"I just want to make sure he's not hemorrhaging to death," I say as my feet carry me quickly toward the exit.

"Right."

The three of us make our way out of the clubhouse, a couple of the wives lending words of encouragement. If I wasn't downright sick over the state of Calvin's health, I'd be celebrating right now.

We reach the locker room door. "Give me a minute to see if your *employer* and *friend* is done getting treatment." Three minutes later he comes out and gives me the nod to enter while he plants himself on the bench next to Sam.

Inside, the object of my concern is sitting in a chair with a grimace that tells me he's in intense pain. My heart lurches and my hands itch to check every square inch of his body to make sure nothing is falling out. Which is why I clench them into tight fists as I close the distance between us. I give myself major props for not sprinting to his side, by the way. His chest is bare and he has an icepack secured to his waist by an ace bandage, his football pants hanging open. I used to laugh at the paperback romance novels I would sneak a peek at while in line at the supermarket. Every time I read something like this, "His masculine beauty took my breath away." I used to think...

A: what kind of a dumbass wrote this dreck.

And B: what kind of dumbass reads this drivel.

And yet, here I stand, making doe eyes at this man, and what am I thinking? His masculine beauty takes my breath away. That's right. Who's the dumbass now?

"I'm taking you home," I say with more steely determination than I'm feeling. He stares back at me unblinking, a small smile tugging his lips up. Then he winces and I can feel his pain as acutely as if it were mine.

"Okay."

That one word propels me into action. Gingerly, I help him into his dress shirt. I don't fail to notice that his eyes are on me the entire time. Concern, however, far outweighs any embarrassment I may feel at being scrutinized so closely.

"Are you okay to walk? Did they give you painkillers? Are you sure I don't need to take you to the hospital?"

His soft gaze takes in my worried face. His silence stops me cold. Something is happening between us. If I wasn't entangled in an array of feelings so contradictory that I'm left paralyzed, I could probably work it out. As it stands though, I'm lost.

"Yes, yes, and yes," he says with a smile in his eyes. "Sam?"

"Outside, waiting with Ethan."

"Tell E to grab my stuff from the locker."

"You got it, Champ." I shift his extra large body to leverage my weight and tuck my shoulder under his pit. He's looking down at me, his expression open, as if he's about to say something of import.

"What is it?"

He licks his lush bottom lip, tugs it between his teeth. And so help me God a missile of heat shoots straight to my groin. Then it pulls a 180 and travels up to my face. No doubt he's noticed the bloom of sweat on my forehead.

"I..." He exhales sharply. In frustration, it sounds like. He catches my eyes again. "Thank you." Whatever else he was about to say, he chooses to keep to himself.

This time, I don't hold back what I'm feeling. That's why I say, "What are friends for?" and unleash a smile that's all for him.

# CHAPTER TWENTY-THREE

"CAMILLA!" THE SHOUT TRAVELS ACROSS the gym to find me in the hallway. He's in the "treatment" room. The man has more medical gadgets than a hospital. He's supposed to be sitting in a tub filled with ice, waiting patiently for my return. "Camillaaaaa!"

Patience has exited the building.

"Stop your bellowing," I scream back from down the hall. When I reach the open doorway, I remember who I'm dealing with. "Are you decent?"

"Course not, but come in anyway." I poke my head into the room and find him in the steel whirlpool, submerged up to his waist. His eyes are closed and his head is tipped back, resting on a bath pillow. "Where'd you go?"

"To get your bathrobe."

"Are you coming in, or are you just going to stand there and stare at me?" A rare, brief smile appears on his face.

"Your eyes are closed. How would you know what I'm doing."

I don't know what's worse that I *was* ogling him, or that the smug bastard knows and is taking pleasure in it. His eyes creep open. Heavy lidded, sulky and beyond sexy, he pins me in place with those pale orbs. All of a sudden, it feels like I'm the one that's naked. But I will not be cowed by a pair of bedroom eyes. No, sir. Therefore, I march into the room holding the bathrobe as a privacy curtain between us, and my gaze directed as far away from him as possible.

"Camilla," he drawls. "Put the robe down. I need your help to get out. If I slip, I could hurt myself even worse." He's right, damn it. "I don't have anything you haven't seen before."

I really wish he would stop exerting his infallible frigging logic on me. "How do you want to do this?" I say, dropping the robe.

"I'll try to push myself up and grab onto you."

Holding onto the sides of the tub, he starts to emerge from the water. My mouth goes bone dry while the rest of me feels like it's being burned at the stake. Droplets cling to his bare chest, onto the sprinkle of dark hair covering it, onto his tight nipples puckered from the cold. I'm in a daze watching him. Who wouldn't be when you have a work of perfection inches from your face. And then he gets to his feet.

*Jesus, Joseph and Mary.* Whatever happened to shrinkage? Because there is definitely none happening here. And if there is, then *what the fuuu..*

"You stare at it any longer, honey, and you'll get more than an eyeful." His voice is quiet and deep, a bit husky, and as rich as molten chocolate. And God help me because I can't stop myself from licking my lips. A sharp intake of breath prompts me to glance up. He shifts and suddenly slips. Instinctively, I grab him around the waist and he clings to my shoulders, our bodies smashing together as we fight to regain our balance. My clothes are soaked. And even though he's been sitting in ice, his body heat is scorching me from my breasts to everything bellow.

"We're going." Mercedes is standing in the open doorway. Her well-groomed brow arches. "Can I bring you two anything to eat?"

"I'm not hungry," I say rather loudly.

"Nothing for me, thanks," Cal adds over me.

"I'll make him something later," I tell her. "Where are you and Sam going to eat?" The ridiculousness of this situation is beyond explanation.

"The Italian restaurant in town." Her eyes narrow just a touch and a smile ghosts across her face. "We'll be an hour—have some clothes on when we get back."

With that, she leaves us alone, standing there clinging to each other. I look up into his smiling face and feel the soft squeeze of his mitts on my shoulders. Holy hell, does it feel good. The warmth, the weight of him. For a moment, I imagine what all that weight would feel like bearing down on me, pushing me into the mattress. *Shiiiiit!!!* Every cell in my body is screaming at me to press closer.

"Let's get you into bed." He smiles wickedly and I give myself a mental slap upside the head. "You're lucky you're injured, buddy," I warn with narrowed eyes and smile of my own.

Locating the robe, I help him get into it, and even manage not to gawk at that championship winning body while I'm doing it. Then we slowly and carefully make our way upstairs to his bedroom, where it takes him a good fifteen minutes to get comfortable on the bed.

\* \* \*

"Motherfudrucker," I mutter under my breath, while I spread the arnica cream on the giant bruise on Calvin's lower back—which is getting larger and darker by the second. A strange and violent protectiveness has me undone. Given the opportunity, I could inflict some serious hurt at the moment. My hands move up his spine, gently kneading every bulging, tense muscle they roam over. "How does that feel?"

"Like heaven, don't stop."

"You're going to have a real hard time getting up and around the next couple of days." His exhausted exhale tells me he knows this. "Somebody needs to take out his knees."

Calvin chuckles. His eyes still closed, he says, "Didn't peg you as the bloodthirsty type."

"Have you seen what your back looks like? You're lucky you don't have a lacerated kidney."

"He's just a kid trying to prove to the team he's worth a first round pick."

"Wow—did someone forget to put their grumpy pants on today?"

"Isn't there some kind of rule about not kicking someone when they're down?" His gentle rebuke makes me suck in a breath. Now I feel like dog shit.

"I didn't mean that," I blurt out. An involuntary reflex has me raking his hair off the side of his face so I can get a better read on him…except the gesture is excruciatingly intimate. Something a lover would do. Both of us realize it at the same time. I'm about to retract my hand when he grabs my wrist.

"Keep doing that." He releases my wrist, but I don't move. "Please." I crumble like a cookie in the face of that sweet, vulnerable plea. Very slowly, my fingers sift through his hair, raking it back. A grumble surges out from deep within his chest. I scratch his scalp and he moans in appreciation. It sounds like Animal Planet has invaded the bedroom. If I didn't already know he was the one making those sounds, I would think an injured lion was hiding under the bed.

"I'm sorry you didn't get to watch the rest of the game."

With his pretty face pressed into the pillow, his eyes are closed and the lines of pain that were marring it a minute ago have gone smooth. And then I need to kick myself because the satisfaction I get knowing that I did that for him is ridiculous.

## WRECKING BALL

"It wasn't as much fun as I thought it'd be...now that I got skin in the game. When I saw you on the ground and in pain, I swear my heart stopped." For some reason, I feel absolutely no desire to lie or dissemble. Maybe because I've been through too much. Maybe because I know life is too short to waste time on subtlety and ambiguity. Either way, I'm not having it. In the past, I spent way too much time keeping shit to myself, not telling Matt how I really felt because I didn't want to rock the boat. Well, fuck the boat. If it sinks under the weight of the truth, then so be it. At least, I can live the rest of my life without regrets.

He wraps his long fingers around my forearm and brings it to his mouth. I feel the soft touch of his lips on the inside of my wrist and my heart begins to thump inside my chest as loudly as an elephant stampede. I study the man that's attached to the pouty lips resting on my pulse. Those impossibly thick and spiky black lashes throw shade on his sharp cheekbones, his breathing deep and even as he descends into sleep. Warm puffs of air hit my skin and radiate pleasure to every point in my body. I try to slowly pull away, but he suddenly wakes.

"No, don't go. Stay...'kay. Hmm. Stay with me," he half mumbles. Sounds like the painkillers have finally caught up with him. When I don't respond, he lifts his head off the pillow and scowls at me. "Don't go."

I chuckle at the look on his face. "Okay, Champ. Relax, I'll stay."

Satisfied, his head falls back on the pillow. I crawl onto the other side of the bed, pull out my iPhone, and click on the Kindle app. Seconds later, he's snoring. I consider leaving for only a moment. I gave him my word; this man that I respect and care about. I can't do that to him. The thought of disappointing, or letting him down in any way is anathema to me. Which is why I push it away and start reading. He shifts, rolling from his stomach to his good side. I hear a soft moan of discomfort before he settles. And then I feel the mattress dipping as he inches backward. Until his spectacular, boxer brief covered ass is resting up against my thigh.

*Oh nooooo. No.no.no.no.no.no.*

A wave of fear breaks over me. It feels like my head is being held underwater and I'm fighting for every bit of oxygen. I recognize this feeling. And I know for a fact it will lead me nowhere good.

\* \* \*

The next day, Mr. Grumpy Pants is back in full grumpy force.

"I can't get comfortable."

"I know. But I can't give you anything for another hour." Grabbing an extra pillow, I fluff the darn thing up and place it under his head. He shifts onto his side, then shifts back onto his stomach.

"Can't you just give it to me now?"

After he did his infrared light therapy and I spread more of the balm on the bruise, he napped on and off most of the day…unfortunately now he's wide awake.

"Sorry. Can't. I'll come back up at eight sharp, okay? Can I get you anything else to drink?"

"You can't leave."

*Mmmm, okay. How to handle this?* He's been growing more and more demanding as the day wears on and now he's become downright obnoxious.

"Calvin, I have to go take a shower. I've been going all day, and I stink like a goat."

This has no effect on him, other than eliciting a mulish expression I've come to know well.

"I don't mind goats," he grumbles.

I get a really bad idea and sit on the edge of the bed.

"Close your eyes." For this, I am treated to a dubious glare. "Do it."

That seems to do the trick. As soon as his eyes close, I start sifting my fingers through his hair. In seconds, his entire face goes slack. He makes a small humming sound and lets out a huge relaxed breath. Ten minutes later, he's asleep. *Hallelujah.* Mission accomplished.

It's nine by the time I get out of the shower. I'm beat with a capital B. Don't know what I would've done if Angelina and Tom hadn't taken Sam for the day. The kid came back with a huge grin on his face so I suppose he had fun.

My cellphone rings with an incoming text.

**Cal: I can't sleep. Where are you?**

*Good grief.* I never figured him to be so high maintenance. And then I suddenly realize that he's probably never had anyone to take care of him. It certainly never happened when he was a kid. Outside of team personnel, who are paid to do it, who else would've? His wife maybe? Truth: she did not look like the mothering type. I would even use the term cold. This does not sit well with me. I text back.

**Me: What can I do for you, dear?**

A second later, I get my answer.

**Cal: You can get your ass over here.**

*Well…okay.* I walk into his bedroom to find him sprawled out haphazardly—in his underwear. Funny how that barely registers anymore; I'm actually more surprised when I see him dressed. His short hair is disheveled and his scruff thick from not shaving. The frustrated look on his face warns me to tread lightly.

"Since you asked so nicely." I walk up and hand him the pills I sequestered yesterday when I found him sneaking an extra one.

"I can't get comfortable, and I can't sleep anymore."

"Wanna watch *Banshee*?"

"The hell is that?" he grunts.

"Only the sickest effing show ever. All the cool kids are watching it, Champ. Welcome to the rest of the world where football isn't the only thing on tv." I crawl onto the bed beside him and grab the remote. "I'm not giving you any spoilers, so don't even bother asking." I fluff two of his mega luxurious goose down pillows, jam them behind my back, and click the *In Demand* button.

We're just settling down to watch, when Calvin shift perpendicular to me and places his head on my thighs, facing the television. Apparently, my thighs are being appropriated and used as a pillow. My heart squeezes a little, it really does. I'm unsure how to react. But I do know that I don't want to scare him off, so I don't say a word.

"Do that scratching thing," he mumbles. And I melt just a little bit more. I can't say no to this man. It's beyond me. Especially when he's being so obnoxiously cute.

*Dang, this is really bad.*

For the next few hours, we watch the show. He asks questions and I tell him to shut up and pay attention. I never stop touching him though. First his hair and his neck. I get sigh after sigh. Then his arm and shoulder. I get hums for that. Anything I can reach gets petted. It keeps him happy and quiet—a win, win. By the end of season two, we're both practically asleep and my thighs are numb.

"Time for night night, Champ." I pat his shoulder twice and he shifts back onto his pillow.

I'm about to scoot off the bed when he reaches around my waist and pulls me back against him. Then he rocks his hips against my big 'ole butt until his dick is completely wedged between my ass cheeks—and getting harder by the second. My eyes go big and wide while every other part of me freezes. All

I'm wearing is a pair of super thin t-shirt pajama shorts. Not much is separating us.

I'm not prepared for this. I'm not at all prepared for this. All this closeness. All the touching is killing me. Because it feels so goddamn good, so good and so comfortable sometimes I feel like he's mine...except he's not. And it's starting to hurt. I try to pull away but he pulls me back, holds me even tighter.

"Cal..."

"Hmmm. Stay."

I feel his nose brush the side of my neck, hear his tired exhale close to my ear. Yup, this is torture. The sweetest torture of all.

# CHAPTER TWENTY-FOUR

I AM VERY RELUCTANTLY FALLING in love, and in good conscience, can no longer deny it to myself. I fought it. Sure I did, dug my heels in and everything. But I never stood a chance. I fought the good fight and lost. This frigging sucks. There's nothing left to do now but man up and discuss it ad nauseam with the only person I trust to give me the unvarnished truth.

"Hold your goddamn horses!" Amber shouts right before her front door flies opens. Her curious stare falls to the pizza box I'm holding.

"John's brick oven?"

"Yes."

"Extra-large pie?" I nod slowly at her query. After a thoughtful pause, she says, "This is serious. What happened?"

"I'm in love with him." I'm whining, I'm flat out whining.

"I knew it!"

I stand there and watch my best friend, the keeper of my secrets and my greatest champion, kiss her biceps.

"Now is not the time for you to gloat."

"Come in," she says with a big shit eating grin and steps aside. Ten minutes later, we're on her couch, stuffing our faces with the greatest pizza ever made.

"I really tried to stop it, I really did," I explain while I grab my third slice and proceed to stuff my already full cheeks with one more bite. The need to drown my sorrows in an insulin rush is overwhelming. Amber is nodding in solidarity at my predicament. "But he's so frigging sweet and helpful and concerned. All. The. Time. And—he holds my hand when I get nervous."

"Uhuh, uhuh." She keeps repeating. The stubborn wrinkle on her brow tells me she's really considering my plight. I stop chewing.

"That's it? Thay thomething?"

"Basically, you're screwed."

I swallow the lump of pizza lodged in my throat. "That's not helpful."

"You're going to have to move out. You can't live with him now. That gives him all the power and leaves you with none. Move in here."

"And live on your pull-out couch? That should really kill any hopes of you dating ever again," I grumble. "I'll just move back in with my parents." Talk about going backwards. The thought is depressing beyond measure. "It's a moot point anyway. I'm not moving out until Amanda comes to pick up Sam, which should happen in the next ten days, with any luck."

"Amanda?"

"Calvin's sister. Sam's mom."

"You're doing it again."

"Doing what?"

"Putting everybody else's needs before your own."

"I can't help it, Ambs."

"Do you think he feels the same way?"

"God, no. He doesn't want a relationship. He's said so repeatedly."

"So you're just going to suffer in silence? Pine from a distance?"

"That's exactly what I intend to do."

*  *  *

Someone keeps pressing the bell on the security box. When I finally make it to the phone to let them in, Cal has already beat me to it. He's been training like a man possessed. If he's not in the gym, he's with his new strength and conditioning coach. I don't think anything is going to stop him from being ready for the first game of the season. Not even a kidney injury. Watching him work, witnessing this level of commitment, I'm getting a master class in what it takes to succeed at the highest level and, quite frankly, it's a little intimidating. If I thought he was training hard before, the level of intensity in his workouts now are on a whole other level.

My favorite baritone is accompanied by a feminine voice talking loudly. Coming from the foyer, the voices draw closer. When Sam doesn't glance up from his bowl of spaghetti, I deduce who it must be. They step into the kitchen and I freeze. She has her arm hanging around the neck of the man I'm in stupid love with.

She's stunning. I thought grumpy pants was pretty, but Amanda Shaw is beyond supermodel gorgeous. And not the barfy stick figure kind that's popular these days. I'm talking glamazon eighties gorgeous. Tall, super fit, and a face that has probably broken a million boy hearts. Her bright blue eyes dart between me and Sam, who by the way, has yet to glance up.

A very uncomfortable feeling descends upon me as they both watch me. Standing before all that perfect DNA makes me, for the first time in my life, feel like a troll. I smile tightly even though every cell in my body screams for me to leave the room.

"Calvin Reginald Shaw, are you gonna just stand there and stare, or are you gonna introduce us?" She has a heavy

## WRECKING BALL

southern accent, which only adds to her hotness...naturally.

*Reginald?*

Reginald smiles at me warmly. "Camilla, this is my pain in the rear end little sister, Amanda."

The goofy smile he shines on me when he says this produces a clump of God knows what that lodges itself in my throat. Meanwhile, she beams adoration at him. There's so much love between these two. That's clear. A strange pang of jealousy hits me...maybe not jealousy, envy then?

"Nice to meet you," I say while I place the pan I was about to wash in the sink. "Can I offer you anything to drink, or eat? We were just finishing up lunch."

"Just water, thanks," she says with her eyes glued to Sam's back. I hide my face in the SubZero and grab a small bottle of Fiji for her.

"Sam, aren't you going to say hi to your mom?" Calvin's voice is gentle, thoughtful...and I'm pretty sure that I just fell deeper into love with him. Sam finishes the last bite of pasta and wipes his mouth on his paper napkin.

"May I please be excused?" He's looking straight at me.

*Oh crap.* Quickly, I glance at Cal and he nods. Smiling, I say, "You're excused." Without a backward glance, Sam goes straight up the stairs. With a pained expression, my gaze meets Amanda's, hers wavering between concern and guilt.

"This is normal," I offer, breaching the uncomfortable silence. "He just needs time to adjust...somebody should go talk to him." Both Shaws stare back at me with matching blank expressions.

"You should," Cal eventually says. I notice Amanda doesn't object. Her gaze falls to the floor.

"Okay." A second later I'm up the stairs and walking into the playroom. Sam is busy working on a new Lego creation. I plop down next to him and start separating pieces. We work for an hour in complete silence.

"Sam—" He looks up at me with nearly the same expression he wore when I first met him. This kid is every reason I want to be a parent. He's stolen a huge chunk of my heart and because of this I can feel his pain as if it were my own. "I know it hurt when your mom had to go to the hospital and leave you. I know how scary that is…but remember what the doctor said? About her having an illness?"

He nods. "I know she's sick."

"She can't help it. She doesn't want to leave you, either."

"How do you know?" He's staring at a car he just put together, spinning the tiny rubber wheels over and over again.

"Because I know that everyone that gets to know you loves you very much, and it's impossible not to miss someone you love." My voice cracks on the last two words and Sam's eyes connect with mine. "I know because I love you, and I'm going to miss you terribly when you go home…and I've only known you a short time. Imagine how your mom felt when she had to go away." He stops spinning the wheels of the Lego car, his expression turning thoughtful. "She feels bad about it. Do you think you can try and talk to her, make her feel welcome?"

Sam nods and what's left of my heart is pulverized into dust. My time here is done. The realization comes crashing down on my head. In a couple of days, these people that I love very much will no longer be part of my life. Another brutal loss. Never in a million years could I have predicted this happening to me again. Except this time, it may break me for good. At the very least, it's going to hurt for a long, long time. Then again, this is my life, a regular barrel of laughs.

*\*\*\**

"She's gorgeous," I murmur into my cell phone. After we all had a *very* silent dinner together, I withdrew to my bedroom while Amanda helped Sam get ready for bed. It wouldn't do to coddle him too much; he's going to be leaving with his mother by the end of the week whether he's ready or not. And he didn't object when Amanda offered to do it. I guess that's good...I'm sulking. I know I'm sulking.

"Like Shana level gorgeous?" Shana, an ex-friend who models. Ex because she dropped me like a bad habit while I was being investigated.

"Yeah, if Shana was ten times hotter. She's like Cindy Crawford in her prime gorgeous, Angelina in *Mr. and Mrs. Smith* level gorgeous."

"How dare she. I hate her already."

"I know. And Cal dotes on her."

"By the way, I had every intention of giving you the silent treatment for at least a week for ditching at intermission. But it seems your loaner boyfriend got us a ton of free press, so I've decided to let you off the hook for this one."

"Thanks, buddy."

"Don't say I never do nothin' for ya—"

"Now back to me. He's so sweet it's making me a little ill to watch them," I whisper hiss.

"You're jealous."

"I'm not jealous—it's his sister." There's a soft knock at the door. "Hold that thought."

It's the first night I'm not on duty. It's also the first night I've shut my door. I glance at the time on my phone. 10:59. It can only be one person. I raise the sheet up to cover my tank top.

"Yes?" I call out.

The door opens. Cal walks in and closes the door behind him. *Closes the door?*

"Amber, there's a man invading my personal space," I say loud enough for him to hear. For this, I get a smirk. "I'll call you tomorrow."

With an exasperated exhale, I state the obvious, "Reginald, you are in my bedroom with nothing but a pair of ratty ass boxers on."

"It's a family name." He walks over to my bed and lies down next to me as if he's done it a million times. Confusion parks itself on my face.

"What are you doing?" I whisper. "And why are you still awake?"

He's on his stomach, fluffing the pillow he then shoves under his head. "What happens next on *Banshee*?"

"It's a school night, Reginald. You have to be up early." There's a strange look on his face I don't recognize. Anticipation? An alert twinkle in his big gray eyes?

"Thank you for talking to Sam. I don't know what you said to him, but it worked. And Mandy really appreciates it." I sink down into the mattress, lying on my side to face him.

"You don't have to thank me. I love that kid. I'd do anything to help him."

"What happens next on *Banshee*? Do they find Job? I don't like what they did to Gordon."

The look on his face is killing me. If he asked for a kidney with that look, I'd give him two.

"I'm not telling. You have to watch it."

"Then let's watch it."

"Reggy—"

Cal rolls his eyes. "That's never going to stop, is it?"

"Not likely." His soft gaze falls to my lips, and I feel it all the way down to my nether region. If I don't say or do something to distract myself, I may end up sexually assaulting him. "Your sister's beautiful. Now I know why your parents had so many kids." His black brow arches in question. "If you and your sister are any indication, they were totally hot as bawls." He snorts at this. "Makes sense that they couldn't keep their hands off each other. I can only imagine what your brothers look like. You guys must've had every chick in high school stalking you."

Something I said makes his amusement fade. The look on his face tells me he wants to say something important so I keep my big mouth shut.

"I never dated in high school. My brothers did, but I couldn't bring another person into that mess...I couldn't risk it." His fingers inch closer to my hand, which is resting between us.

"Risk it?"

"Getting someone pregnant." He was so petrified of having a baby he was abstinent all throughout high school? *Please make the pain stop.* "My parents were seventeen when they had me."

*Slay me now. Just put me out of my misery.* It feels like I just stepped on a land mine called Calvin Shaw and he's blown my poor, tender heart to smithereens. It never crossed my mind that I could love this way again—all consuming and without a shred of self-preservation. Unfortunately, I was very wrong, very frigging wrong.

"I can't even imagine how hard that was for you," I murmur.

"It was either get the bottles ready and change diapers, or listen to the boys cry while I was trying to sleep, or study. Mandy helped."

"She's the second oldest, right?" Cal nods. His hand covers mine so they're palm to palm. I thought I had long fingers, but his dwarf mine. The warmth of his hand seeps in and spreads all the way to my heart. Shifting, he's on his side, only a foot separating us, so close I can feel the heat radiating from him, smell the scent of his shampoo and deodorant. It's so familiar to me now. Like he's mine. Except he's not.

"When is she driving back to Virginia?"

"Hopefully in a couple of days. Why?"

"I have to let my parents know when I'm moving back in." His frown is immediate. "Why?"

"Why do I have to let them know?" I chuckle. "Because I have manners, you dope." It's a reflex move, done without thought or premeditation, I reach out my index finger and poke this nose. He doesn't waste the opportunity. Grasping my wrist, he pulls it in, pulling until I'm forced to scoot closer.

Still wearing a very determined scowl, he says, "No, I mean why do you have to leave?"

"Calvin..." Again, he's staring at my lips with a hunger in his eyes that I'm not too far gone to notice. He looks like he's a hair's breadth away from diving onto me. Something's holding him back, though. My heart speeds up, pounding inside my chest. He drops my wrist and rakes his fingers through my hair, gripping at the root. My entire body shudders from the pleasure. And then his soft, pouty lips are on mine. The kiss is tentative, exploratory. He's trying to figure out what I like, and when I sigh and sag against him, he slants his mouth and deepens the kiss.

I've only kissed one person my entire life. Technically, two if I count that drunk dude in college that grabbed me as I was leaving a frat party and stuck his tongue so far down my throat I could feel it in my gut. And yet this feels...well, it feels familiar. And it feels right. It feels so right it scares the living shit out of me because this is no *fugazi*. This is the real thing.

He pulls me closer. He's stopped fighting it, whatever it was that was holding him back. He's a man possessed now, making love to my mouth like he's been dying to do it, like I'm everything he's ever wanted. And all that keeps running through my mind is *yes, yes, yes!* Shifting, I roll onto my back and he follows me, settling between my thighs with remarkable agility.

*Oh dear, oh dear, oh dear.* His erection is rock solid and pushing against the inside of my thigh. I mean…I knew he was hung but the feel of him is something else altogether. It lights me up, calling into action every cell in my sex starved body. I run my hands over the amazing landscape of his back, every muscle hard and hot—like the rest of him. They move down to the swells of the most perfect ass the good Lord has ever created. I squeeze twice because I can, damn it. And in return, he rolls his hips, hitting me in just the right spot.

*Holy frigging crap!!*

"Cal," I whisper-moan. His big hand covers my breast. Two fingers pluck at my nipple and I almost shoot off the bed. I feel his lips smile on the skin of my throat. Right before he scrapes it possessively with his teeth, then licks the abrasion. That's going to leave a mark. Doesn't matter. Does. Not. Matter. There's so much desire bleeding through me at the moment, I'm at risk of forgetting my first name. His hips have mine pinned to the mattress, his dick pressing right into my sweet spot. And I am lost, drunk on the delicious sensation of his weight and smell and touch. His head comes up. My eyes flutter open, and the sexy beast staring down at me with a wicked grin and a mischievous sparkle in his eyes circles his hips. I gasp, my eyes wide and rolling back in my head. He covers my mouth with his hand.

"Stay with me."

*Huh?* Did I just hear that right? I come to my senses for a super brief moment and meet his eyes. Uh oh, he has that look, the one that's won him championships and—stuff. He rubs against me again and a shiver races up my spine and curls my toes.

"You don't have to leave. Stay here."

"Wha bu I iss." I peel his hand away from my mouth and stare into the eyes of the man I love. The determination and anticipation I find there kills me. Because in those crystal clear eyes rimmed in steel blue, I also see my destruction.

My heart starts to pull back, retreat. It knows it's in danger of being broken. Irreparably, this time. I'm in trouble, deep shit actually. I don't ever remember exploding into love with Matt like this. Our progress was slow and methodical. It started as puppy love and stayed the course until we inevitably got married. I never questioned when, or how we fell in love. It seemed to me like I'd always been in love with Matt. But it never felt like this. This is something else entirely. I can't stay. If I stay, he'll ruin me. I'm still trying to wrap my brain around the fact that he's attracted to me. I just can't mistake this for anything other than lust. He doesn't want a relationship. He doesn't want a family. And who can blame him.

"Calvin—" My voice is soaked in regret and yearning. Nothing to be done for it. He kisses me passionately, swallowing up whatever else I am about to say.

"Don't decide now. Think about it. Now shut off the light."

*Huh?* He turns me away from him as easily as if he were handling a pillow. Then he pulls my hips back into his groin. He's still hard. His erection nestles between the rounded cheeks of my rear end and I want to scream from the empty ache pulsing between my thighs. So close and yet so far away. He has the sexual self-control of a frigging ascetic. It's simply astonishing. Breathing out a relaxed sigh, he buries his nose in my hair. *No way can he just fall asleep like this? Right?*

"Turn off the light, Cam. I have to be up by five."

I reach up and turn off the bedside lamp, immersing the room in total darkness, while I remain immersed in unspent desire.

# CHAPTER TWENTY-FIVE

THE NEXT DAY, I LEAVE Amanda and Sam to get reacquainted while Calvin heads off to practice. Tomorrow being the season home opener, he's laser focused on the impending game and not noticing much else. At my parents' house, I find my father outside gardening.

"How's your blood pressure, Dad?"

He looks up from pruning the rose bushes. "Your mother's got me taking this slow class at the American Legion."

"You mean qigong?"

"I don't know what that is. I'm doing the slow exercise."

Curling my lips between my teeth, I fight the urge to laugh 'cause I can tell Tom is getting irritated and God forbid that DeSantis temper sparks. "I'll be moving back in soon." My face feels tight as I speak.

He steps away from the bushes and wipes his hands on a rag. "Feel like a beer? I feel like a beer."

Five minutes later, we're kicking back on the freshly painted navy Adirondack chairs, gazing out at the marvel that is my father's green thumb.

"You outdid yourself this summer. The trellis of climbing roses is breathtaking."

He takes a sip of his cold beer. "I've been meaning to plant that for the past two years. Nothing like a health scare to remind you not to waste time."

I turn to take him in. So stoic, my father. "Were you scared?"

He turns and holds my gaze. "Of course, I was...but not for myself—for you and your mother. Who's going to take care of my girls if I'm gone?" The side of his mouth curves up, and his soft brown eyes crinkle at the corners.

"You know you don't have to worry about me. And Mom is much tougher than you give her credit for. All the same, we still need you...especially to referee."

"You two disagree because you're so alike." Heavy skepticism is all over my face. "You'll figure it out, eventually." We sit for some time just enjoying each other's company, neither one of us needing to fill it with garbage talk.

"Are you coming tomorrow? Cal gave me passes to the clubhouse and field for you."

"Wouldn't miss it for the world. So—are you gonna tell him?"

I stiffen at the casual query. "Tell him what?" I ask. My father being part bloodhound, I know he won't be so easily distracted.

He shoots me a knowing smile. "How you feel." Apparently, how I feel is no secret—to all seven billion people who inhabit planet Earth. Dissembling is pointless.

"It's not that simple."

"Punkin', take it from an old man. It's never as complicated as you imagine it to be."

\* \* \*

I spend the rest of the afternoon getting my room ready. Which suddenly seems about as big as a broom closet since I've been living at the *Ritz* for the past four months. It's early evening when I get back to Cal's.

"Where the hell have you been?" He's on me as soon as I

step into the side door that leads to the kitchen. Like he was listening for the car to enter the garage.

"Easy there, big guy. I went to see my parents." I place my hand on his chest, to push him away since he's all up in my business, and fail. Mistake. Big mistake. He takes it hostage, trapping it in place, and cages me against the wall with the rest of his body parts—his very nice body parts. Then, as if he has a right to, he grabs my face and kisses me…really kisses me.

I am instantly swamped by a tidal wave of lust and longing. The longing is the bad one. I can't entertain the lust because of it. I love this man. I am in stupid love. And because of it, I cannot let myself enjoy one minute of the desire smoldering between us. On tippy toes, I grip his t-shirt and press my hips against the steel pole hiding under his silky track pants. One big mitt leaves my face and he slips it into the back pocket of my jean shorts, pulling me even harder against him. And I. Am. Done for. My mind draws a complete blank from the heat and pleasure spreading through me.

A double cough comes from the end of the hallway. Cal flinches. He pulls away, but doesn't let me go.

"Yes?" Could he make his annoyance any clearer? That's a hard no.

"Dinner's ready," Amanda announces. I bite the inside of my cheek as I watch his eyes narrow.

"Give us a minute," he snaps.

"Okay—we'll wait for you," she replies, her tone instantly apologetic.

As soon as her soft footsteps fade away, he leans in and places a gentle kiss on my neck. Trying to push him off gets me nowhere.

"Did you think about it?"

"I can't."

He presses his hips into me again and I gasp, my eyes

practically rolling to the back of my head.

"Yes, you can. We'll discuss it later."

"No, Calvin—" He pushes off the wall and is down the hall, headed to the kitchen, before I can get another word in.

Amanda has cooked a remarkably juicy roast chicken. I can tell she's nervous so I make a big deal about complimenting the food. It seems to relax her a little. Her eyes are constantly jumping between Sam and Calvin, measuring their responses. Cal is quiet throughout dinner. He's back to communicating in grunts and nods.

"The couscous is delicious Amanda. The blonde raisins give it a nice flavor."

"Thanks," she says, her eyes still on Sam.

"Isn't this food delicious, Sam?"

"I guess," is his surly reply. He's been doing a lot of that the last couple of days, wavering between wanting to be nice and remembering how angry he is at her.

"I'd love to have you all over at my parents for dinner before you leave."

At this, Calvin glances up. "There won't be time."

The words come flying out sharp and quick. Everyone at the table not named Calvin is kind of taken aback. I don't see what the problem is? He likes my parents. I know he does. And they couldn't love him more, not to mention how crazy they are about Sam. "Why not?"

"Because they're leaving day after tomorrow."

*Christ, he's being a dick. What's his deal tonight?* And then I remember he's playing tomorrow, so I cut him some slack and drop the glare I'm wearing.

"I was thinking we could hang out for another week," Amanda offers casually.

"No." He practically shouts. Now we all turn to stare in his direction. "Sam has to get back to school. He's already gonna miss a few days." Cal's flat out glowering.

Amanda's gaze falls to the food she's dissecting into tiny pieces just like her brother does. "Yeah, you're right," she agrees in a small voice.

As soon as we're done, Calvin disappears into his office to go over game tapes of Arizona. I insist on washing the dishes since Amanda cooked. With a little encouragement, she and Sam go upstairs to watch tv.

Two hours later, I'm getting out of the shower when a I hear a soft knock at the door. Throwing on my cotton robe, I prepare to deal with my visitor.

"Now is not a good time, Cal." I rip open the door to find Amanda standing there.

"Not Calvin," she says, her lips briefly curving up.

Aaaand my face goes up in flames. "Is everything okay?"

"Can I come in for a minute?"

What is it with these Shaws and their late night visits? "Sure," I say even though I'm kind of uneasy about it; I make a point to leave the door open.

"It won't take long. I just want to thank you for everything you've done for Sam…for me." She glides in, taking in the room. "I stayed in this room when Kim was still around." Kim's name ignites a spark of serious irritation. The last thing I want to do at this hour, or any hour for that matter, is hear about Calvin's ex-wife.

"You don't have to thank me. I love Sam. He's absolutely wonderful…You're very lucky." That last bit was meant to remind her she's responsible for a life. God knows, I envy her.

"Camilla…there's something else I need to say." Turning, she meets my gaze squarely. "There's only one person that's as precious to me as Sam is, and that's Calvin." I'm not surprised. By the way she's been watching us since she got here, it was only a matter of time. "What happened with Kim almost

## WRECKING BALL

destroyed him. I don't know what your intentions are, but I know my brother and he's rarely interested in someone. If this is anything other than mutual, then be warned. I don't respond well to him being hurt."

I could go on a long monologue about how I would never hurt anyone, let alone someone I love. I could…but I don't.

"No need to worry. I'm moving out day after tomorrow. And the only thing between your brother and me is friendship. I want children. I always have. And after spending so much time with Sam, I couldn't be any more certain of it. Like I said, you're very lucky. Your brother doesn't want a family. He's made it abundantly clear—end of story." She's taken aback at my directness. Mission accomplished. Awkwardness hangs in the silence. "If you don't mind, I'm exhausted."

"Oh yeah, sure."

Standing by the door, I wait for her to leave. She finally realizes she's being kicked out and exits. As soon as she steps out into the hall, I say goodnight and shut the door.

I guess I can't fault her for worrying about her brother. However, something else keeps nagging me. My gut instincts tell me that she needs Calvin to be whole so she can fall apart. I don't like it one bit…except he's not mine to protect, or worry about.

I put on my tank top and pajama shorts. I crawl into bed and shut off the light. Two minutes later, the door opens and closes. The mattress dips. He scoots closer, curving his hips around mine. I don't say a word because I don't know what to say. I hate that he's here. And I love it, crave it. A burst of pure joy rips through me every time I see him, smell him, feel him pressing that body that won't quit against mine. He wraps his arm around my waist and digs his nose in my hair.

"Seriously?"

"Shhh, go to sleep. We'll talk tomorrow."

I do as he asks. Because really, what choice do I have? My heart has already chosen.

# CHAPTER TWENTY-SIX

I'M NERVOUS. LIKE, REALLY NERVOUS. I went from being a major bloodthirsty football fan, to whimpering lovestruck nervous nelly in a matter of four months. Every time someone comes within touching distance of Cal, I hold my breath and cringe. Football is officially no longer fun for me. Everyone else seems to be having a great time, though. My Dad is busy entertaining Sam and Amanda with his corny jokes during commercial breaks. They're all laughing and carrying on—no sweat. Amber's been getting her kicks by taunting poor Ethan, who happens to be handling it like a true gentleman. Me? I'm living on adrenaline.

By the end of the third quarter, I'm beyond drained. Add insult to injury, the game is a nail bitter. It comes down to the last possession. The Titans get the ball on their own ten yard line and have to drive the length of the field for the game winning field goal. On second and five, Cal ends up getting sacked. The next second I'm on my feet, screaming, "Get off of him, you fat fuck!"

Not my best moment. I'll admit it. Needless to say, I draw a bunch of attention and some applause. In the end, the Titans squeak out a victory. Hallelujah.

Ethan orders me to wait for Calvin and commandeers the Yukon to drive everyone home. This does not sit well with me.

I'm not even sure Calvin won't go straight to his car. As I contemplate the horror of sitting here by myself while every other family member departs with a corresponding player, my spirits steadily sink. I feel more and more unsure with each passing minute I don't see that beautiful face appear in the doorway. And then, in an instant, all doubt disappears.

He steps into the room and scans the area, his eyes quickly moving across the crowd. His hair is still wet and his face clean shaven. His suit is impeccable. He's so beautiful it stops my heart. No really, I feel it skip a couple of beats.

Finally, he finds me standing behind a group of people headed for the door of the clubhouse. Quite a few curious glances turn his way. Some people pat his arm and congratulate him on a good game, but he doesn't acknowledge them; his attention is all for me. He's crossing the room, heading in my direction. Without hesitation, he takes my face in his hands and kisses me as if we aren't standing in a room full of people watching us. And he doesn't stop. Not when someone wolf whistles, not when someone laughingly shouts, "Get a room."

Pulling away, he says, "Ready to go home?"

I nod. It isn't my home, but I don't have it in me to correct him. When he hangs his arm around my neck, I catch him wincing. My frown is immediate.

"What's wrong?" he asks.

"It's official. I hate football."

\* \* \*

I open the door to my bedroom and find Calvin tucked into my bed, snoring…I am so screwed. He soaked in ice as soon as we got home. Then he practically crawled upstairs. Since Amanda and Sam are leaving tomorrow, I spent some time with them, talking and watching tv—saying our goodbyes. I'm going to miss Sam so much I can't even bear to think about it.

# WRECKING BALL

Cal looks so peaceful in sleep, even though I know for a fact how banged up he is. Saw it for myself when he asked me to get his sweats out of the closet and didn't bother to warn me that he'd dropped his towel. I was so upset about the bruise on his ribs I almost didn't notice the rest of him.

The urge to touch him, to run my hands over every inch of that delicious body to make sure he's not permanently maimed is overwhelming. Slowly, I lower myself next to his hip and sift my fingers through his hair. A muffled sigh greets me. His eyes slow blink open and take me in, his expression so serious it checks me.

"Come here." He doesn't wait for me to answer, or act. He wraps those game winning hands around my arms and pulls me down, rolling us over until I'm on my back and he's in-between my thighs. And good heavens does my body approve. His hips press into mine and it's my turn to sigh. *How the heck can he be this hard already?*

This is happening. I don't give a single shit what the consequences are. It's a given my heart is getting broken, therefore, I might as well enjoy the hot sex that goes with it. Because it will be hot—there's absolutely no doubt about it.

"How much longer are you going to torture me?" I whisper. His lazy smile and bedroom eyes lay waste to every coherent thought in my head. I think my eggs just got fertilized by that look alone.

"Until tomorrow. As soon as the people in the next two rooms get the hell out of my house. Then you're mine."

There goes my heart again, doing backflips like a dolphin at Sea World.

"Now be real quiet while I get a taste."

"What?"

I don't have time to say anything else. He sinks down and kisses a path down my neck, over my collarbone, headed straight for my breasts. In one swift move, he rips my tank top over my head. Then he comes up on his elbows and stares. The expression on his face is…pained. He looks like he's in pain.

"How are your ribs? Maybe we should wait until you heal?"

"Honey, there's only one way to make this pain go away." He lowers himself back down and cups my breasts. Fastening his mouth onto my nipple, he licks and pulls. His other hand quickly covers my mouth before the scream can leave my lips. *Sweet baby Jezuz.* That feels so good I may die of pleasure. "They're even better than I imagined."

His hand leaves my mouth and skates down my body, caressing everywhere it travels. Those hands that know how to measure and calibrate the millimeters it takes to win a championship are busy learning me. A burning need pulses between my thighs. "Calvin…Calvin."

He shifts, rocking his erection against my aching lady parts and I have to bite my lip to stop from crying out. I'm being teased into madness while his discipline could rival that of a Buddhist monk. His big warm hand slips inside my shorts and underwear. One hand teases and tugs at my nipple while the other plays between my thighs. He kisses the corners of my mouth, my lips as I whimper and beg for more.

"Shhhh." He covers my mouth again with his palm. Skilled fingers pet and stroke me, push inside of me until I'm nearly dying with the need to come. Until I fall into an orgasm that has me bowing off the bed and digging my nails into his massive biceps. Keeping the pressure steady, he eases me down gently, expertly. The feel of his his soft lips on my neck makes me shiver, makes me yearn for more, keeps me in a suspended state of longing and lust. This isn't sex. He's making love to me, showing me how he feels, proving how important my pleasure is to him.

# WRECKING BALL

My eyes blink open to find his face inches from mine, watching me with total fascination. The pressure in my throat intensifies. Swallowing does nothing to get rid of it. I can't hide from him any longer. What's the point? It is, what it is—and nothing's going to change that. I'm in love with a man I can't have. The quicker I come to terms with that, the quicker the recovery. Cupping his face, I let everything that's in my heart shine openly in my eyes.

"Stay with me," he murmurs.

My hand falls between us, measuring the shape of him over his boxer briefs. He's so hard it has *got* to be painful. His brow furrows. I scrape my short nails up and down his erection and he groans harshly.

"Let me take care of you."

Calvin plants a heartfelt kiss on my mouth, lingering awhile to taste me, brushing his lips back and forth on mine. Pulling back, he holds my gaze, the gravity of the moment apparent in his expression.

"I haven't made love in a very long time. If I get started, I'm not gonna be able to stop."

*Made love?* Good Lord, I'm dead. Or something like it. I'm officially dying of love for this man.

His fingers gently brush my hair back while he takes in my reaction. "Tomorrow you're mine."

He shifts, returning to his spot next to me. Then he wraps his arm around my waist and buries his face in the curve of my neck, exhaling one long relaxed breath. There isn't any part of us that isn't touching. Like he can't bear to have even an inch separating us, like he's afraid I'll sneak away.

I'm so close to proclaiming my love out loud that I have to forcibly bite my tongue. Instead, I pet and stroke up and down his arm, place tender kisses all over his face, squeeze him tight. In answer, he grumbles his appreciation and snuggles closer.

Not ten minutes after that I hear his soft snore. It's suddenly the dearest sound in the world to me. In my excitement, I almost forgot he played a game today. But tomorrow… tomorrow he's mine.

*  *  *

The next morning I walk into the kitchen to find Calvin cooking breakfast—I kid you not. I'm actually surprised he didn't pack their bags and put them out on the front doorsteps. Sam and Amanda are at the kitchen table, digging into…are those pancakes triangular?

"Mercedes?" I ask the chef.

With a lethal smirk, he says, "Gave her the day off."

I take a seat at the table and load my plate with scrambled eggs.

"Would you like some triangular pancakes?" Amanda queries. My eyes connect with hers over the rim of her coffee cup and we both chuckle.

After we all have breakfast together, Cal and I help Amanda load her Mercedes with all of Sam's Lego sets, which takes much longer than Cal anticipated. By noon, I think he's ready to have an honest to goodness meltdown. We all say our goodbyes. I hug Sam tightly, almost incapable of letting go, and tell him I love him and I'll miss him and make sure he has my number so he can call any time he wishes. They'll be coming up for Christmas and we make plans to get together.

Amanda is in her car, about to drive off, when Ethan's Audi comes up the driveway. Before he even parks the car, Calvin is waving his arms in the air.

"Hell no! Go home, Ethan. Can a man get some goddamn time alone with his girlfriend!"

The smirk Ethan levels at me is one of pure victory. With that, Amanda drives off and Ethan follows immediately afterward. Cal has his arm around my neck as we watch them disappear down the driveway. He looks down at me and what I find on his face makes my heart leap inside my chest. There's lust, a lot of it. But more importantly, there's reverence and wonder. And there's love. Plenty of love. I have no doubt because I know what it looks like, and I know it's all over my face, too.

"You wreck me...every time I look at you." He searches my face to see the effects of his words. The effect is that I can't see the beginning or end of my love for him. It's a constant never-ending thing. How did this happen? How did we get here? Not too long ago we were barely able to tolerate each other. He snuck up on me, this sex on a stick, six foot four, two hundred and thirty pound man, snuck up on me and stole my heart.

\* \* \*

I've only ever had sex with one person. I'm so nervous right now I'm practically vibrating out of my skin. Taking my wrist, he drags me into the foyer and doesn't make it much farther. We've waited far too long to do this. Desire explodes between us, making us both impatient and clumsy, out of control. He wraps his hands around my face and devours my mouth, kissing me like his life depends on it.

Rising on my toes, I shove my fingers into his hair and hold him in place. He grabs my ass and pulls me against the baseball bat he has hidden under his favorite black track pants. *Goodness gracious.* It ignites a fire in my belly, awakening every primal instinct in my body, which is currently screaming, 'Now! Do it now!'

He rips my long sleeve henley off. I return the favor with his t-shirt. Then I jump and wrap my legs around his waist, hooking my ankles while he carries me to the stairs. Thank fuck they're covered with carpeting. Although at this point, nothing short of a fatal wound is gonna stop me. Placing me down on the stairs, he whisks off my jeans in a nanosecond and rears back to inspect his handiwork. His intense gaze takes in every inch of skin the daylight reveals. I've never seen his expression so…taken, awestruck—and hungry. I've never seen anyone look at me this way.

"Do you trust me?"

I do. I trust him as implicitly as I do my parents and Amber. "Yes."

"I haven't been with anyone since Kim and I broke up. We take blood every couple of months to check for PEDs. I'm clean and I know you are." Oh, yeah—the 'contagious disease' test. "I don't want anything between us. But I'll grab a condom if you want me to."

"I don't want anything between us, either." The smile that comes over him is spectacular. He takes my bra off gingerly, as if he's savoring every minute. My panties come next. I'm sprawled out naked on the stairs. His eyes are on me wide and unblinking. "You're so goddamn beautiful. You're the most beautiful thing I've ever seen."

Standing, he pushes his pants down and I suck in a breath. My God…was there ever a more perfect figure of man than this. Those traps. Lord have mercy. They make my mouth water every time they make an appearance. His dick is so thick and hard it practically reaches his belly button. I can't take my eyes off of it. I'm…mesmerized.

"If you stare at it any longer, Honey, I'm going to go off before the fun begins." My eyes meet his and he smiles a little knowing smile that makes all sorts of deliciously filthy promises. Then he picks me up off the stairs. "Not on the stairs…maybe later, though," he says with a sexy smirk.

I kiss him over and over while he carries me into the den.

"Not on the new couch!" I screech. "I'd like to see you explain the mess to Mercedes."

# WRECKING BALL

Without pausing, he keeps going up the stairs, headed to his bedroom. Planting me on his bed, he makes a place for himself between my thighs. Everywhere our skin touches, it's like an electric charge runs through me. The precum leaking from his erection slips over and in between my body. I scream when he hits my clit over and over again. There's no time, or need for a slow seduction. The foreplay has been going on for weeks. I can't take anymore. That's why I hook my leg around his waist and on the next rock of his hips he slides right into me. I can hardly breathe I'm so full.

"Jezuz Christ," he groans. "Don't move, or I'll come. You're so tight, Honey. Don't move."

I need him to move, or I will die. One squeeze of my kegels and he shouts out his release, his face crumbling as if he just took a hit of the best drug ever created. His forehead falls onto the mattress next to me as he basks in the afterglow of his orgasm. I feel his soft lips on my neck, his hands weave into my hair. He licks my earlobe and nibbles it. Little by little, I can feel him growing harder inside of me and I slowly. Lose. My. Mind. His hips start rocking. His movements determined, in control. There's no hesitation in the way Cal makes love. He knows exactly what he wants and how to go about getting it. His thrusts come harder now. His hand, heavy and warm on my breast, brushes back and forth on my nipple. I'm close, so bloody close. I grab his ass and dig my fingers into the dents of his cheeks. He grunts and thrusts faster. He angles his hips a fraction and his hair rubs me in just the right spot. One more stroke and I go off like it's the Fourth of frigging July all over again, except this time the fireworks are happening inside my body. The climax keeps going and going in pulsing waves that never seem to end. Cal keeps thrusting, milking my orgasm for every drop, not wasting even a bit of it. He pinches my nipple hard and it launches me into another one. He's my anchor and

I cling to him because I am lost in a sea of bliss. So lost I may never be found again.

*  *  *

After the bed gets destroyed, he decides he needs to take me from behind on the stairs. The rug burns on my knees will last for weeks. I returned the favor by riding him hard and slow on the marble of the kitchen island. I think he may have bruised a vertebra. By ten, after a fortifying meal of pizza, we debate for a second whether we should both ice up and decide to go back to bed instead.

My head rests on his chest while he plays with my hair. The sense of satisfaction I'm feeling right now is in a class by itself. I could stay like this forever and not want for anything else.

"Can I ask you something?" I say looking up at him.

"You know you can."

"What's up with the cow comment?" I have been dyyyyiiing to ask this for months. I have got to know. His lips curl between his teeth. Then he blows out a deep breath. "You don't have to be embarrassed. We're way past that, don't you think?" I chuckle, glancing down at our entwined bodies, sweaty and sticky from a marathon of fucking, 'scuse me, *making love*.

Placing a hand behind his head, he stares up at the ceiling. "I already told you." His answer only confuses me more. I scan his face to get a better read on him. "When I saw you that day, staring back at me with those big brown eyes—you hit me like a wrecking ball...I panicked."

*What code are we speaking in?* "I don't get it."

"I've felt that way only one other time in my life," he confesses. Those expressive gray eyes meet mine and it dawns on me.

"With your ex," I finish for him. He answers with a small

nod. His admission feels about as good as someone scratching my corneas. "I'm not Kim," I groan. Is this not clear enough? I roll over, off of him, and his body follows mine. He wraps his arms around me and presses closer. His chest blankets my back, my rear end wedged against his groin. Not a breath of air separates us.

"I know you're not," he murmurs in my ear, seducing me out of my now sour mood with his skilled fingers between my legs. Rolling his hips, he makes me feel how hard he is for me, how much he wants me again. "You wouldn't force me to accept something I don't want any part of," he murmurs with his mouth latched onto the sensitive skin of my throat.

Yup, there it is—the insurmountable wall that's standing in our way. I knew this about him. Of course, I knew this. But it was a nonissue until this very moment. He was my friend, the man I was reluctantly in love with. Not my lover. *Not my lover.* I sit up abruptly and cover my breasts with the edge of the sheet like I'm a virgin in a Victorian melodrama.

"What's wrong?" the caveman next to me asks while he rips the sheet off. His big hand strokes up and down my spine. *Feeels sooo good.* I almost forget why I'm upset. What do I say? 'Thanks for the best sex of my life. I love you beyond measure, but you don't want kids so sayonara.'

"Cam?"

I know what I have to do and it kills me, it absolutely kills me. Because while I'm explaining, I know he'll be thinking about his ex-wife.

"This was a mistake." Those words are razor blades leaving my mouth. Over my shoulder, I chance a glance at his face. It's like a sheet of ice has crystalized over him. He just stares at me like he's seen a ghost.

"Why?" he says an eternity later. I'm dying inside by slow inches. He's the last person on the planet I want to hurt, and yet I know this is going to hurt both of us.

"I don't do casual sex. You know that."

"Who said anything about casual?"

I need to be dressed for this. I'm out of bed and walking down the hall to my room a second later. He's on me before I reach my door, hugging me from behind and kissing my neck. I don't fight him. I let him hold me until he relaxes his grip because I don't want him to think I'm doing this out of anger, or regret. That's the thing—I *don't* regret it. I just can't continue any further. If I stop this now, I may be able to salvage our friendship. That's the best I can hope for now.

"Let me throw on some clothes and we can talk."

Releasing me, he follows me into my bedroom. Mr. Modesty lounges naked on my bed like he doesn't have a care in the world while I throw on a tank top and leggings. He's propped up on an elbow, his long legs crossed at the ankles. My eyes do a slow glide from his perfect dick, thick and soft and long, asleep on his thigh, to his heavy lidded gray gaze. He's unequivocally the sexiest man on the planet. Period. Full stop. His expression is warm and affectionate again, a naughty smirk playing on his lips. I know what it means; he thinks he can change my mind. Not this time, though. This time I won't fold and I can't compromise. It wouldn't be fair to either one of us.

"This isn't casual, Cam. You know me better than that."

I do. I definitely do.

"I know...but the thing is—" By the look on his face, I know he's getting ready to argue. "The thing is...I want kids. I can't be with you if there isn't even the slightest chance of you not changing your mind. And I know you won't. You've said so often enough." The silence drags on. I can't look at him. I'm afraid of what I'll find. Anger. Contempt. Or worse, his indifference.

## WRECKING BALL

He exhales a deep breath and sits up, throwing his legs over the side of the bed. With his back to me, he says, "You're right, I won't change my mind."

"Would it be so bad?" I dare to ask. The muscles of his back turn to stone. He tips his head back and chuckles without humor. It's the saddest, most hopeless laugh I've ever heard.

"Yeah," he says harshly. "It would be. Do you have any idea what it's like to be a fourteen year old boy and have to strap a baby to your chest in a carrier—a carrier I had to rig up because we couldn't afford the store bought kind, and go to the supermarket to get formula because the woman that's supposed to be taking care of us hadn't been home in three days?" *Jesus, Mary, and Joseph.* Tears glaze my eyes. "A baby that I had to bathe and change and stay up all night with because he had an upset stomach. And then go to school the next day." As his voice grows more weary, my chest caves at the weight pressing down on it. "Do you?"

"No, I don't," I answer timidly. I can feel his pain and frustration in the marrow of my bones. I can't even begin to fathom what it must've been like for him. Me, an only child spoiled and suffocated with love and support. What would I know about that kind of sacrifice? Nada. And I love him even more for being strong and responsible when all the adults around him weren't. For carrying the burdens of an entire family on his shoulders—and he's still doing it.

"I've raised kids already. I've raised kids, but I've never been one. This isn't something I've thought about lightly."

I'm fully crying now. He's right. I know how much thought he's put into this. And I'm so mad for him. So mad for the childhood he was robbed of, of the joy he never had growing up, of the feeling of safety he never experienced. It's also robbed him of the chance to experience his own children—because he will *never* have them.

"I love you very much…you should know that," I say through a blur of tears. He turns swiftly to face me, his expression one of utter shock. "I'm not saying that to coerce you. I'm saying it because I want you to know that if I felt only a small fraction of what I feel for you then maybe I could carry on. But I can't, not with you. I love you too much to pretend that I would be happy with your terms. And leaving you later would only hurt more…I'm going back to my parents tomorrow morning. I hope we can remain friends, you mean the world to me, but I'll understand if you can't."

I can feel him pulling away from me already. I can see the distance in his eyes. And I know it's self-preservation, though it hurts all the same.

"You don't have to leave," he says quietly, so quietly.

"Yes, I do." Without another word, he walks out of the room—taking my heart with him.

# CHAPTER TWENTY-SEVEN

I'M PRETTY SURE THERE ARE only a certain number of tears each person is allotted in a lifetime and I have hit my quota. The next day, I moved back into my parents' house, got under the covers, and cried for three days straight. That was a week ago. I haven't shed a tear since.

I miss him. I miss him like I miss the heart I left behind. In its place there's a vacuum now, a frigging supernova that sucks up everything good in the world and devours it. I feel nothing other than this gnawing hunger for him. And I know it'll be with me for far longer than the shame and guilt I felt for Matt because this time there's no anger to direct at the agent of my misery. There are no villains in this piece. We're both justified in what we want.

I check my phone in case I missed a text. Pathetic—I know.

**Cal: Mercedes wants to know what you marinate the pork chops with.**

That's from earlier today. Texts from him started coming in the day after I left. Usually inane questions, or random information. As transparent as his intentions for sending them are, I don't tell him to stop. I can't bring myself to sever that last thread of hope.

**Cal: Sam asked about you today. Mandy is doing great.**

Ughhh, it's horrible. Every time I think I'm turning a

corner, thinking of him less, I get a text from him and it sends me straight back into the bowels of emotional hell. I haven't slept through the night once since I left his house and tonight is more of the same. It's two a.m., and after tossing and turning for two hours, I've given up hope. Not even a new novel from one of my favorite dark romance authors can hold my attention. My iPhone vibrates with a text and my head jerks off the pillow. My heart drums fast and hard inside my chest in anticipation of who might be texting me at this late hour. If it's Amber, I'll kill her for giving me false hope.

**Cal: Are you awake? I'm outside.**

Am I awake? I may never sleep ever again. I text back immediately.

**Me: I'll be down in a sec.**

After throwing on a tank top and lounge pants, I grab my flip-flops and creep downstairs. I have no idea what to expect or what I'll say, but at the moment a driving need to see him lays waste to everything else. Through the glass of the front door, I spot him. Hair disheveled, a week's worth of stubble covering the bottom half of his face—and still the most gorgeous creature on the face of this planet. The dark circles hanging under his eyes are the mirror image of mine.

When I open the front door, the look of relief that comes over him makes my heart swell to the point of pain. I love this man. It's just an endless supply of love on tap. There's absolutely no danger of me ever running out of it.

He takes his hands out of the pockets of his track pants and grabs me like I have no choice. Wrapping those long, skilled fingers around my biceps, he pulls me into his body. Top to bottom, there isn't any part of us that isn't touching. I encircle my arms around his waist and bury my face in his chest. He holds me so tightly for a minute I fear it may be my last breath.

Exhaling heavily, he murmurs, "Goddamn this feels good."

*I'm not going to cry. I'm not going to cry. Breathe in, breathe out.*

His fingers sift through my loose hair, his lips rest on the top of my head. He grips the roots possessively and tugs. I'm forced to look up at him, and holy hell if I don't get instantly turned on. His expression is a fairly even mix of devastation and determination.

"You're killin' me."

"I don't mean to. If it makes you feel any better, I haven't slept a single night since I moved out."

"I don't want you not sleeping. I want you sleeping next to me."

*Fuck, I'm going to cry.* Eyes brimming with unshed tears, I go for honesty—it's all I have left. "Do you think this is easy for me? It's frigging impossible." I try and put some space between us but he won't allow it, tightening his grip on me even more. "Why are you here, Cal?"

"Brought you something."

"You brought me something?" Okay, now I'm confused. I don't have time to mull this over, though. Taking my hand hostage, he drags me over to the Range Rover. Once he's got the passenger side door open, he picks me up by the waist and places me in the seat—literally picks me up. Then he leans in, pushing his hips in between my bent legs, grabs my face, and kisses me. We're all lips and tongues, licking, sucking, devouring each other as if it may be the last time and all I keep thinking is, *'Please don't let this be the last time. I'll be good, God, I swear, just don't take him away from me.'*

We break apart panting and he closes the door. Then he gets in on the driver's side. The atmosphere is crackling with pent up sexual tension. Neither one of us moves a hair. And then I turn to look at him. Smoky gray locks onto simple brown and not even the army of the devil himself can stop us. We dive at each other. I grab his t-shirt, yank and yank until he helps me peel it off of him. He takes my tank top and has it over my head before I even know what's what. Not for a second have we stopped kissing. I'm eating his face. Seriously, he may not have a face once we're done; I'm going Hannibal Lector on his ass. As a matter of fact, I may not have one either because his scruff feels like I'm cleaning my cheeks with steel wool. Until his big warm hand covers my breast and pinches my nipple. Then all thought ceases and only sensation exists.

God almighty this man knows how to push all the right buttons. When the warmth of his palm leaves my breast, I whimper. Not for long. Not for long, thank heavens, because he grabs me around the waist and pulls me onto his lap. Without objection, I swing my leg over and straddle him, our groins coming together suddenly. His dick, so hard I'm afraid it may cause him permanent injury, pushes up against me and I have to scream from the wanting, from the overwhelming hunger I have for him. I swear I'm ten seconds from going mental from it. Reaching down between us, I stroke him over his pants and feel a wet stain. I dig my short nails into the swollen head of his erection, scratch lightly over the slippery fabric, and he sucks in a sharp breath.

"I have pants on," I say in a huff.

"No problem," the sexy bastard murmurs. He takes the crotch of my lounge pants between his fingers and rips the seam open as easily as if he were opening a bag of chips. I've never been grateful for tinted windows before, however, at the moment they're the best thing mankind has ever invented. At my astonishment, he smiles...smiles like he never has before. It's big and white and stretches from ear to ear and all I can think is that I want to make him smile like that at least once a day for the rest of our lives. Lifting his hips, he pushes his pants down his thighs and his gorgeous dick springs free. I sigh...I sigh because I know what he can do with that gorgeous dick and a stupid smile grows on my face, too.

His hand reached between us while his gaze, burning brightly even in the dark, holds mine. He pets me slow and steady, his touch determined, like his whole purpose in life is to get me off. God, how I wish that were true. It feels like every ounce of blood in my body has traveled south. The man's got some mad skills. He knows exactly how to get what he wants. He wasn't exaggerating in the least. He spreads the slickness he finds between my legs over me and himself. Then, canting his hips, he pushes inside of me, never once breaking eye contact. The air in my lungs rushes out of me. We sit there, wedged together, without moving for a minute. I'm so filled up I have no leverage.

"I love you." The words are pushed out of me as easily as he pushed in, with zero resistance. Because what's the point of holding back? He either feels the same, or he doesn't—either way, no regrets.

Grabbing my face again, he kisses me as if kisses are words and everything he wants to say is on his lips. And then I can't wait another second, I hook my arms around his neck and bury my face on the side of his throat. He digs his fingers into the soft curve of my butt and begins to jack his hips up and down powerfully. It doesn't take long for me to come. He follows immediately afterward. We stay wrapped up in each other for a long time, joined in every way we can possibly be. Now that I think of it, even when we're not touching it feels like we're joined. Maybe that's why it hurts so much when we're apart.

The film of sweat between us cools, leaving me cold and vulnerable. Without a word, he grabs his t-shirt and slips it over my head. The feather on the Seminole logo falls over my nipple and he runs the pad of his thumb over it, my entire body shuddering in response. He cups my face and tilts my chin up, our eyes tangling.

I'm not a fan of words. Not since the man I thought I would spend my life with used them to deceive me the last five years of our marriage. In my experience, words are cheap and disposable. Give me action instead. I'll even take silence over promises that risk being broken. The fact that Cal hasn't yet told me how he feels doesn't bother me. He can keep those words tucked inside all he wants because his eyes are screaming his love for me.

"What was it that you had to give me?"

Surprise flashes across his face, followed closely by a lazy grin. He reaches into the back seat and grabs…

A sports bra. *A sports bra?*

"You came here…at two thirty in the morning…to return a sports bra?"

"I thought you might need it."

"I thought you said—" I brush my lips on his. "You were going to burn all my bras because it was a crime to hide these," I say, pointing to my boobs. And then I positively melt at the goofy grin he gives me. Mooning over a gorgeous man? Hmm, sounds familiar. Maybe I am my mother's daughter after all.

"Come home with me," he murmurs. The smile slides off his face and his expression turns seriously intense. It's my turn to cup his face, to brush my thumbs gently across his cheeks.

"You know why I can't." He looks so torn it breaks my heart. "I'm not trying to punish you. But I can't compromise on this. I won't let someone else's needs kill mine—not anymore. I'm different now, and you have something to do with that."

He exhales harshly and brushes his face with his palm.

## WRECKING BALL

Then he pats my hip in a signal to scoot over. I slide off his lap, back onto the passenger seat, while his body slips out of mine; the messy evidence of our lovemaking everywhere. Inadvertently, I catch a glimpse of myself in the rear view mirror and gasp. My hair looks like it's been dry humped by a squirrel while my face looks like it's undergone a chemical peel. *Real nice.* I make a half-assed attempt to tame my hair, my fingers snagging on multiple knots, as I gather strength for what I'm about to say.

"We can't do this anymore, Calvin. You can't text, or call. I can't see you. It's too hard, I'm too weak, and I love you too damn much."

A sideways glance reveals his stony countenance directed straight ahead. He's working hard to measure his breathing. His Adam's apple rises and falls, as if he's fighting to keep something locked down. Still, he remains silent. I open the door and get out. I don't say goodbye, and I don't look back. Because that, most of all, is too damn hard.

*  *  *

The next day, I open the front door to find Mercedes looking like the harbinger of doom.

"Mercedes? How are you? Is something wrong?" Not the slightest lift of the corners of her mouth, nor an explanation. I'm starting to worry. "Is Cal okay?" I hold the door open in a gesture to welcome her in.

"You need to come home," she announces in that thick Spanish accent of hers.

Lost, I look around for clues. "Uhhh, I am home."

"Where you belong," she clarifies.

I usher her in and she follows me without objection. "Mercedes—it's complicated." I pinch the bridge of my nose, a headache threatening.

"You are a woman, he is a man. It is not that complicated."

*Oh, jeez.*

Angelina walks into the foyer and I introduce the two women. That was my first mistake. Two hours and three cups of coffee later, the two women are still commiserating about their faithless daughters and their inexplicable love lives. It turns out that Mercedes' daughter, Stella is a very successful trader and has absolutely no wish to ever get married. Angelina trumps her easily with stories of my criminally minded deceased spouse. Listening to these two go on and on, I'm pretty sure I've hit rock bottom. By the time I'm ushering Mercedes back out, she's resigned to the fact that I'm not budging.

"Men say these things. They don't know what they want until you make them want it," she adds, in a last ditch effort.

I'm shaking my head before I even speak. "No. No, I won't do that to him. I won't be another person that forces something on him. He's too good a person. He'll give me what I want at his expense."

Now that I hear it said out loud, it dawns on me that we're exactly alike. *Holy crap, how did I miss this?*

"How is he?"

"Not good. He's not eating well. He barely speaks. He's depressed, Camilla. How do you feel?"

"Depressed. Not eating well. Barely speaking."

She grips my chin and kisses me on the cheek, leaving me standing on the front steps of my parents' house with a heavy heart.

# CHAPTER TWENTY-EIGHT

Radio silence lasted all of two days. Part of me was thrilled to hear the sound of the *Monday Night Football* theme I've assigned to him. The rest of me hated it. The man is a world champion, for heaven's sake. Where I'm a champion of... nothing, other than myself. Given time, it's safe to assume who would eventually win this battle of wills. That's why when he texted that he was on his way over to my parents' house because he needed to "talk", I did the only thing I could, I packed my bags and took Amber up on her offer to stay at her place until I could find another job. That was ten days ago. Ten days of texts and messages I don't dare look at because I know I'll cave.

"My boobs hurt." I say this in a very small voice. Cue ten years later, I finally get a response.

"That's nice," my *consiglieri* absently murmurs. On her nights off from the club, Amber is always on the couch watching her favorite shows.

"Amber...Ambs?" Crickets. "Paging Amber Isabelle Jones. Yo there, Miss Jones."

Her blonde head turns towards me. "It's *Scandal*! I can't have this convo during *Scandal*."

"I said—" and I say this very slowly and meaningfully. "That my boobies hurt. They also happen to be as large as an inflatable raft—two inflatable rafts to be precise."

"Stop bragging," she bites out, shooting me a look of feigned contempt. "You're due for your period."

"I was due two weeks ago."

That's when she peels her eyes off of the television and slowly, ever so slowly—like in the *The Exorcist* when Linda Blair's head does a 360—well Amber's head does a ninety degree turn to face me.

"Store. We need to go to the store immediately."

For two weeks, I've been talking myself out of believing it. The excuses have run the gamut from stress, to uterine cancer, to early menopause. And yet the P word never once came up. Lies, all lies I told myself because the truth could very well be more frightening than early menopause, though clearly not more so than uterine cancer. The look on Amber's face is like a slap upside the head.

We scrabble off her couch, jam on our flip-flops, and run out the door. With my hair a rats nest from the humidity and hers on top of her head in a messy bun, we look like complete and total train wrecks as we run to the corner store.

"Which one should I buy," I ask, confused at all the varieties of at-home preggers tests stacked on the shelf. "Words, or symbols?" I hold them up for her inspection.

"All of them," she answers, nodding. "We need all of them."

To call it awkward when the elderly gentleman at the register rings up fifteen home pregnancy tests would be a gross understatement. "We just want to be sure," I blurt out loudly, for him and anyone else that may be interested. Once we get back to Amber's apartment, the shit really hits the fan— and winds up all over me.

"Did you check the expiration date on that one?" We're both crowded into her tiny bathroom, ten *positive* tests lined up on her sink.

"I'm pretty sure they're not all expired," the wise ass also known as my best friend says.

"Now is not the time for sarcasm!" My emotions go back and forth violently from ecstatic to scared shitless like someone's playing an aggressive game of ping pong with my heart. I can't settle on one. "What do I do?" Amber stares back blankly. For once, she's speechless. "Now is not the time for you to be quiet!"

"I'm thinking you need to tell your baby daddy."

Ughhhhh, just the sound of that makes me want to hurl. I walk out of the bathroom and into her bedroom, falling face down on the bed. She's right behind me, pressing her case. "I don't see what the drama's about. It's not the first time a professional athlete's knocked up his girlfriend…and you're a couple of months shy of dirty thirty one. Not like you two are under age pups."

"You don't understand," I moan. How do I explain to her that Cal had a vasectomy specifically to avoid something like this from happening? Good grief, the man has atomic sperm. How the heck does one get knocked up by a man who's had a vasectomy?!! I make a mental note to Google this miracle ASAP. I can't decide if I'm the luckiest lady on the planet, or arguably the unluckiest. Matt and I went the last couple of years without protection and nothing happened…I suddenly realize that the thought of Matt doesn't hurt anymore. His memory has settled in a place inside of me that I can look at without feeling pain or guilt or anger. All I feel is warmth and love. My elation at this discovery lasts for all of a nanosecond. As soon as my mind shoots back to Cal, fear fills my gut. I have no idea how I'm going to tell him, and it's pretty obvious that this news won't be celebrated as it should.

\* \* \*

It's early evening and I'm busy scanning job sites on Amber's computer when Justin walks out of her bedroom, grabs a bottle of water from the fridge, and bids me farewell. This is a mystery I have yet to solve. Justin has been coming over at least a few times a week in the last month. They never go out. He just comes over, they disappear into her bedroom, and then—nothing. Total silence. Not a peep, except for hushed whispers. I mean, what the hell are they doing in there? Playing *Scrabble*? 'Cause if there is any sexy time, it's certainly not vigorous. I haven't broached the subject yet with my little blonde friend, though the time is fast approaching.

There's a heavy pounding at the door and Amber comes flying out of her room fully dressed. "He's here."

That didn't take long. He must've realized I wasn't at my parents' place anymore. If he doesn't stop pounding on the steel front door, I'm pretty sure one of Amber's nosy neighbors will call the cops. I can see the breaking news now…

*Super Bowl MVP is arrested for stalking baby momma. Gets karate chopped in the balls by spunky best friend.*

"Want me to get rid of him for you?" she says with a creepy, gleeful look in her eyes. Nnnnnnoooo. I definitely cannot unleash Amber on him—yet.

"I have to deal with this. It's time. The stubborn ass won't stop until I do."

"You need to tell him before he finds out some other way."

Just the thought has me hyperventilating. "I'm scared."

"I know." She grabs my hand and squeezes. "I'm here for you."

I jerk open the front door to find him standing there with his hand hanging in the air. He's so frigging handsome—it's just so unfair. How did I ever think he was pretty? Or cold? That's love for you.

"Did I just see Harper leaving?" he asks with a puzzled

frown.

"Yes." I turn and walk into the living room. Then I cross my arms under my now giant breasts. I've already moved up a bra size. The pregnancy has had an immediate and visible effect on my body. Mostly my boobs. Though I feel puffy all over. Even in a loose t-shirt and cut off jean shorts, I think I look different. Sitting on the couch, he looks around absently. He's restless, infused with nervous energy. His eyes return to me filled with manifold sentiments: relief, affection, joy…love. There's so much love. His gaze moves over me, hitting all the salient points on my face and body.

"Why have you been avoiding me?"

"You know why."

"You look…great," he says wistfully. His words burrow in and wrap around my heart. Can he tell? Maybe this will go better than expected…maybe. Missing him has become so much a part of me that now that he's here, all I want to do is drink in the sight of him. With his hair cut short and scruff covering his firm jaw, the changes are noticeable. In less than a month, he seems to have lost the weight I gained. His eyes look dim. The dark circles painted under them are still there.

"You look like shit." I'm sure it's written all over my face how much it bothers me to see him like this. He gives me a nod and a sad smile, which makes my chest feel tight and my throat close up.

*I will not cry. I will not cry. I will not cry.*

I love him so much. More than I could ever have imagined after what I've suffered through. And it's an honest love. I see him for who he really is, and love him even more for all his moles and warts, out in the open, not hiding under the veneer of his good looks or fame or any other crap that I may have once found fascinating but now couldn't give a lick about.

"I feel like shit."

"I've been watching the games. You're playing well." Lost in thought, he nods absently. "Looks like you guys may have a playoff team this year," I manage through the thick chunk of emotion clogging my throat.

His warm eyes flicker to my stomach. A determined look enters them as he stands. He stuffs his hands in the pockets of his black work out pants, and shrugs up his big shoulders. Then he takes them out and crosses them in front of the wide breadth of his chest. Finally, he drops them to his sides. All this in the span of seconds.

"I can't sleep. I can't focus. I can't even eat." Slowly walking toward me, he continues speaking softly. "I need you to come back." I put up a hand to stop him. If I touch him, if I let him hold me, I will lose it. And right now, I can't let that happen—too much is at stake. "I'll beg if you want me to."

"Nothing has changed, Cal. You don't want kids and the thing is—I get it. I understand why you don't. I can't imagine how difficult it must've been to have all that responsibility fall on your shoulders. But kids are extremely important to me. The most important thing. It would come between us later, and I won't do that to either of us. It wouldn't be fair."

He rubs his brow and pinches the bridge of his nose. "What if...I compromised? What if I said I'd have one with you?"

"We both know you would be agreeing under duress." Blowing out a deep breath, he pins me with an exasperated look.

"I'm tryin' here, damn it. Give me somethin' to work with." His twang is back, which means his emotions are getting the best of him. The fact that he didn't deny what I just said stabs my gut while tears sting my eyes, the influx of hormones running in my blood making me weepy. I can't help him make this decision. I know what I have to do—for both of us. It's the only way to discover his true feelings.

"I'm pregnant."

"What?" Intense and unblinking, his gaze snaps to mine.

"I said, I'm pregnant." I do my best to hold the eye contact for as long as I can, which happens to be not very long at all.

"The fuck…" he murmurs. His eyes move over me again, looking for evidence. And then slowly, ever so slowly, they climb back up to mine…and turn into two chips of ice.

"Whose is it?"

His voice has descended to an inhuman growl. The vein at his temple is throbbing. Everything I have been dreading for weeks is coming to fruition before my eyes. I can no longer hold back the tears. They slip down my cheeks unimpeded. I try like hell to keep my voice steady as I speak.

"If you're asking if I'm pregnant with *our* baby, then the answer is yes."

"This can't be happening to me again," he mutters to himself. "It's Harper's, isn't it?" His voice is harsh, clipped. His eyes look wild. I must still be in possession of my heart because the stake he just drove through it wouldn't hurt this much if I wasn't. Breathing harshly, his hands on his hips, he turns his back to me.

"It's yours," I say more calmly than I'm feeling, and quickly wipe the tears away. His head whips around in my direction.

"I'm supposed to believe that? I don't know what's worse, that you got knocked up and are trying to extort money from me, or that you think I'm stupid enough to believe you."

It takes all the willpower I possess to moderate my voice, to try to remain rational. After a deep breath, I say, "I know you're shocked right now, Cal. I was shocked too, trust me, I was *shocked*. But don't say another word—you'll regret it later."

"I'm not the one that's going to regret anything." He's seething with anger. "You are."

A moment later, he stalks out of the room and out the front door. The loud bang that reverberates throughout the apartment makes me jerk. The pain I'm feeling sinks down to my bones. I can feel the blood drain from my face and pool at my feet. I'm rooted to the floor in the middle of the room for a full fifteen minutes, every muscle in my body trembling.

"Are you okay?" Amber's voice is soft. I turn to find her standing in the open doorway. All I can do is shake my head, anything else and I will crumble. Quietly, she comes over and hugs me tightly. "We'll get through this together. You're not alone."

Those words ring true and familiar. And after a beat, I recall why. Those were the exact same words she said to me the night Matt drove his car into a watery grave.

\* \* \*

Two days later, I feel marginally human again. I spent the last forty eight hours simultaneously stuffing my face with any carb I could get my hands on and bawling my eyes out. That out of the way, I determine it's time to let my parents in on the fun.

"What is it?" my mother screeches when she sees me walk into the kitchen with a look of utter desolation on my face.

"Where's Dad?" I am composed with a capital C. Gotta keep it together even though every hormone in my body is staging a riot.

"At the store. What is it Camilla? You're making me nervous."

"I wanted to tell you two together…I guess it can't wait." Angelina presses a hand to her sternum. She looks truly panicked now, so I get it out quickly before she has a heart attack. "I'm pregnant."

## WRECKING BALL

Her face is a carousel of emotions. Shock, curiosity, suspicion, joy, elation. Take your pick—there's one of every flavor. She settles on hope.

"You're sure?"

"Went to the OBGYN this morning and confirmed it."

A slow, very slow smile starts to creep across my mother's face, until it nearly breaks in two. "A baby...we're going to have a baby. God has answered my prayers."

I'm not sharing her enthusiasm just yet.

"You're not...mad?"

Her blue eyes slam into mine. "Why would I be mad?"

"I don't know...I'm not married. I don't have a job. This isn't exactly a good time to be having a baby."

"Camilla, you're my daughter. I love you more than the next breath of air I'll take into my lungs. But you need to stop expecting the worst, for everyone to disappoint you. Are you happy about this baby?"

Those words hit their intended mark. I feel them not only in my head, but also in my heart. I did expect the worst from her...and from Cal, for that matter.

"Very happy."

"Then that's all that matters. I've lived enough life to know the rest will work itself out."

"Before you get too happy, Ma, you should know that Calvin doesn't want any part of it. He told me many times he never wanted children, so I can't fault him. This was...kind of a miracle."

"What's a miracle?" My father queries as he walks into the kitchen with two shopping bags.

"Put those down, Tom. This is important."

My father's alert and inquisitive gaze finds me. "What is it?"

"I'm pregnant."

It takes my father a minute. "This is great news," he announces with a bright white smile.

"Calvin has cold feet," my mother adds.

"He does not have cold feet, Ma. He flat out does not want children. He's told me a million times."

"He should've thought of that before—"

"Thomas," my mother cuts in.

"It's not his fault, Dad. You see…uhhh…well, Calvin had a vasectomy. We're both shocked that this happened."

Confusion blankets my father's face. "Is this a prank? Is this some kind of *Youtube* challenge thing?"

"This is not a prank, Dad. Nor is it a *Youtube challenge thing*. Sometimes, after a vasectomy, an opening can develop in the…umm…vasa that allows sperm to get through."

*Shit, this is awkward.*

"So we're going to have a baby?" Dad reiterates.

"Yes."

"Calvin will come around. You'll see."

"Don't count on it, Ma. He's very stubborn and very committed to what he wants. He doesn't take this lightly. I don't want you to blame him if he never comes around."

"Camilla, sometimes people don't know what they want until they have it."

"I hope you're right, Ma. I really hope so."

# CHAPTER TWENTY-NINE

Hot September nights roll into brisk October days. All along the Palisades, high above the mighty Hudson River, trees are turning so many different shades of red to yellow that they put Pantone to shame. Shortly after Cal's visit, the Titans' started losing. Although their season isn't a total loss just yet; they're still in second place within their division.

I know Cal is training hard, focusing on work, doing what he's always done to manage all the emotion he has no idea what to do with. Most days I love and miss and worry about him, praying that in time he'll come to his senses. Other days I want to buy a ski mask, dress in black, and break into his house to gut him like a feral pig.

Over three weeks have past since the scene at Amber's place. Meanwhile, I haven't received a single text, or email from him. My mother's convinced he just needs time to have his 'come to Jesus' moment. I'm not so sure. If Calvin is anything, he's stubborn and committed. When he makes his mind up about something, nothing gets in the way. That's what worries me most.

"Camilla Ava Maria DeSantis."

I turn at the sound of a sexy masculine voice. Chuckling, I counter with, "Ethan Fancy McButterPants Vaughn." I get a heated glare for using Amber's new nickname for him.

He walks up and hugs me, throwing a heavy arm around my neck as we stroll lazily through Central Park on the way to Sarabeth's.

Ethan's been great. I'm not sure if Cal put him up to it, but he found me a part time teaching gig. And I've already been on a couple of interviews for full time positions. When I explained what an impossible feat that was, he smirked and said I needed to stop underestimating people. He may be right.

"You're getting fat," he says and rubs my teeny tiny bump. I slap his hand away.

"If I didn't love you so much, I'd get Amber to kick you in the nuts." He feigns fright and I laugh at his dramatics. "That's how we became best friends, you know. She beat up Jimmy Murphy for me. I'm sure he's still feeling it."

"How's the job?" The part time gig is at a tiny, uptown private school. It pays well, and more importantly, I'm back to doing what I love. With the baby coming, time and money will be in short supply.

Central Park is packed. All around us, skaters and cyclist zip by, women push designer strollers while jogging, and people parade their dogs around. I can't help noticing all the couples out with their kids. Ethan notices it, too.

"Amazing. I can't ever thank you enough."

"Don't worry, I'll find a way for you to thank me." He smirks suggestively, and I swat him. Avoiding his perceptive gaze, I say, "Are you going to make me ask?"

Ethan exhales loudly and rubs the back of his neck. "Not good. He got in a fight with Harper the other day at practice." At this, my head snaps in his direction, shock splashed across my face. For all of Calvin's grumpiness, he never gets violent. There could be mayhem swirling around him and he remains calm and in control, no doubt it has something to do with growing up with eight siblings in a doublewide trailer. "I've never seen him like this, not even when he found out Kim was screwing around."

"What happened?"

"Don't know. He barely speaks to me. He's not returning any of Barry's calls, either. It's starting to worry his teammates." Ethan stops walking and turns to look at me. "Let me force the paternity test. Come on, Cam."

"No." I start walking again. There's no way I'm going to coerce an apology, or a reconciliation with a paternity test. He has to come to that decision on his own. "He needs to trust me. If he can't do that then he doesn't know me. And if he doesn't know me, he doesn't really love me."

Cal and I have glaring trust issues, no surprise there—with our pasts, it's impossible not to—however, I've made a conscious effort not to let it influence my future. I would never make Cal pay for what Matt did, and I sure as shit am not about to pay for Kim's sins either. I turn when I realize Ethan is no longer walking next to me. "Are you coming?"

"I have a charity thing Saturday night," he grumbles. "Will you be my date?"

"How the heck are you ever going to get laid when you show up to an event with a pregnant woman on your arm?" Life's sense of humor makes an appearance with impeccable timing. A tall, blond chick with a perfect body rollerblades past us, her head swiveling to get a good look at my smokin' hot friend. "Hey, baby," she croons.

"Who says I'm not getting laid?"

The look of pure delighted surprise on my face checks him.

"Oooo, tell me all the sordid details," I purr, wringing my hands. "And don't leave out any of really filthy parts." At this, he looks pained.

"They're not really all that filthy."

"Well then make some up, for goodness sake!"

He throws his arm around my shoulders and says, "Okay, but I need fuel if I'm gonna do this right."

I practically jog to Sarabeth's. Because single and desperately horny pregnant women need to get it any way they can.

*  *  *

"Do I look fat?"

"Only around the belly," says my best friend. I give her the finger because I can. I'm allowed to be irritable when I'm feeling vulnerable and large and being forced to dress up. Looking in the floor length mirror, I decide that this is as good as it's going to get. The black jersey Donna Karan gown that fit me perfectly for years still does—everywhere except the middle. I left my hair down. Though I don't think it's going to distract from the girth.

"Wassup, Fancy McButterPants," Amber shouts at poor Ethan, who is patiently waiting for me to find my cellphone. She walks from her bedroom to the kitchen in a pair of super small t-shirt shorts and a thin tank top. She's always been pretty carefree about her body because there isn't much of it.

As I'm digging into my tote for my cellphone, I watch Ethan's eyes track her across the room with an equal mix of naked fear and fascination on his face. He thinks he's being discreet about it. Yeah, as discreet as a sledgehammer. *Men, smh.* Before Amber can do irreparable damage to Ethan's self worth, I grab my purse and push him out the door.

"What event is this again?" I ask him once I'm safely buckled in his Audi and we're on our way.

"You know—the event for pediatrics cancer research. You've never looked more beautiful, by the way." Something in my gut churns uncomfortably and it's not a baby. More like

# WRECKING BALL

suspicion.

"Nice try, counselor. But you know those shenanigans don't work on me." His grin spreads from ear to ear. "The one Mrs. Davis founded?" Mrs. Davis—the wife of the owner of the Titans. I get a small nod in reply. As soon as we step into the Metropolitan Club, my suspicion is confirmed. Many of the Titans players are in attendance.

"What the hell is going on? Why are the guys here?"

Ethan has the grace to look guilty. "Mrs. Davis planned it for the bye week."

Across the room, a man as beautiful as sin stands in a corner by himself, staring absently into space—the weight of the world on his broad shoulders.

*Oh for the love of...*

His head turns and a pair of unblinking crystal clear gray eyes take me in from head to toe. My stomach flips just looking at him. No one ever tells you that being in love feels a heck of a lot like food poisoning. He needs a haircut again, it's curling around his ears, and his jaw is covered with scruff. God forbid he should actually use a razor. I can't take my eyes off of him, of course.

"I'm going to the bar," Ethan mumbles. I don't even have time to lay into him; the coward leaves skid marks. As Cal gets closer, I can see the faint yellow-green ring around his eye. Looks like Harper got a good shot in. I'm secretly pleased at this. Before Cal reaches me, the wife of one of the younger players approaches, a very bubbly blond I remember meeting at the charity carnival held at team facilities. She chatters on, jumping from topic to topic while her eyes flicker to my stomach. It was either wear a dress that shows off the bump, or a tent that makes me look like a whale. I sense when she can no longer pretend she doesn't see it.

"Are you...are you pregnant?"

*Awkward.* What do I say when the congratulations start? And do I admit it's Calvin's? Right about now, I want to take a running start and punch Ethan in the face.

"Eight weeks," I answer and hope she leaves it at that. Scanning the room, I find Ethan and head over to the bar area. "Cindy, will you excuse me for a moment? I have to ask my date something." I'm gone before she has a chance to respond, undoubtedly leaving behind a wake of confusion.

At the bar, I tap Ethan on the elbow. The bartender hands him a beer and, turning, he drapes his arm around my neck. For the first time ever, his open show of affection makes me a tad uncomfortable, seeing that we're under surveillance.

"He's watching," I murmur.

"I know," he whispers in my ear. Goodness this man is devious. I really need to get him and Amber together. Although that may be like pairing up chaos and mayhem, or shock and awe…or Cagney and Lacy.

"I don't think that's a good idea." My eyes are glued to the stormy expression on Cal's face as he stalks in our direction. One of the defensive players is about to say something to Ethan when Cal reaches us.

"Beat it, Simms." The glare does the trick. Simms walks away shaking his head. His eyes skip between Ethan's arm and me. "What the hell is going on here?"

*Oh no, he didn't…*

He's standing with his legs spread apart and his arms crossed, his biceps bulging through the fine wool of his suit. At the moment, I'm not sure what I want most, to kiss him senseless, or castrate him and wear his balls around my neck.

"Cal—"

"Shut up, E." His scowl, though, remains directed at me. "Ethan go away."

"Ethan don't you dare."

"I haven't heard from your lawyer, yet."

And there it is, the opening salvo. If he was trying to get a rise out of me, he just succeeded. "Really? You want to do this here? With Mr. and Mrs. Davis watching?" I say through gritted teeth.

"Wasn't that your plan?"

I can't…I can't keep trying to deal rationally with an irrational man.

"My plan?" Rage is taking over. I can feel it. I'm going Hulk on his ass. "My plan was to live a quiet, drama free life. But then you come along with your perfect ass, and your sulky mouth, and your goddamn leaky pipes! You wanna blame someone, Cal? Blame your shoddy surgeon!"

I'm so frigging angry and frustrated right now that I may do and say something I'll regret, so I turn to Ethan and say, "I'm out of here. Please tell this larger-than-life-size prick that he can take every red cent he has and shove it. Any further communication can be sent through you." Then I turn to the prick in question, point to Ethan, and say, "Meet my lawyer," and walk away.

I get as far as the coat check when the noise of a large man moving fast finds me. He swipes my coat from the poor coat check girl with one hand, startling her, and grabs my arm with the other.

"Get your filthy hands off of me." He rears back a little and releases my arm. I grab my coat from him and he follows me out onto the sidewalk. Except for the limos and SUVs lining the street, it's blessedly empty.

"I'll drive you home." His attitude is much more subdued.

*Good choice.*

"The hell, you will," I say raising my arm to hail a cab.

"Don't be stupid. You're not riding in a cab in your condition."

"What condition would that be?!"

"Calm down."

*Whhhhyyyyy?* Why would anyone in his or her right mind say *calm down* to an angry hormonal woman?

"Did Harper knock the last bit of sense out of you? Don't tell me to calm down when you've been acting like a frigging lunatic for two months now!"

His fingers go to the bruise under his eye, touching it gingerly. He doesn't respond, just stares like he's waiting for something. An inspiration from God? Who the hell knows what goes on inside this man's head, but the silence continues. In exasperation, I turn my back to him.

*Where the hell are all the cabs in Manhattan when you need one?*

"I miss you." His voice is low and quiet. *I will not cry. I will not cry. I will not cry.* "Did you hear me? I miss you so much it's physically painful."

"Whose fault is that?" Okay, so I'm being bitchy. But come on…after what he's put me through. He's standing close, radiating body heat and a surfeit of emotion.

"How do you feel?"

The urge to turn and drink in the sight of him is greater than my willpower and my common sense. He looks so forlorn that I almost feel bad for him. Almost. I love this man, this man that may never come around, may never realize what a gift we've been given. I try to cross my arms in front and find it impossible with my new gargantuan breasts so I drop them.

"Fine. Just…swollen," I grumble.

"You look…" He takes a deep breath, his nostrils flaring. "You've never looked more beautiful."

Why doesn't he just punch me in the heart? It couldn't have hurt more. This man does not hand out compliments. I've accepted that about him. And, quite frankly, respect the heck out of it because the ones he does so meagerly dole out, mean that much more.

We stand there quietly a little longer; I refuse to be the one to cave. In the meantime, his eyes move over every inch of me, noting all the changes. His hands tighten into fists by his sides. Then, before I can even consider what to allow or not allow, he reaches for me, slips his warm hand around my neck, and holds me in place for the sweetest kiss he's ever given me.

It's tentative and searching, tasting of raw pain and love. My brain short circuits. I completely lose the ability to reason and melt in his arms. With all his faults, I still love him more than is wise and more than my pride. However, love can't thrive without trust and the thought of him not trusting me kills my amorous mood. I pull away and he lets me. Watching me intently, he waits for me to speak. It's now or never.

"You know what hurts the most? That you don't know me, that you believe I would deceive you for money—*for money,* Cal." He's shaking his head before I even finish the sentence. He runs his fingers through his hair and rubs his temples.

"I was mad. I know you wouldn't—"

"Calvin," I say, cutting him off. "I love you beyond measure. I know I'm hanging out on a limb here, but I'm willing to risk the fall because I can't live with regret. I've lived with too much of it already and the cost is too rich for my blood. Regardless of the past, I *choose* to trust you. I'm making that choice knowing that you're human and you may disappoint and hurt me, and that's okay too because you're worth it.

"I certainly didn't plan for this baby. But I'm not gonna lie, I couldn't be any happier about it. Now you can either get on board, or walk away for good. The choice is yours. But make no mistake, nothing will stop me from ensuring that this kid feels loved and treasured—I will not have you fuck with that.

Got it? Make a choice and commit to it."

A myriad of emotions cross Cal's face. Lady Luck is on my side tonight. I'm about to walk away when a cab pulls up. With his hands shoved in the pockets of his pants, he doesn't make a move or say anything as I shut the door. And yet, something tells me that my words will remain with him long after I'm gone.

# CHAPTER THIRTY

Two days later, Amber and I are kicking back on her couch, eating dinner while we wait for *Monday Night Football* to start. While she's flipping through channels at warp speed, I'm busy inhaling my pasta with broccoli with one hand and rubbing my bump with the other. I've been doing a lot of that lately. What's that about? Anyhow, I'm busy doing stuff when a familiar voice grabs my attention. Not missing a thing, my very clever friend flips back to *ESPN*.

"My legacy?" Calvin murmurs to the reporter. He's dressed in his practice uniform, the helmet hanging from his fingertips. He wipes his sweaty brow and squints in the distance. He looks lost, rudderless and adrift. Unhappy. It kills me to see him like this. "That's not up to me to decide. My legacy is how I'm remembered by everyone else...by the people I love, and the ones that love me."

*Did I just hear him right?* The bottom has fallen out of my stomach. The pasta doesn't taste nearly as good on the way up as it did on the way down.

"Did I just hear him right?" I say, covering my mouth.

"If you're referring to the *people I love* comment, then yes," Amber faithfully reports.

He's looking directly into the camera, and it feels like, directly at me. Then he walks off screen, leaving the reporter stunned at his sudden departure.

"Men are so fucking dumb. No wonder they believe they rule the world."

Chuckling, I wipe the tear that's escaped down my cheek. I turn to get an eyeful of my little blond friend and find her cheeks stuffed with food.

"I don't get why you're still single."

"Because I'm smart, that's why," she says, still chewing her pizza. "Who needs this drama?" I can't argue with her there. I'm no fan of drama myself. As a matter of fact, I've already had more than I can bear in a lifetime. "I predict that turkey—" she points a greasy finger at the television screen, "will be banging down my door three days hence."

Such a smart mouth. I laugh, of course. "I hope you're right…I just hope he does it for the right reason."

Amber drops the cynical mask. "I get it," she says, the mood serious all of a sudden.

If I know one thing, it's that we all learn at our own pace. You can show someone the way, though ultimately they have to figure it out for themselves. It may be wishful thinking, however, it seems that Cal is starting to figure it out.

\* \* \*

"For realz? That's what you're wearing?" Amber says, throwing herself down on the bed with a script in hand.

"All the teachers are dressing up. What else am I supposed to go as? Sexy maid? Sexy kitten? Or beached whale?" I finish painting the square pink nose and the white stripe down my face. "What time is your audition?"

Stella, Mercedes' daughter, did me a favor and got Amber an audition for a hot new television series that's about time travel. Turns out, her best friend is Delia Law, the best selling romance author whose books the show has been adapted from, so she was able to pull some strings.

"Ten...I'm nervous. And I'm never nervous for these things."

"Could be a good omen if this feels different." She looks up at me, vulnerable and unsure—something Amber rarely is. "Ambs, you deserve it. You deserve something really wonderful to happen to you. It's just a matter of time." Just then the pressure that's been steadily growing in my gut since I had breakfast spikes. I rub my tiny bulge in slow circles and measure my breathing.

Her delicate features twist into a frown. "What's wrong?"

"It's probably nothing, but I've had this ache growing since breakfast. And I feel a lot of pressure...probably nothing."

Twenty minutes later, as I'm about to leave for work, I can no longer ignore the pain. "Amber, I have to go to the hospital. Call the school and tell them I can't make it in. And call Ange."

"I'm coming with you."

"No. Just make the calls. You have to go over your lines and get ready for the audition. Besides, the hospital is only five blocks away."

Grabbing my purse and keys, I make my way outside and hail a cab.

"NYU Medical Center." The cab driver cranes his neck and gives me a bright grin.

"Nice costume."

"Thanks," I squeak out because the pain and pressure have been growing exponentially since I left the apartment.

"Are you okay, lady?"

"Of course not! Why do you think I'm headed to the hospital?" I shout while I'm doubled over, sweating bullets and scared out of my mind. That prompts him to drive at warp speed. Two minutes later, we pull up in front of the emergency room. Needless to say, it's a miracle I'm still in one piece.

Today is my lucky day apparently because the emergency room is empty—something that never ever happens in New York City. Let's hope the winning streak continues.

After I check in and tell them who my OBGYN is, I'm whisked off for tests. For the first time since I left the apartment, I entertain the thought that I may be losing this baby and a terror, the dimensions of which I can't even begin to measure, gets a hold of me.

*Breathe in, breathe out, breath in, breathe out. God, please, I'll be good. I promise. Just don't take this baby away from me.*

\* \* \*

"Abdominal distention, excessive flatus volume and smell… symptoms were clear," says Dr. Levine, my OBGYN, a lovely man in his late sixties. He's standing next to the emergency room doctor, who happens to be crazy hot. *Holy Moses.* Sharp cheekbones and sharper jaw, a mess of disheveled brown hair and sleeves of tattoos that travel up both his arms and disappear under his scrubs. Great. Why couldn't I get some old toothless dude seeing me at my worst.

They're both smirking. I'm feeling a ton better since they administered the medication.

"What did you eat this morning?" says Doctor Hotness.

"Cantaloupe and whole wheat toast."

"How much cantaloupe?"

"A lot."

He smirks again, his bright green eyes turning into crescents. "Cool costume."

"Thanks…so you're saying I had to fart?" No point in acting coy about it. Gotta face the embarrassment head on.

"I prefer the clinical term, but yes. The cantaloupe is the culprit. It ferments and turns into gas. That's not uncommon in pregnant women."

"Camilla!!!" The shout is so loud I can hear it over the

chaos typical of emergency rooms. Then, a scuffling sound. "Get the fuck off of me!" More scuffling. Doctor Hotness scowls while my doctor pushes the curtain aside to see what the commotion is about. And that's when I spot him.

His eyes are huge in his face. Even the dark scruff can't hide the pallor of his skin. Without once breaking eye contact, he rushes toward me, two security officers fast on his heels. I glance around. The entire emergency room is watching this play out.

"I got here as soon as I could—" he rushes in. I can see that. He's still wearing his entire practice uniform, cleats and all. He's also soaked in sweat.

"Sir, you can't leave your car in front of the emergency room like that," says officer number one.

"Then tow it! Can't you see my wife needs me!"

*Wife? The fuck?*

Calvin takes a step closer and Doctor Hotness steps in between us. "Whoa, buddy." After which, Calvin levels Doctor Hotness with his most lethal Prince of Darkness glare.

"It's okay, doc. He's tame—mostly."

Calvin walks up to me and cups my face gently, as if I'm something fragile, as if he's afraid to hurt me. He looks like he might rip at the seams...like he's about to cry.

"I love you. I love you so much I can't remember what it's like not to love you. And I'm the biggest ass in the world for not telling you sooner, but I..." Looking over his shoulder, he scowls at the group congregating around us. "Can we have some privacy?"

The crowd disperses at once.

He gets down on his knees in front of the gurney I'm sitting on. "I was scared." He bites his bottom lip and I want to soothe it for him with mine. "I was scared of the power you have over me. Because you do—" he says, nodding. "You do.

I…I've never felt like this before. The thing is…you're the best person I know. You give everything, and you never ask for anything in return and…"

"Calvin—"

"I'm not done," he says and plants a quick kiss on me. "I thought I was an adult. I thought taking care of shit, being responsible made me a man—but I was wrong. You did… loving you made a man out me." He blinks repeatedly, fighting the tears tracking down his cheeks, his jaw tight. For a moment, I fear it may shatter. "I'm sorry you lost the baby. We can try again as soon as you're ready…if you still want me. Please say you still want me."

I wipe the tears away from his face and place a kiss on each cheek, his nose, his lips. He crushes me to his chest and holds me so tightly I have to push him away before he cuts off my oxygen supply.

Looking into his glazed eyes, I say, "I didn't lose the baby. How do you feel about that?"

His expression morphs from shock, to wonder, to joy in a split second. "You're not messing with me, right?"

"It's Halloween, not April Fool's. No—I'm not messing with you," I say, holding his face in my hands.

"Thank God," he mumbles, exhaling deeply. And it's like the floodgates of love open all at once. I'm assaulted with kisses. I'm hugged and squeezed, his hands sliding over every square inch of black and white fur. Then, hauling me onto his lap, he hides his face in the curve of my costume covered neck.

"Nice costume," he mumbles an eternity later.

"You like it?"

"I fucking love cows."

"Reginald?"

"What, Honey?"

"Why'd you think I lost the baby?"

# WRECKING BALL

"Amber called. She said you were having a miscarriage and it was all my fault. Then she said she hopes I get gang raped in a dark alley by a herd of homosexual mules."

"She's very creative."

"She's never allowed to babysit."

I kiss the man I love more than life itself. "Are you mine now?"

"I've been yours since the minute I laid eyes on you, my little wrecking ball."

"And you're okay with being a father?"

He pulls back and his solemn eyes meet mine. He nods twice. "Yes. Because I'm doing it with you. All my life, I've felt like something was dragging me down. But when I'm with you, that weight's gone." Cal stands us up and bends down to kiss my pink cow udders. "Marry me?"

My smile spreads from ear to ear. "Boobear—I thought you'd never ask."

# EPILOGUE

"What's it gonna take?" he says, his voice low and sexy.

My gaze slides over the traps I love to nibble on, across the broad chest that keeps me warm every night, down to the corrugated muscles of his stomach. How am I supposed to form a cohesive thought when I have his wonder for the senses distracting me? And let's not forget that not much is covering the rest of him.

No surprise, he's parading around in a pair of tattered boxer briefs old enough to be considered a relic. Some things never change. I tried to throw them away one day and wound up getting spanked for it. Can't say I won't try that again very soon. His big hand strokes and pats my daughter's back, who looks like a tiny beanbag snuggled between his shoulder and neck.

"Babe, she's asleep. Go put her down."

"In a little while."

"What's it going to take for you to give me another one?" The wicked smile curving those sensual lips does not bode well for me.

"Something you don't possess—the ability to breastfeed." Bending down, he plants a sweet kiss on my lips and starts to pull away. I can't resist threading my fingers through his hair and keeping him in place for one more. When my daughter stirs awake, we break apart. Gently, he pets the silky black hair that's standing up straight, her fine features and coloring an exact replica of her daddy's.

Of all the ways this man has managed to surprise me, the way he took on fatherhood was by far the most shocking. He didn't miss a single beat. As soon as our son came into this world, he took one look at that baby, shed two tears, and took charge. For the first few months, I had to threaten him to hand the baby over so I could breastfeed. Then he went and reversed the vasectomy.

He has one more year left on his contract with the Titans. Retirement soon to follow. Is it terrible to admit how relieved I am? At first, I was worried about how much he'd miss the work, the camaraderie with the guys. However, when he told me he wanted to go into coaching, I knew he was going to be fine. That Team Shaw would be fine.

When I asked him if he regrets not winning another championship, he told me he was done wanting anything for himself, said he was looking forward to helping other people make their dreams come true. He says life has a funny way of showing you what you want before you even know you want it. I have to agree.

"We just had this one."

His pushiness used to make me crazy. Now I think it's cute. Insert eye roll. But that's love for you. It'll take your world, turn it upside down, and have you smiling while the g-force takes your breath away.

"We haven't done it in the hammock in a while," he murmurs in that ridiculously sexy voice that's gotten me into trouble more than once. A slight lift of a black eyebrow follows. "Kids are asleep."

"You and I both know you're no good in a hammock. It got dangerous last time."

"That's because we were trying to give Connor and Christian a little brother—"

"Sister. *Sister*. And just so we're clear, no more penises in this house, EVER again. Got it?" Needless to say, the boys are more than a handful.

"Point is, I needed better leverage."

"You almost gave yourself a concussion."

"Are you questioning my abilities, woman? 'Cause I'm ready to provide a demonstration."

"No one is disputing your ability to make babies, my love." I can't help the giggle that bubbles up when he begins a stealthy crawl toward our bed. "Reginald—don't you dare wake that baby."

"You're payin' for that." Ten minutes later, after he's put Caroline in her crib, he returns wearing a look that warns me good things are coming. "Now where were we? Oh yeah, I was going to torture you with my tongue."

I giggle as he pounces on me. And then I breathe out a relaxed sigh as the weight of him settles between my thighs. "Just remember, no more penises," I whisper in his ear.

"I'll do my best, Honey."

And I know he means it. This amazing man would never give anything other than his best.

# ABOUT THE AUTHOR

P. Dangelico loves romance in all forms, shapes, and sizes, cuddly creatures (four legged and two), brick oven pizza, the NY Jets (although she may rethink that after this season), and to while away the day at the barn. What she's not enamored with is referring to herself in the third person and social media but she'll give you the links anyway.

www.pdangelico.com
Facebook- PDangelicoAuthor
Instagram- PDangelicoAuthor
Goodreads–P.DangelicoAuthor

Manufactured by Amazon.ca
Bolton, ON

45051315R00178